THE HUNTED

Resources for Men and Women
from the Best-Selling Every Man Series

Every Man's Battle
Every Man's Marriage
Every Man, God's Man
Preparing Your Son for Every Man's Battle
Every Man's Challenge
Every Day for Every Man

Every Woman's Battle
Every Heart Restored
Preparing Your Daughter for Every Woman's Battle
Every Woman, Every Day
Every Woman's Marriage

an everyman novel

THE HUNTED

FRED STOEKER AND DEAN WESLEY SMITH

WATERBROOK
PRESS

THE HUNTED
PUBLISHED BY WATERBROOK PRESS
12265 Oracle Boulevard, Suite 200
Colorado Springs, Colorado 80921
A division of Random House Inc.

The characters and events in this book are fictional, and any resemblance to actual persons or events is coincidental.

ISBN 1-4000-7038-4

Library of Congress Cataloging-in-Publication Data
Stoeker, Fred.
    The hunted : an every man novel / by Fred Stoeker and Dean Wesley Smith.— 1st ed.
        p. cm.
    ISBN 1-4000-7038-4
    1. Thailand—Fiction.   I. Smith, Dean Wesley.   II. Title.
    PS3619.T6426H86 2006
    813'.6—dc22

                                                2006002881

Printed in the United States of America
2006— First Edition

10 9 8 7 6 5 4 3 2 1

ACKNOWLEDGMENTS

Give everyone what you owe him:
If you owe taxes, pay taxes; if revenue, then revenue;
if respect, then respect; *if honor, then honor.*
ROMANS 13:17 (emphasis added)

A few years ago, Stephen Arterburn and WaterBrook Press began brainstorming new ways to promote the message of sexual purity that I first advanced in our book *Every Man's Battle.* My role in the ministry was already clear: I was to keep working on the eight nonfiction books that eventually became the Every Man series, including *Every Man's Marriage, Preparing Your Son for Every Man's Battle,* and *Every Man's Challenge.*

But we felt there was also a place in our ministry for fiction books—entertaining novels that would weave the message of sexual purity throughout their pages. As frequent airline travelers, Steve and I were well aware of the great need for good, clean novels that could help Christian fliers pass the time they spent crisscrossing the country. When WaterBrook Press agreed that this concept had merit, the Every Man novels were born.

I'm not a novelist—all honor goes to Dean Wesley Smith as the writer of this book. He took some of the concepts from *Every Man's Battle* and shaped a wonderfully exciting and entertaining story. Thanks to him for the many long hours of work spent on this manuscript!

I'm grateful for the voice God has granted me to help advance the message of sexual purity throughout His kingdom in various ways. May God strengthen your heart in purity's battle as you read *The Hunted.*

He will cover you with His pinions,
And under His wings you may seek refuge;
His faithfulness is a shield and bulwark.

PSALM 91:4, NASB

11:40 p.m., November 14
Mae Hong Son Province, Northern Thailand

SCARED. THE WORD DIDN'T EVEN BEGIN TO DESCRIBE HOW
I was feeling. Words like *frightened, terrified,* and *sheer panic*
came closer. Yet, somehow, I tried to catch my breath and stay
silent at the same time as my heart raced and every cell in
my body told me to run. Beside me, my best friend, Mike,
crouched next to the tree I was hiding behind, peering back
into the darkness.

The black Thailand jungle pushed in on all sides. Earlier in the day, the jungle had looked exciting to me, full of promise, mystery, and things to explore. Now, at just a little before midnight, it had become a humid, terror-filled nightmare.

My two other rafting buddies, Hollis and Dave, were hiding ten feet away behind another tree. I could see only their vague shapes in the faint moonlight, and I couldn't hear them at all over the pounding of my own heart.

Dear Lord, I don't want to die. I repeated the thought, like a prayer. *Dear Lord, please don't let me die. Not now. Not here.*

The men who had been our guides, and who now wanted to kill us, crashed through the brush. It sounded to me like they were very close behind us. The noise they made seemed fantastically loud, like they were giant horror movie monsters.

My mouth was completely dry, and I wanted to throw up what was left of the fish dinner I'd eaten a few hours ago, back when everything was still wonderful, still a happy adventure. But I knew that if I did, they'd hear me. They'd find me. They'd find my friends. And our lives would be over.

I took shallow breaths, trying to be as quiet as I could, working to calm myself, listening to every sound around me, no matter how small.

A mosquito buzzed at my ear. I stopped myself from brushing it away.

Swearing echoed through the trees, followed by shouting in a Thai dialect I didn't understand. Of course, I didn't understand anything but the most basic Thai words and phrases, just what I'd picked up listening to a language tape for a few hours here and there over the last couple of months.

Two months ago, I hadn't even planned on coming here.

"John, we have to move," Mike whispered, but his voice sounded more like a shout in my ears.

The faint light of the half moon through the jungle canopy made everything seem surreal, almost dreamlike. I could tell the men who were after us were coming, somehow following us, crashing through the Mae Hong Son Province jungle like elephants on a stampede.

I wanted to hold my hand against my chest to silence my pounding heart for fear that the men with the guns could hear it.

"John," Mike whispered again.

"If we move, they'll hear us," I mouthed back, my thread of a voice sounding to my ears like a shout telling everyone our location.

Calm down! The thought, a warning ringing inside my head, helped me.

Calm. Calm. Think.

"Doesn't matter. They'll find us here," Mike said. "We have to keep moving. You ready?"

I glanced back in the direction of the men chasing us. I couldn't see them, but I could hear them. There were at least ten of them.

We were supposed to be sleeping. They had planned to

wait for us to go to sleep before they tried to kidnap us. But Mike had overheard two of our guides talking about it earlier, thinking we didn't understand them. Lucky for us, Mike knew just enough of the Thai language to get the gist of what they were saying. He had traveled all over the world on his rafting expeditions, and he had picked up bits and pieces of all kinds of languages along the way. He had kept quiet, watched them, warned us, and then gotten all of us out of camp just in time.

Right now, I wasn't sure what good that would do us.

The men who were chasing us knew this jungle. I didn't. Neither did Mike or Hollis or Dave. I was a city guy. My wilderness experience was limited to the Cascade Mountains back home in Oregon. And I'd spent time in a few elk-hunting areas my father had taken me to years ago. But I knew nothing about the mountains and jungles of northern Thailand.

Nothing.

Except for studying a few maps of the river area we planned on rafting, we had left all the rest up to our guides. The same guides who had turned on us and were searching for us now.

I heard one of the guys I was with take a step.

Suddenly it seemed like the world around me exploded.

Two of our would-be captors, or their friends, opened fire with their AK-47s, spraying the trees and brush like they were trying to mow down everything in front of them.

We were in front of them.

With a sickening thud, a bullet smacked into the tree right beside my head, sending bark and splinters into the side of my face before I even had time to react.

Hollis yelled, "Run!" and took off away from the gunfire.

Dave followed him quickly.

So much for my plan of hiding. I stayed firmly planted behind the tree, and Mike crouched at my knees as another blast of gunfire from our former guides tore through the trees and underbrush.

"Now," Mike said. "Follow Hollis."

As a team, just as we had worked on so many other things over the years, Mike and I moved at the same time, sprinting through the brush following our two panicked rafting buddies. The brush ripped at my arms, branches jabbed at my legs, and the rough ground beneath my feet threatened to trip me with every movement.

Somehow, both Mike and I managed to stay on our feet and running, the shapes of the looming trees of the jungle nothing but dark shadows to be passed under and around.

Behind us, more gunfire cut through the trees. Another shot came frighteningly close. I saw it cut off a branch beside me.

It seemed the people who at first had wanted to kidnap us to gain appropriate international publicity now just plain wanted us dead. They didn't seem to care about their earlier plans. Apparently we had made them angry by escaping and messing with their agenda.

After what felt like an eternity of slashing our way through the brush, bullets flying after us, we caught up with John and Hollis. Hollis, overweight and out of shape, had stopped and was fighting to catch his breath. Even though he owned a sporting goods store in Hood River, right at the base of Mount Hood, and snow skied all winter, he still was in bad condition. Mike and I had worried about him a great deal through the years on our tougher rafting trips. In this heat, running on this terrain, he wasn't going to make it very far.

The faint light from the half moon seemed far brighter than it should. Full-blown panic throttled all of us. I knew panic never got a person anything but killed, no matter what the situation was. And that's exactly what panic would do to us now. We had to calm down and think carefully, as clearly as was possible under the circumstances. Otherwise, we were going to be listed as missing tourists in the remote northern regions of Thailand, and no one but our families and friends would care.

I was sweating like I had just finished a hard workout at the gym. I took two long, deep breaths, making sure to exhale completely. My mouth tasted like paper. Which brought up another point. We were going to need water, and soon, at this rate. Mike had rousted us out of the camp so quickly and silently that I hadn't thought to bring anything except what was in my waterproof fanny pack. No water.

Of course, if we hadn't moved as fast as we had, we would be kidnapped by now. Or dead.

I glanced at the other three. Mike had only his emergency fanny pack as well, strapped to the small of his back. Dave had a small daypack, and Hollis had nothing.

"You all right?" Mike whispered to Hollis. Hollis only nodded, his breathing sounding like he might keel over at any moment.

I stood up straight and forced myself to think and to continue to breathe deeply. We had to figure out where we were, and then outsmart the men following us.

Somehow.

I glimpsed the slice of moon shining through the trees.

"The river's to our right," I whispered to Mike. "We're headed upstream and toward it slightly. We're going to be too easy to follow at this rate."

Mike stood from where he had been kneeling beside Hollis and looked around. "You're right. The way we're crashing through the jungle, a blind man could follow us without a cane."

"We can't keep this up," I whispered, glancing at Hollis. It was clear he wasn't going to be running much farther.

"They'll expect us to keep going the way we're going," Mike whispered back. "Or to head for the river to try to follow it back into town."

"Agreed," I said.

"We go left then," Mike said. "As slowly and as quietly as we can. Let them go by us."

More gunfire sprayed the jungle, not as close as it had been but still sounding far louder than I wanted to think about. We had to do something, and do it soon.

"The road's to the left," Dave said. "Won't they expect us to go back there to try to get out?"

"We go under the road," Mike said. "And keep going. There's a bridge over a stream about a half mile above the camp. Remember? We get into the water and go up that stream and find a place to hide in the mountain area. They won't look for us up there."

I nodded, remembering the large bridge and running water I had seen just after we made camp this afternoon. The bridge was a good thirty feet over the streambed, and the stream itself had looked shallow enough to wade in. "It might work. Let's do it."

Mike put his hand on Hollis's shoulder. "Can you move?"

"I'm fine," Hollis said, brushing off Mike's hand.

I knew that Hollis and Mike were having trouble dealing with each other, especially after what happened in Bangkok the previous night. Their relationship had been sorely strained. They might not ever work it out fully. But we had to get out of here alive, so they had to deal with each other now, like it or not.

Actually, after last night, I was still uncomfortable around Hollis. I knew it wasn't very Christian of me, but there were times I found it easier to just walk away than face up to things. I knew that I was in the wrong, but I was finding the concept of forgiveness and grace a bit difficult under the circumstances.

After Hollis confessed his sins to us, I hoped time would heal the wounds. After all, we had been rafting companions since college fifteen years before. I wanted to get over my anger and lingering sense of betrayal.

Maybe that was optimistic. After all, we might not have much time left.

"We go as slowly and silently as we can," Mike said. "Try not to break any branches, leave any trail."

"Yeah, right," Dave said.

I agreed with Dave. Four men from Portland, Oregon, sneaking around in Thailand's jungles not leaving a trail. Not possible.

"I'll lead," Mike said. "Hollis, stay close to me. Dave and John, bring up the rear."

Without waiting for an argument from Hollis, Mike started off to the left, headed at an angle away from the men following us and back toward the Mae Hong Son Loop. That road was the only way in and out of the hundreds of miles of northern Thailand's mountains and jungles. It connected the town of Mae Hong Son and the capital of the province, Chiang Mai. We had flown in from Bangkok to Chiang Mai early this morning. That now seemed like a lifetime ago, an eternity.

Behind us to the left, more machine gun fire cut into the

jungle, more shouting in a language I didn't understand. What were four adult men from the Pacific Northwest doing here?

How had it come to this?

A stray bullet smashed through the brush between Dave and me, thudding into the ground and sending up a spray of dirt. It froze me for a moment. I could have been standing there. Really, it would only have taken an extra step, just a second of difference one way or another.

I might have died right in that spot.

But I didn't have time to think about that now.

Dave disappeared ahead of me, and I forced myself to keep moving, stepping quickly past the place the shot had hit.

Dear God, please help us.

In the dark jungle of northern Thailand, with men chasing us with machine guns, it felt to me like God had forgotten us. I sure hoped I was wrong.

2

Pride goes before destruction,
and a haughty spirit before a fall.

PROVERBS 16:18, RSV

5:32 p.m., September 8
Beaverton, a suburb of Portland, Oregon

I KNEW HOW I'D GOTTEN TO THAT SPOT IN THE JUNGLE. IN
fact I could remember the exact minute I'd started aiming
myself at this point. My road here had started more than a
month ago, back in my house in Oregon. Lorraine Stevens,
my fiancée, had kissed me softly on the cheek, her wonderful
honey smell wrapping around me like it always did. Then she
looked up at me with those fantastic brown eyes of hers. "John,

are you sure you don't want me to stay and feed you guys? I could stay in the kitchen most of the time."

I pointed to the coffee table sitting in front of the big-screen television behind me in the living room. "Chips, dip, bottles of soda, bowls of peanuts, hot dogs, pizza on order. What more could four grown men want, anyway?"

She laughed and shook her head, sending waves of movement down her long, brown hair. "I won't answer that question."

I laughed with her. "Good idea. Safer that way."

This time she pulled my head down and kissed me full on the lips and held me like that for a few long seconds. I loved her, loved when she kissed me like that. The world just seemed right when we kissed.

Then she held me at arm's length, a frown crossing her beautiful face. "Are you sure you're all right?"

I shrugged. "Bothered a little. We'll continue the discussion later, if you wouldn't mind."

"I don't mind," she said. "Anytime, you know that." Lorraine looked at me with that look I knew would make her a good attorney someday, the look that seemed to stare into my very soul. "I just didn't want to upset you, that's all. Not with your party tonight."

"I'm all right," I said, trying to reassure her. "And besides, it's just the guys. I'll call you after they leave."

Of course, I was sure she saw right through me. Her words in our discussion over the last hour or so had really stung.

Actually, they had done more than sting; they had gone in deep and left wounds. But it would take me some time, and maybe some more discussion with her, to understand exactly what she was talking about.

In the meantime, the guys—my three rafting buddies—were due here at any moment for our traditional rafting end-of-season party and Monday Night Football game.

She kissed me again. "Have a good time. I'll talk to you later, and I'll see you after work tomorrow. My turn to cook at my place."

"Great," I said, "since it's going to take me a few days to clean up after tonight, I'm sure."

She laughed, and I watched her five-foot-three frame almost float down the sidewalk toward her blue '96 Saab, then I closed the door.

Every time she left, I felt a little hollow. In March, she wouldn't be leaving anymore to go back to her apartment. We were getting married on March 12, and as far as I was concerned, that date was too far away. I wanted to spend the rest of my life with her, and the rest-of-my-life part couldn't start soon enough.

I'd had three major girlfriends since high school, one who became an actual fiancée right after I had finished my master's degree in communication. But not one of them had felt right like Lorraine did. I couldn't imagine loving a person any more than I loved her.

I moved into the living room and grabbed a handful of potato chips and crunched away while I thought about my earlier conversation with Lorraine. For some reason, as we cleaned, we had started talking about faith again. Lorraine was extremely faithful, as was my best friend, Mike, and his wife, Dusty. The four of us often went to church together, and we often talked about the Bible and the meaning of Christ's sacrifice for us and how it should shape our struggles to lead godly lives.

But today, just an hour ago, Lorraine had called my faith shallow.

When I had asked her to explain, she'd looked pained. She had even asked me if I really wanted to know what she meant. I told her to go on. So she tried to put her feelings into words.

"John," she had said, "you live a more Christian life than most, and your job of finding grants for nonprofits is a very admirable way to make a living. But you really don't understand true faith. Your faith has never been challenged, and you've applied God's teachings to your actions without ever taking them into your heart."

Wow, those words had hurt. Especially coming from her. I had always thought of myself as following Jesus's teachings, as having a very deep faith. I had been raised in the church, and I had told Lorraine that loudly.

She had just smiled at me and said, "That's the same thing the C & E Christians say to their friends."

That statement had actually made me mad. I wasn't a

Christmas and Easter Christian. I went to church regularly. My faith was much more than a convenience to me.

But I'd learned the hard way to listen to Lorraine. She was generally right—especially when it came to me. I clearly needed to look at why I got so angry. By the time the conversation had ended, I had told her that much, and she had agreed.

The doorbell rang. Before I could get there, Mike pushed open the front door. "Fast-Food Boy arriving," he shouted, poking his head in and holding up a six-pack of soda and a fragrant bag of everything from monster burgers to fries to onion rings for me to see.

"Put the swag on the stove by the microwave," I said.

Part of the ritual of these year-end rafting parties was for us to put on a junk-food paradise. All of us had learned the hard way what eating like a teenager could do to us. Most of us had put the brakes on the habit years ago—but we really enjoyed falling off the wagon at our gatherings.

"I waved at Lorraine at the end of the street," Mike said, heading for the kitchen. "Did she get the afternoon off?"

"Yeah. She wanted to help me make sure the place was clean for you animals."

Mike laughed. "As if we would notice."

"It was nice of her," I said.

"And you would expect anything different from Lorraine?" Mike asked, putting his soda in the fridge beside the six-pack I had bought earlier.

"Good point," I said.

I followed Mike back into the living room. He had been my best friend since all four of us rafting buddies had ended up living in the same apartment complex in Eugene during college. We all called him Mighty Mike because he stands only five-three but is stronger than two normal men. Just out of college, he married his childhood sweetheart, Dusty, and now they had two wonderful kids.

Mike is the one who got us all started rafting and suggested we spend time each spring and summer on different rivers, challenging ourselves. We had done most of the class-three whitewater from Alaska to New Mexico in the last ten years. And even a few stretches of class-four stuff.

I loved the experience of rafting, but I enjoyed even more getting outside, being challenged by the rivers, and spending time with my good friends.

For the last ten years, while Dusty worked as an RN in Portland, Mike had spent his springs, summers, and early falls taking clients on different rafting adventures, running the growing and now successful whitewater rafting business out of his home with Dusty's bookkeeping help. He loved the job, even though he worried that it kept him away from his kids too much of the time.

A moment later the doorbell rang. This time it was Dave who pushed the door open and shouted, "Anyone home?"

Dave had a bag of groceries in his arms, with a large bag of barbecue chips sticking out the top. He was the only person who liked the things, and he always brought his own bag. And every party, we ribbed him for how they smelled. He never seemed to care.

Actually, not much seemed to bother Dave. He stood about my height at six foot, but he was skinnier than I was since he seldom worked out and clearly didn't eat well or often. He was the reader type, hoping to someday finish the novel he'd been working on for the past decade since he completed his English degree.

In the meantime, he worked as a freelance stock trader from an office in his home, an old house he had remodeled himself in the west Portland hills. He never seemed to hurt for money and never talked about his trading, only answering questions about stocks when pushed by one of us.

Dave was the only one of the four of us who was divorced. He had one child from his previous marriage, a cute second grader named Barb whom he loved very much but didn't see as often as he wanted since she lived with his ex-wife in Seattle.

"Hollis is right behind me," Dave said, leaving the door open to the wonderful, warm fall evening. I had had the air conditioning on all day, but for the moment it didn't seem to be running.

Hollis came in, closing the door with his heel. "Greetings, gentlemen of the big city."

He always said that, since for the last five years he had lived up the Columbia Gorge in the small town of Hood River. He had started a sports shop there, specializing in windsurfing and snow skiing equipment and rentals. He and his girlfriend, Susan, had bought a house there four years ago, and he seemed to love it. They were a couple, but they weren't married. Ever since they'd bought the house, I had been bothered a great deal by the two of them living in sin. I had talked to Mike about it, but neither of us said anything about our concerns to Hollis. I think we both just expected them to get married one day and make the situation right. Like the Bible said, "Judge not." Judging was God's job. So we kept our mouths shut and led by example.

Hollis also had a large bag of food in his arms.

"And Lorraine was worried we wouldn't have enough to eat," I said, shaking my head as Hollis dropped his bag next to Dave's on the dining room table.

"Never happen as long as I'm around," Hollis said, dumping out two bags of pretzels, a can of Pringles Salt and Vinegar chips, and two large containers, both full of garlic dip.

"Be sure and try the dip," he said. "A lady up in the Gorge makes it. It's fantastic, my favorite."

I shook my head and said nothing. Mike and I had tried to get Hollis to lose some weight last spring before the summer rafting season. Even though he was a couple of inches shorter than I was and skied all winter, he still outweighed me by a good forty pounds. In a trouble situation on a river, those forty pounds might make the difference between life and death. But no amount of our talking could convince him of that. He loved his food, he said. Starving, he often told us, was overrated.

Dave put out his food supplies on the dining room table next to Hollis's, then opened his bag of barbecue chips, breathing deep as the mesquite odor fill the room. "You know, I'm going to miss these parties. I don't get this kind of excuse to eat junk food that often."

"We'll still have them," I said.

For the last four years, ever since Lorraine had helped me find and buy this house, rafting end-of-season parties and the beginning-of-season planning parties had been held here. I had the biggest place, and since Lorraine and I had decided to not live together until marriage, I was elected to put up with the inevitable after-party mess. The consensus was that I lived alone so I didn't have to get permission to trash the place.

Mike had two kids, so parties at his house would be interrupted by the sounds of little feet and loud voices. Hollis lived with his significant other far away in Hood River, forty-plus miles outside of the city, and Dave lived alone, but he swore he never cleaned since no one but him ever saw the inside of his place. After the one time I had been to his house, I tended to believe that statement.

So my house, clean and empty of additional occupants, had been elected.

"Yeah, right," Dave said. "I've been married before, remember. Trust me, this is it."

Mike just laughed. "Marriage has its advantages. Dusty and I are prime examples. She's sent me all around the world with a smile. You know, we could have next year's beginning-of-season planning party at my place."

"I'll get my place cleaned by next fall," Dave said. "Honest."

"Hey, guys," I said, heading to the kitchen for a drink. "Lorraine is a supporter of these parties. She was here this afternoon helping me set up for this bash."

"Oh, so that's why I can see myself in this tabletop," Dave said, bending over and staring into the oak dining room table.

"Nah," I said. "You're just looking at a knot in the wood."

Mike and Hollis both laughed.

Dave just glared at me with mock anger. "Funny."

It felt good having the guys here. But part of me knew that Dave was right. I, too, had a feeling that this would be the last party with the four of us. I just didn't know why.

3

Put on God's whole armor (the armor of a
heavy-armed soldier which God supplies), that
you may be able successfully to stand up against
(all) the strategies and the deceits of the devil.

EPHESIANS 6:11, AMP

12:09 a.m., November 15
Mae Hong Son Province, Northern Thailand

SOMEHOW, MIKE HAD MANAGED TO LEAD US SLOWLY AWAY
from the men chasing us, back toward the road and the bridge
over the stream. The clear night and the half moon had helped.
But Mike just seemed to have a knack for finding the easiest,
and the quietest, path.

Gunfire had continued to cut through the brush, but after the first few close calls, most of it had been aimed away from us, somewhere up the river. Clearly our attackers still thought we were headed in that direction. For the moment, we had gotten lucky, but I had no doubt that could change quickly. Our trail through the jungle would be laughably easy to follow once the sun came up.

I knew that because at one point, I had been forced to stop and hide in some thick brush, trying not to move or breathe or fight off a swarm of buzzing insects as one of the guides who had turned on us passed within twenty steps of me.

He hadn't seen me.

That left me far behind the others. They were out of sight completely. But even in the faint light from the moon, I could follow where they had gone.

If a greenhorn like me could find our trail in moonlight, our ex-guides would be after us as soon as the sun rose. That is, if we didn't come up with a plan to prevent it pretty soon.

Near where I thought we should be running into the road, Mike had stopped and waited for me to catch up. When I joined them, Hollis was sitting on the ground, his head down, breathing hard. Clearly his being overweight and out of shape as well as his hard night in Bangkok were taking their toll. I wasn't sure how much farther he would make it.

I wasn't faring that well myself. I had cuts and scrapes and insect bites over a large part of my skin, and I was thirsty. Very thirsty. I would need water pretty soon to survive in the warm, humid air.

Dave crouched next to Hollis, clearly trying to listen to the sounds of our pursuers behind and now mostly to the right of us. They still sounded loud, especially the gunfire and shouting, but I was getting used to the sounds of the jungle, and I could tell they were a good two, maybe even three hundred yards away.

"We're leaving a very clear trail," I whispered to Mike.

"I know." He pulled me down so that I was kneeling beside him and Hollis, then pointed ahead. "Bridge is there," he whispered. "If we go into the water here, they might think we went downstream toward the river."

"We need to leave a false trail a little downstream," I whispered, "as if we came out there and kept going that way."

"Good idea," Dave whispered. "Then we go upstream and under the bridge."

"We need to find out where the guards on the road are," I whispered. "I don't want to wade that stream only to get shot by a guard on the bridge right over us."

"Agreed," Mike said. "Stay here with Hollis. Dave, let's go take a look."

After Mike and Dave had disappeared off into the dark, I touched Hollis on the back. "Better that you sit against the tree. You'll get more air to your lungs leaning back than hunched over like that."

Hollis brushed off my hand, but he did as I suggested, moving until he was sitting with his head up and back against the base of a large teak tree. Massive areas of these mountains had seen the teak trees logged off by the hill tribes. One of the reasons the guides had us camp for the night in this area was because the huge teak trees here hadn't been logged. And now, since they were government protected, they never would be. For the moment, I was very glad they had picked this place. Running and hiding would have been much, much harder, if not impossible, on one of the plantations, or in a logged-out area.

After a moment, Hollis opened his eyes and spoke softly. "You want to tell me why this is happening?"

"I've been asking myself that same question since they started firing at us," I whispered. "I can't answer it. Clearly, they thought we might get them something they wanted—publicity, money, notoriety. Who knows what they were thinking? But now I think they just want us dead."

"But who are *they?*"

"No idea. And I'd just as soon not have the chance to ask them."

But Hollis had brought up something that I, too, had been wondering about. We had been warned by the tour agency about a few remaining bands of opium smugglers working this area of the hill tribes. But, according to the agency, they usually left tourists alone unless somebody stumbled into something they shouldn't see. To the south in Thailand, a radical Muslim group called the Jemaah Islamiah had bombed and kidnapped people on their quest to form a pan-Islamic state across Southeast Asia. But they didn't operate here in the north. This part of Thailand was an up-and-coming ecotourist magnet, one the country desperately needed after the tsunami had wrecked so many of the coastal resorts. It was supposed to be safe.

Maybe our would-be captors' original plan was meant as a signal to the Thailand government that no part of the country was safe anymore from the Jemaah Islamiah. Or maybe the opium smugglers had decided that tourists were in the way, and they wanted the jungles to themselves again. Or maybe our ringleaders were working alone and had decided to collect ransom from the families of "rich American tourists." It didn't much matter now why we had been targeted for kidnapping. Since we had escaped from our erstwhile guides, they clearly wanted us dead.

Suddenly and silently Mike and Dave appeared out of the brush.

"There's a guard a hundred paces down the road from the bridge," Mike whispered. "If we do this quietly, I think we can make it."

"And then what do we do?" Hollis asked.

"We figure that out when we're away from the gunfire," I said.

"Agreed," Mike said. He stood and helped Hollis to his feet. "Stay close to me. And watch your footing on the bank down into the stream."

"Dave and I will set the false trail downstream, okay?" I said. "You and Hollis try to make good time upstream. We'll catch up."

Mike nodded.

Twenty paces later, we eased out of the trees and jungle and into an open area above the stream. In the light of the moon, I could clearly see the log bridge structure spanning the creek.

The slope in front of us was covered with tung buatong flowers that looked amazingly like the wild sunflowers in the States. They bloomed here only in October and November, and earlier in the day, the sight of fields of them was stunning. One guide had told us that the plants stood taller than any man. Because it was night, the blossoms had curled in on themselves, making the hill look like it was covered in pale dots, the bright yellow color of the flowers washed out by the faint moonlight.

Mike started down, disappearing under the flowers almost instantly.

Hollis stayed close behind him, with Dave following him, and me following Dave.

The moment I got into the hillside of flowers, it seemed almost pitch black, as what little light there had been was blocked by the luxuriant leaves and blooms. I put both hands out ahead of me and used them to feel my way, moving downward slowly, making sure of my footing while brushing flower stems to one side or the other.

The entire hill smelled of a thick, green mint. The heavy scent, combined with the heat and humidity, made it even harder for me to breathe. The fragrance was so strong it almost made me choke.

I stayed as close as I could to Dave. Even though I couldn't see him, I could hear him. And every sound that I made sounded loud enough to me to be heard thirty miles back down the road in Mae Hong Son.

Finally I broke out of the flower field on the edge of a stream that seemed to literally roar over the rocks as it fell toward the river. I had spent enough time on rivers over the past few years that the sound of running water actually calmed me.

I stopped and let myself take a couple of deep breaths, clearing the thick mintlike smell of the flowers out of my nostrils. To my left, the wooden underside of the bridge loomed over us, like some ancient monument to a lost deity. They had clearly built the bridge, made of huge logs, a long time ago. I wondered when the last time was that someone had actually been under it.

Mike and Hollis had already waded into the water and were moving upstream, picking their footing carefully.

"You all right?" Dave whispered, glancing back at me.

"Fine."

Actually, I didn't want to think about how I was really doing right at that moment. Who knew how many bugs were crawling on me, how many times I had scratched myself on brush and logs? I did know that the cuts would become infected fast in the heat and humidity if I didn't do something about them. But that wasn't a problem worth worrying about right now.

All four of us were in the same shape, reduced by the threat of death to survival mode.

I glanced at my watch, the luminous dials making it easy to read. It had been just over thirty minutes since we had escaped camp and they had started after us.

It felt longer than forever.

In thirty minutes we had gone from a long-anticipated camping and rafting trip to a life-and-death struggle.

Yes, it seemed much, much longer than that.

Dave turned and eased himself down into the water, making sure of his footing with each step.

I followed, letting the cold water of the creek sweep up around my feet and ankles. The rocks under my boots were slick with moss, rounded after many years of wearing by the water, but it was fairly easy to find good footing, and after another minute or so, I was under the bridge.

Mike and Hollis were a good fifty paces up the streambed on the other side, continuing on. I could tell that Hollis was struggling, but Mike was helping him push forward. Mike knew, just as I did, that we had to go far enough up the stream before leaving it so that it would be difficult for the guys with the guns to track us.

Dave and I turned downstream. About thirty paces later, there was a muddy area on the far side of the creek where it looked like animals came regularly to get water. Above the muddy area was a rock slope that seemed to stretch for a pretty good distance along the river.

I touched Dave on the back and pointed first at the mud, then at the rocks.

He nodded and headed that way. We both climbed up through the mud and then went about thirty paces up the rocks, leaving distinct footprints until the mud was gone from our boots. Then we moved to one side of the rocks, got our boots muddy again, and went back, walking backward on the rocks, retracing our steps to make it seem like four men climbed out of the stream and onto the rocks right at this point.

By the time we got back into the stream, Mike and Hollis were no longer in view. Moving silently, but as quickly as we both could on the slippery rocks, we waded back upstream and under the bridge.

The entire time, I kept expecting to hear shouting from above us, then gunfire. Thankfully, I heard nothing but the sounds of the water cascading down over the rocks.

By the time the bridge had disappeared behind me, my feet were numb and I was having a harder and harder time finding my footing. The hill was getting steeper and the water moving faster as well. At least twice I had ended up on my hands and knees in the icy cold water, its source snowmelt from the high mountains. In front of me, Dave had gone down twice as well. Once he'd bumped his head hard against a rock, scaring me. But he was all right. Just stunned for a moment.

I had used one of my slips into the stream as an opportunity to wash the sweat off my face and some of the bugs out of my hair. The quick bath made me feel a little better, but I was still hesitant to drink any of the water, even though I was incredibly thirsty. Who knew what bacteria lurked in it—but I was willing to bet some of them were unfriendly. I would rather get as high up the stream as possible before drinking. But no matter how high we went, it wouldn't be long until we all wouldn't have a choice but to drink the water. Otherwise our choice would be between certain death from dehydration and possible death from dysentery. I, at least, planned to take my chances on the river.

The creek had turned to the right, blocking any view of the bridge and the road with a good hundred yards of forest and jungle. Ahead, in the darkness, it sounded like there was a monster growling and rumbling in the night. But this sounded like a very familiar monster. More than likely our stream would run us right into a waterfall, and we wouldn't have any choice but to leave the water and maybe try to climb around it if we wanted to keep going higher. I wasn't certain, considering the steepness of the mountains, how much higher we would want to climb. We weren't in shape for it, we didn't have the equipment for it, and it was dark. Mountaineering was not, in my opinion, our best option for escape. But our options were fairly limited. I could only hope we'd find some better way out of this.

Finally we rounded a corner, and ahead of us was a pool with a fairly impressive waterfall crashing into the upper end of it, sending up spray swirling in the faint light. The moon reflected off the surface of the pool, making the opening in the jungle seem almost bright.

I studied the falls and the cliff face it came over. The rock face had to be a good ten stories tall, if not more. No way Hollis was climbing over that. And it didn't look as if there was an easy way around it. It seemed we had backed ourselves up against a wall. I sure hoped our little decoy route worked. Otherwise, we were going to be in big trouble very shortly.

As if we weren't already in enough trouble.

I could see that Mike and Hollis had managed to skirt around the edge of the pool, staying in the water, before climbing out on the other side on some rocks. Hollis was again sitting with his head down, his knees up, the worst possible position to catch his breath. It was clear he was near the end of his rope.

Dave and I splashed around toward our friends. I finally climbed out of the cold water and dropped onto a fairly flat rock beside them. My face and upper body were sweating; my legs from the knees down were numb with cold.

I wanted to ask Mike what we should do next, but the loud roaring of the waterfall made anything but shouting almost impossible. And shouting wasn't a good idea, considering how noise and voices carried in the mountains. I estimated we were no more than a quarter mile above the road. I wondered just how close the men who wanted us dead were.

Mike stood and motioned that I should follow him.

I did, patting Dave on the shoulder as I went and indicating that he should keep an eye on Hollis. He nodded and said nothing.

Mike went back into the water, and I did the same, moving toward the base of the waterfall. As we got closer, I could feel the mist against my face, cooling my skin.

By the time Mike stopped, I was soaking wet from the splashing and spray. He pointed through the edge of the waterfall and then went ahead, staying out of the main thrust of the falling water, but ducking under the edge of it.

I followed him.

The incredible sound of the falls occupied every pore of my body. It penetrated my bones, like an intense vibration, making it hard for me to move, hard to even think.

Somehow, I followed Mike, ducking under the pounding water, letting it hit my head and shoulders like punches from a prizefighter. And this was only the edge of the waterfall. The force of the entire stream in the center of it would crush a car in an instant.

As I stepped through the pounding, it amazingly became

muted, as if the sound from the water smashing into the pool was all directed outward. Behind the waterfall, in the faint moonlight coming through the water, I could see Mike climb over rocks up toward a black shadow behind the falls.

No, not a shadow.

A cave.

There was a cave behind the falls.

My heart leaped.

Now, if it was only deep enough to be dry, and our guides didn't know about it, we might have a good hiding spot.

Mike disappeared from sight ahead of me, and I kept following, carefully feeling my way over the rocks in the darkness. The last thing either of us needed at this point was to twist an ankle or break a leg.

Suddenly I heard a metallic clicking sound up ahead. Mike had lit his lighter, exposing a small opening in the back of the area hollowed out by the waterfall.

With the light to guide me, I joined him. He used his body to shade the light from the sight of anyone below. I sure hoped the waterfall blocked most of the remaining light. It seemed incredibly bright to me after stumbling around in the dark for so long.

As I got to him, he ducked and went into the cave, holding his lighter out in front of him like a torch.

Inside, the cave turned to the left and opened up into a

fairly large area. There were two other tunnel-like exits that seemed to go deeper into the cliff face, but I had no desire to explore those at the moment.

Clearly, at some point in the past, someone else had been in here. There was a very old fire ring near the center of the cave. Mike saw the ring at the same time as I did and held his lighter up, staring at the ceiling. The rocks above me had been charred black by the smoke from a number of fires, and near one side it was clear there was a crack in the roof. A slight breeze flickered Mike's lighter flame.

"I'm going to shut this off for a moment," Mike said, his voice echoing loudly in the cave.

He clicked the lighter closed, and we both stood there in the pitch darkness, waiting for our eyes to adjust.

The sound from the waterfall at the mouth of the cave was a distant rumbling, and my breathing seemed extra loud to my ears.

I could see the opening of the tunnel, faintly outlined in the moonlight coming through the waterfall. In the daylight, that light would be considerably brighter.

Above us, there was no sign of light at all.

"Looks like the good Lord has given us a place to hide in the midst of our enemies," Mike said. "Thank You, God."

I joined in the prayer—I couldn't have agreed more.

4

But certainly God has heard me;
He has attended to the voice of my prayer.
PSALM 66:19, NKJV

7:12 p.m., September 8
Beaverton, Oregon

THE PARTY WAS ONE OF OUR NORMAL GATHERINGS, BUT
I wasn't feeling normal that night. All during the first half of
the Monday Night Football game, I kept going back in my
mind to what Lorraine had said, how she had called my faith
shallow.

Two things bothered me about that comment of hers. After five years together, I had come to trust her judgment. She
had a clear eye for things I sometimes didn't see. She'd saved

me from real trouble more than once. Since then, I had always listened very closely to all of Lorraine's observations. I came to trust them almost more than my own. And this time, she was making an observation about my faith.

Her comment had hit home in some way, but I honestly had no idea why or how. I considered myself a person of faith. I tried to live my life in that manner. Lorraine and I hadn't slept together, and I hadn't slept with any other woman since I met her.

I did good works and went to church. I tried to be the best person I could be. What more was there? Not understanding why she called my faith shallow really bothered me.

At halftime, in the kitchen, Mike turned to me as he dug a soda out of the fridge. "Man, you're a thousand miles away tonight."

I munched on a pretzel while leaning back against my kitchen counter. Dave and Hollis were still in the living room, watching the halftime program and arguing over the chances of Dallas going all the way this year.

"I guess I am," I said. "I'm just thinking about a conversation Lorraine and I had today."

"Lovers' quarrel?" Mike asked. "You're not getting cold feet about the marriage, are you?"

"Absolutely not," I said, not even wanting to think about the idea of not marrying Lorraine. "I wish the wedding was tomorrow instead of next March, to be honest with you. But March works the best for all the families involved, so we're sticking with the date."

"So what's the problem?" Mike asked, dropping down onto a chair in the small kitchen nook that looked out over the barren backyard. Lorraine and I planned to work that into shape next summer, after she moved in and would be here all the time.

I stared at Mike for a moment as he cracked open his soda and dug a chip into one of the containers of dip that Hollis had brought. I considered Mike one of the most devoted men I had ever met, and my best friend. I knew that Dusty and Lorraine could talk at levels of faith that I often found impossible to follow. Maybe Mike could help me understand what I was missing in all this.

"Lorraine called my faith shallow. I'm having a heck of a time figuring out what she meant."

Mike just nodded, not laughing as I had half expected him to, but also not coming instantly to my side as I had hoped he would.

"Is it?" I asked. "You know me better than just about anyone. I live by my faith, I attend regular services, I follow Jesus's teachings. Don't I?"

Mike nodded again. "You do all that."

"So what was she talking about?"

This time Mike did laugh, and I didn't much like the sound of it. Sort of like a parent laughing at a question a child asked that would have no answer the child could understand.

"I'm not so sure I would call your faith shallow," Mike said. "I think a better term for it would be *unrealized*."

"Help me here." I shook my head. "I have no idea what that means."

Mike nodded. "I know. And sometimes, knowledge like this can't be pushed. Lorraine didn't push you in any way, did she?"

"No, she didn't," I said.

"And she won't, either," Mike said. "She knows you enough, trusts you enough, loves you enough to want to marry you. She is going to trust in God to lead you to your complete faith in one way or another."

I went over and dropped down into the chair across from Mike, the one that Lorraine usually sat in while she was in the kitchen with me. It felt sort of weird, actually, to be using her chair. Often, during the evenings, she would sit in her chair and watch me cook while we talked about the events of the day. Or, if she was cooking here, I would sit in my chair and do the same. But despite the familiar place, I felt all shook up inside.

"Not understanding, are you?" Mike asked.

"Not a clue," I said.

"This is one of those many things you just need to trust to God. The answer will be very clear to you when He shows it to you."

"Great," I said. "And until then, I just stew about it, right?"

"No," Mike said. "You don't stew at all. You trust in God."

"Are you two talking religion again?" Hollis asked, coming into the kitchen and heading for the fridge.

Hollis was the least religious of our group, even though he claimed to be a Christian when he was pushed on the subject. "My parents were pillars in the Presbyterian Church," he would say. "They were enough to make me plenty Christian."

Neither Mike nor I had tried to talk any kind of faith with him in years, figuring he would know who to turn to if he needed some questions answered or wanted to shoot the breeze on the subject.

"Not really," Mike said. "Just talking about life in general."

Mike glanced at me. He hadn't lied. What we had been talking about was life. And living life with faith.

"Speaking of life in general," Dave said, entering the kitchen and joining us, "you know we've never gotten around to that really big adventure trip we used to talk about back in college."

"Yeah," Hollis said, "with old John here shackling on the anchor, now we're never going to get to it."

I bristled at anyone referring to Lorraine as an anchor. She was far from that to me. She was a partner and a support for everything I did.

"Lorraine doesn't mind my rafting trips," I said, deciding not to engage Hollis any more than that. As the years had gone by, I was glad he had moved out of the city. The only time I saw him was at these planning parties and on the rafting trips themselves in the summer. He was a nice enough guy, and we had a lot of years of history, but we had grown apart. More specifically, I had accepted Jesus into my life and he hadn't. That difference came up in so many small ways, it was becoming painful to me. I had asked for God's help in bringing him into the fold, but so far the right opportunity had never presented itself to me.

"So, Mike," Dave said, leaning against the island in the middle of my kitchen, "what's a great river we haven't run yet?"

"There are a lot of them," Mike said, smiling at the understatement. "More than we're going to be able to do in an entire lifetime, I promise you."

"Remote," Hollis said. "A real adventure kind of trip, like we used to talk about."

Mike shrugged. "Any of the big rivers in China. Really hard to get to, though. Years of permissions and planning."

"Something we can do soon," Dave said. "A really big one. Who knows? This might be our last big rafting trip."

"Hey," I said. "Just because I'm getting married, it doesn't mean I'm falling off the face of the earth."

"Oh, we know that," Dave said. "But none of us are getting any younger or any lighter."

"I'll drink to that," Hollis said. He took a sip out of his cup and rolled with the jab from Dave like a good boxer.

"That really big adventure we always talked about has just kept getting pushed back and back and back," Dave said. "I don't want to get too old, too busy, or too comfortable to actually do it."

All three of us stared at Dave. Could he actually be suggesting what I thought he was suggesting? I had forgotten all about those nights of planning back in college, the maps, the excitement of thinking about the one river that was as remote from the Pacific Northwest as a person could get.

"Are you talking about the Pai River?" Hollis asked.

"Bingo," Dave said. "When we were still in college, that was about as remote and dangerous a river as we could imagine."

"It still is," Mike said. "There are some rafting companies who take people on the Pai, but those upper canyons are dangerous, the rapids are at least class three, and on the longer trips, you might even run into some class-four water if you don't watch the levels. Different kind of stuff than we're used to out here."

"And, if I remember right," I said, "the season there is from July to January. Any other time and that river's either not high enough or it's too high to run."

"Can we get equipment there, or would we need to haul our own rafts?" Dave asked.

Mike shrugged. "We could get it out there. Not as good as our own stuff, but still professional level."

"Are we really thinking about this?" Mike asked, glancing at me.

"I have to admit, we aren't getting any younger," I said. I knew I could make it. Most of my work for the year had been done, or would be done, by November. I would talk to Lorraine about it, but I was sure she would be supportive. The trip could be sort of a last bachelor blast for me.

"It would be a real kick," Hollis said. "As long as we could go before the snow flies on Mount Hood and I hit my busy season."

Mike looked at me, then at the other two. "That river has always been a dream of mine," he said.

"Could you make it?" I asked him.

"I think so," Mike said. "It would be a good chance for me to get in contact with some of the guides there and set up some business for next year for a few of my customers here. But I would still want to check with Dusty."

"Dave?" I asked.

"Anytime is fine by me."

"It would have to be in the middle of November," Mike said. "Best water."

"Works for me," Hollis said.

"Same here," Dave said.

"I'll check with Lorraine," I said, "but I'm sure I'm fine as well."

"Are we actually going to do the Pai River?" Mike asked, a tone of almost reverence in his words.

"We are," Hollis said, lifting his glass in a mock toast. "To one of the most frightening and remote stretches of whitewater on the planet. Here we come."

We all drank to that, and soon the excited feeling of our college planning days, the days when we'd dreamed of this adventure, were back.

For the first time in a decade, I felt as young as a student again, and free from the shackles of everyday life. Even my worries about my faith were shelved for the moment, overshadowed by my growing excitement about taking the trip of a lifetime.

Of course, I had no idea just how much excitement I was setting myself up for.

5

Be careful—watch out for attacks
from Satan, your great enemy. He prowls
around like a hungry, roaring lion,
looking for some victim to tear apart.

1 PETER 5:8, TLB

12:44 a.m., November 15
Mae Hong Son Province, Northern Thailand

I DUG AROUND IN THE FIRE RING, WORKING AT SEVERAL
charred logs in the dusty soot. It had been a very long time
since fire had been set here. A very, very long time, which
made me feel better about our chances of not being found by
our pursuers.

I had looked through the cave for anything that might

burn while Mike had gone back out through the waterfall to get Hollis and Dave. Using Mike's lighter, I explored a short distance up both tunnels leading off the main room, finding nothing but sand and rocks. The only things fit to burn in the cave were the old charred logs still in the fire ring. With luck, I might be able to get one of them started.

However, I did make a good find about thirty paces up one tunnel. A spring bubbled out of one wall into a small pool, draining out of the cave in some hidden way. Fresh water. And more than likely clear of any parasites after filtering through the local stone.

The cave wasn't cold, but the night still had hours to go yet. A fire to help dry out some of our clothes and give us some light would be nice. Otherwise, we were going to be sitting wet and cold in the dark until daybreak. Which was preferable to being hunted in the jungle, of course. But I was willing to work hard to improve upon our situation.

I went back to digging at the fire ring, working on one log to scrape away the burned wood and to find a place to light the charred surface.

"Good job," Dave said, brushing water out of his hair as he entered the big room of the cave. I had set Mike's lighter open and burning on the rock beside me, so Dave and Hollis could see.

"We're trapped like rats in a cage if they find us here," Hollis said.

"It's not going to matter where we are if they find us," I said. "In here, at least we can stay dry and get warm. And they won't see us easily."

"Or track us," Mike said. "We left no sign that we came in here. Unless one of the guides knows about this cave, they won't think to look behind the waterfall."

"Someone knows this cave is here," Hollis said, pointing at the fire ring.

"It's old," I said. "Probably older than those guides." One of the logs finally broke apart in my hand, exposing unburned wood.

I used Mike's lighter to start a flame up the side of the crumbling log after pulling the other logs to one side for later. We didn't need much of a fire. Just enough to keep the place lit up for a short time.

After a moment, the log was burning, giving the cave a flickering, yellow look, filling the air with the smell of burning wood. The slight stream of smoke from the very dry wood flowed up toward the ceiling and out.

I tossed Mike back his lighter.

"I hope the breeze out there is away from the road," Dave said after watching the smoke disappear for a moment.

"Will they be able to track the smoke?" Hollis asked, dropping onto the cave floor and resting his back against a large stone someone else had used for a seat beside the fire in some long ago time.

"You'd be surprised what some people can track," Mike said. "But it's unlikely. It should dissipate well before it gets outside."

The light crackling off the small fire filled the cave. For the moment we all remained quiet with our own thoughts.

I kept wondering how this had happened, how a simple trip could go so wrong, first in Bangkok and now this. Was this one of God's tests for me that Lorraine and I had talked about? I knew almost getting killed tonight had tested me, that was for sure. And it scared me something awful.

I was pretty sure that the image of dirt being kicked up by a bullet right where I was about to step would be something I would have nightmares about for years to come.

If I lived that long.

But I was equally sure that God had sent me a signal out there. Now I needed to work out what the signal meant. I knew that I felt all alone spiritually. Shouldn't the Lord be with me here, like He was with Daniel in the lion's den? I was beginning to get a handle on what Lorraine meant about my faith being shallow. I really was being tested. God was using my adventures in the wilderness to show me something I needed to know.

I needed to find God. I knew He was here, no matter how far away He seemed from me right now. The flaw was in me, not God. But I also needed to live through this if I hoped to learn my lesson. Maybe it was time to tune in to reality. I turned my attention back to my buddies around the fire.

"Okay," Mike said, "we've got a good hiding place and light now. While it lasts, we need to treat cuts and scrapes, make sure nothing gets infected."

He reached into his pouch and pulled out a small bottle of antiseptic, putting it on the rock beside him.

"You happen to have any water in there?" Dave asked. "Otherwise, I'm about to take a drink from that waterfall."

"You don't need to," I said. I pointed to the tunnel on the left. "There's a small spring back there about twenty steps. Looks like it has fresh water coming right up out of the rocks. I bet it's as pure as water can be."

"I'll test it," Mike said, pulling out of his pouch the small test kit we always took on our rafting trips. Clearly, Mike had been thinking ahead and had snuck into his small pouch whatever survival equipment that he could once he knew we were in danger.

He hadn't alerted the rest of us about the kidnapping plot until we were settling in for the night to sleep because that was the first moment a guide wasn't with us. So we had only taken what we could grab and carry easily as we crept out of camp.

We almost hadn't made it out of camp at all.

At first Hollis didn't believe Mike. It was only when the three of us started to leave him there that he had decided to come along.

In my fanny pack, I had a small bottle of DEET insect

repellant that I hadn't had a chance to put on, some toilet tissue wrapped in plastic, and some Advil in case one of my migraines came on. I'd had a little more notice than Hollis and Dave to pack. But it hadn't done me much good. Too much of what I wanted was trapped in the guides' vans. And my fanny pack was too small.

"I've got an empty bottle in here," Dave said, pulling off his small backpack and digging it out. "Planned on filling it in the morning before we started upriver."

He tossed Mike the empty bottle, and Mike headed toward the back of the cave.

I picked up the small, half-filled bottle of hydrogen peroxide Mike had produced, then ripped a small bit of cloth from the bottom of my shirt. "Dave?"

"Cut on my leg that has me worried a little," he said, pulling up his pants leg to show a pretty good cut indeed, washed clean by the cold water of the stream, but still bleeding slightly.

I treated it, then the other scrapes he had on his arms and neck, then turned to Hollis.

"Nothing to worry about," Hollis said, waving me off.

I could see one pretty good cut on his cheek and another on his right forearm, but I wasn't going to force the issue. I finished taking care of my cuts just as Mike came back and handed me the water bottle.

"Clean as it gets," Mike said.

I took a large drink, then handed the bottle to Dave, who took a drink and handed it to Hollis, who finished it.

"I'll make the trip this time," Dave said, taking the empty bottle from Hollis.

Mike tossed him the lighter, and Dave vanished back into the dark. I handed Mike the bottle of hydrogen peroxide and the small piece of cloth, and he started to treat his own cuts and scrapes.

I pulled off my shirt and twisted it, ringing what water I could out of it. Then I used it like a twisted-up towel to wipe down my back, hoping to knock off all the bugs I imagined were crawling around there. I don't think there actually were any, but I didn't want to take any chances. I hated bugs of all types. Especially mosquitoes.

I flapped out my shirt and laid it over a rock near the fire. The night was warm enough that I didn't need to put a wet shirt back on just yet.

"Man, that's some good water back there," Dave said, emerging from the tunnel and handing Mike the bottle.

"Got enough on my run," Mike said, passing it to Hollis.

Hollis drank about half, then without getting off the ground, made a motion to hand it to me.

"Finish it," I said. "I'll make the next run back."

Hollis nodded and finished the bottle.

Mike flipped me the lighter, and I took the bottle from

Hollis and went back down the tunnel to the spring I had found. I filled the bottle first, downed it, filled it again, then spent a minute washing off my face and hair and arms. After I got back near the fire, I would treat my cuts again, then put on some DEET.

"We got lucky finding this place," Dave was saying as I came back into the larger cavern. The fire was still flickering, burning slowly through the first log. My three rafting companions all looked like silhouettes in the faint light, shadow people in an ancient cave.

Like real cave men, not city guys out of their depth.

The half bath and deep drink of water had made me feel a great deal better. But I sure wasn't feeling lucky at the moment. More confused about why this had happened and scared about what might happen next. *God, I'm in trouble. Where are You?*

"You think we're lucky?" I asked Dave.

"He's right. We are," Mike said. "We're alive, we got enough warning to get out before they had us trapped, and now we've found a decent hiding place. If things had gone like our guides had planned, we'd be in a lot more trouble. God's been watching out for us. But I've been doing some thinking. I think we have to figure out how to get back to Pai and report what happened last night to the authorities."

"Weren't you Mr. Sit-and-Wait-Them-Out Guy?" Hollis asked.

"I was, but I may have been wrong," Mike said. "I'm worried about our lack of food supplies. We can't stay here for long."

"I doubt the guides are going to just let us walk down the road and get help," Dave said.

"Won't they give up by sunrise?" Hollis asked. "There should be some traffic on that road by then."

"Not much traffic," Mike said. "We didn't meet any yesterday. So I doubt the guides are going to go anywhere at sunrise."

I thought back over the ride out from Pai to our first night's camping site. He was right. We hadn't met a car. Not one in over an hour. We had come to this area of Thailand for its rivers and the adventure of it being so remote. One of the most remote places in the world. Now we were paying for that choice.

"Not good," Hollis said, shaking his head in disgust and looking down.

"So we have to get to Pai on our own," I said. "From here, the river runs right into town. How far is it?"

Mike shrugged. "By foot, I'm guessing it's all of thirty miles."

"A bunch of pretty big hills in those thirty miles," Dave said.

"Yeah, going down the river would be our best bet," Mike said.

"And what are we going to do for a raft?" Hollis asked.

"Maybe they've left the camp unguarded," Dave said. "We could dig one of the emergency inflatables out of the supply van."

"I'm not sure we need to take that risk. We could use wood to hold onto if we have to," Mike said. "The river between here and Pai is pretty flat, from what I remember from studying the maps. It has a few class-two rapids and maybe one almost class three. We should be able to body float those if we had to. And walk around the worst ones."

"Surely they're going to be watching for us along the river," Dave said.

"Yeah. It would be like shooting ducks on a pond," Hollis said. "And I'm a pretty big duck."

"Not if we get in at night," Mike said. "And get out of their range by sunup. Remember, the river veers away from the road about two miles downstream. They're not going to get too far from their only escape route."

I had to admit, Mike had a pretty good plan. Only a few major problems with it, of which the biggest would be getting back down the stream and into the river without being seen. The idea of floating in the dark, in a Thai river, with guys with guns hunting me in the nearby woods, didn't thrill me, to say the least. But neither did sitting here until I starved. Or returning to our campsite and getting shot.

"Why don't we just sit in here until someone comes looking for us?" Hollis asked. It looked like he'd been doing some thinking as well. "Seems a bunch safer."

"It's the morning of November 15," Mike said. "We were

scheduled to get back in the van today and head up a side road, then camp tonight about twenty miles higher up the Pai River, then spend tomorrow hiking another fifteen miles higher, then the next two days rafting back into Pai."

In the faint light of the slowly dying fire, Dave and I both nodded.

"Oh," Hollis said. "So no one is even going to know we're missing until we don't show up for our plane flight back to Bangkok."

"Exactly," Mike said. "And even then, I bet it would be a few more days before anyone official would start looking for us, no matter how much our folks back home complained."

"And even if they did look," Dave said, "where would they start? The schedule we gave to the police has us covering a big chunk of northern Thailand."

"I got it, I got it," Hollis said. "Sit here and starve, or get shot going for help. Great options."

The last of the small flame I'd made flickered and went out, leaving the cave lit by only the glowing coals of the one log I had lit. I didn't move to start a second log. It just didn't seem to be worth the effort. And we might need it for later.

No one else moved to restart the fire either.

I eased down to the ground with my back against a rock near the cave wall. I tried to meditate on what God wanted me to learn from this, but my thoughts were filled with Lorraine, and how worried she had been about me going on this trip. Far more worried than she had ever been on any other rafting trip I had ever taken.

Her wonderful, smiling face filled my mind. I so wanted to marry her, create a family with her, plan our future together. Now, sitting here in a dark cave in a remote area of Thailand, that future seemed like a dream.

Trust the Lord, she had told me before I left, after one of our many conversations. *He will be there for you.* If feeling totally bereft and forgotten by God showed a lack of faith, then my faith was indeed shallow.

I closed my eyes and tried to let the Lord in, but all that kept coming to mind was Lorraine's beaming smile, her wonderful honey smell, and the calmness I felt being with her.

That, and the memory of that bullet smashing through the place I was about to step.

6

House and wealth are
an inheritance from fathers,
But a prudent wife is from the LORD.
PROVERBS 19:14, NASB

6:42 p.m., November 10
Hunan Restaurant, Beaverton, Oregon

LORRAINE WALKED INTO THE RESTAURANT, GLANCED
around, then saw me and smiled. I felt like someone had
turned up the lights in the building. Her smile could make me
do just about anything and not care. She had to be the most
beautiful woman I had ever known, both inside and out. I
sometimes wondered what she saw in me. I was just glad she
loved me.

57

She had on a light jacket over a soft sweater and middle-length skirt. Since finishing her degree in political science at the University of Oregon, she had been working as a legal secretary to save enough money to go back to law school the next fall. While she was in school, we planned to rent a cheap apartment in Eugene and come back home to Portland on the weekends. Since I could work from almost anywhere doing the funding grants, we figured it would work out fine, although I had no doubt that by the end of the three years, we would come to hate the two-hour drive between the cities.

"You all packed?" she asked, giving me a kiss on the cheek as I stood to greet her.

"What there is to pack," I said, easing down into my chair across the table from her. "A number of changes of clothes, bug spray, and travel food. Everything else is going to be furnished by the river guides Mike hired."

"Good," she said, nodding and then picking up her menu. "I'm famished."

We came here often, since it was near her office, and I already knew what I wanted. Staring out the restaurant window, I gave her a moment to look.

The final stage of the Portland commute was winding down, and the nightlife and dinner crowds were starting to show up on the streets. I loved Portland, loved just about everything about it, from the fact that it had more acres of parks in the city limits than any other city in the country to the fact that the downtown area was vast, safe, and full of great bookstores and restaurants.

The restaurant we sat in was in the heart of the city, just a few blocks from Powell's Books, and everything around the restaurant felt alive and active. This was a long, long way from a remote river in the northern mountains and jungles of Thailand. It felt odd, somehow, that in four days I would be on that river instead of sitting across from the woman I loved.

Over the past month, since Lorraine and I agreed the trip was something I should take, I had spent a great deal of time reading about Thailand. Bangkok, southern Thailand, and Phuket, the area hit so hard by the huge Christmas tsunami, were the normal tourist destinations. But I came to like northern Thailand the more I read about it.

Remote from anywhere in the world, including the rest of Thailand, the region had vast mountains and angry rivers, elephants working for the tourists, and massive national park areas. All the tourist books I read said it was cooler, far more laid-back than the rest of the country, and just slightly dangerous. When Dave asked Mike about the dangerous part, he had just waved the comment away.

"A number of years back, the king cleaned up all the opium armies running in the north and in the triangle," Mike had said. "Our guides will keep us out of troubled areas. And we won't get near any of the hill tribes that live there."

Chiang Mai, an old capital of an ancient civilization called

Lanna, was the main city in the northern region. We planned on one day and two nights in Bangkok to rest, then a quick fly-in to Chiang Mai, where we would load up in two vans and head north. Since we were doing almost no tourist activities on this trip, I hoped that someday Lorraine and I could go back, maybe after she got out of law school. There were a bunch of things I wanted to see and do in Thailand that there just wouldn't be time for on this rafting trip. Besides, it would be a lot more fun sharing the sightseeing with Lorraine.

When I had suggested it, she loved the idea. Actually, she loved traveling in just about any form. I'd learned that soon after we first met.

She finally put her menu down and smiled at me across the table. "I'm going to miss you."

"I'm going to miss you too," I said. It was a complete understatement. I was already regretting going on the trip because I would have to be away from her for a week. *Missing her* didn't begin to express how I really felt.

Suddenly she got a worried look on her face. "I'll pray for your safety every night."

I stared at her for a moment, trying to read what she meant from the look on her face. She had never said anything like that before any of my other rafting trips. Of course, on those, I wasn't going halfway around the world and then traveling up into an extremely remote area to raft. If something went wrong on the Pai River, help was a long, long way away. I would be praying for her safety too, if our roles were reversed.

"Thank you," I said. "I'll do my best to stay safe."

"I know you will," she said. "I'm just worried."

I reached across the table and touched her hand gently. "I can stay here if you think I should."

She shook her head and smiled. "Of course I want you to stay, but that's just because I'm going to miss you and am feeling selfish."

"Are you sure?"

She nodded. "I'm sure. I just get worried, that's all."

There was something about the way she said that, but before I could respond, the waiter came and took our order.

"So," she said after he left, "you're flying out in the morning, changing planes in Los Angeles, then going direct to Bangkok. Right?"

"Right. I'm not looking forward to that much time in coach, let me tell you. Almost a twenty-hour flight. Ugh." I mimed moving like a Frankenstein monster, which I would undoubtedly be doing for real when I got off the plane in Bangkok.

She laughed and I tried to memorize the laugh so that it would get me through some of the fitful sleeping I was planning on during all those hours in the air.

"Can you call me from Bangkok?"

"I'm planning on it. I've checked with my cell phone

company and my phone will work there, at least in the Bangkok and Chiang Mai areas. Once we head out of Chiang Mai, it won't work."

"So call me from both cities," she said. "And then again when you get off the river and back to Chiang Mai. If you wouldn't mind."

"Mind?" I laughed. "Try to stop me. But the call might have to be at the office, or late at night. We'll be halfway around the world, and in a hugely different time zone."

This time it was her turn to reach across the table and touch my hand. "I keep telling you, I'm a light sleeper. Something you're going to have to get used to in March."

She smiled, and right at that moment, March couldn't get here fast enough for me.

"Thank heavens I don't snore," I said.

She smiled. "And how would you know?"

"I sleep in tents with the guys every summer, remember?" I said. "Hollis snores like he's got a log caught in his throat, and Dave makes grunting snores. Mike says I don't snore, and Mike only makes heavy breathing sounds when he sleeps."

"Are you going to be sharing tents this trip?"

"Nope, the company that's furnishing all the gear says we'll have single-man tents that will be put up ahead of time at each camping site. And they do all the cooking as well, so we don't have to suffer any more of Dave's chili attempts."

Lorraine laughed. "Someday, you're going to have to get

him to cook that chili at a party. I can't believe it's as awful as you describe it."

"Not a chance," I said, remembering the dreadful and never-the-same-twice taste of Dave's chili.

Our dinner showed up about then, and Lorraine and I clasped hands and gave silent prayers of thanks. I also included a silent prayer to keep her safe while I was gone. I might be going into a remote jungle to take on some rough whitewater, but she would still be here in Portland, with all the traffic and things that can go wrong in a big city.

A couple hours later, after a leisurely dinner and a few cups of hot tea afterward, I walked her to her car. There, she kissed me, pushing me back against her car. Then, holding me at arm's length and looking up into my eyes, she said, "Put your trust in God. Listen for His still small voice. He'll bring you home to me."

"I can stay home."

"No. Just remember what I said."

With that, she kissed me again, then climbed into her car and with a wave headed for her apartment up in Northwest Hills on Quincy.

Right at that moment, I almost called off the trip.

Almost.

But by the time I had reached my own car and driven over the hill to my house, I was excited about the trip again, writing off Lorraine's worry as just the natural feelings of a woman in love. I would worry about her as well while I was gone. Of course she would worry about me.

When any couple was in love and apart, that's the way it should be.

Of course, I didn't know then that her advice would provide my only hope of saving my life and my soul.

7

We have this as a sure and steadfast
anchor of the soul, a hope…
HEBREWS 6:19, RSV

1:23 a.m., November 15
A cave in the Mae Hong Son Province

MIKE HAD STARTED THE FIRE BACK UP, BREAKING APART
another charred log to get to the unburned center. The yellow,
flickering light, the cool, but not cold air temperature, and the
smell of a burning campfire made the cave almost comfortable.
Under other circumstances, it would have been idyllic, a great
place to camp and spend the night.

But an overlay of terror sucked the hominess right out of
the air.

I was still shirtless, and my pants were still wet from wading up the creek. I thought I felt bugs crawling on me, even when there weren't any, and after the long day of travel, all I wanted was a safe, warm bed and a long night's sleep. But for me, there could be no sleep tonight. Not with the threat that men with machine guns might come bursting into the cave at any moment.

I worked to breathe regularly to keep the panic I was feeling from reaching any higher. I needed to stay calm to survive this, and to help my friends as well.

And I needed God's help if I wasn't going to freak out. Like Lorraine had told me, I needed to hear the still small voice of my Savior. I prayed, asking for calmness, asking for the safety of my friends, asking for guidance. Asking for Christ to help me through the wilderness and bring me closer to Him.

For what seemed like a long time after Mike got the fire going, we had all just sat in silence. Hollis even started snoring, fast asleep sitting up.

Mike just shook his head and stared at the cave mouth and listened to the low rumble of the waterfall guarding the entrance. I had no doubt that Mike was praying as well.

Dave sat against a rock, also staring at the cave opening. I wasn't sure what he was thinking.

I leaned against the cave wall, staring into the darkness and imagining Lorraine and that wonderful smile and laugh of hers. More than anything, I wanted to be with her right now, instead of afraid for my life, hiding in the dirt. I wondered if she'd had some kind of premonition when she'd worried so about me.

Why was this happening? Why us? Why now? When Lorraine had called my faith shallow, had she known how badly I would need it out here? Speaking of faith, why was God testing us like this? Was I so in need of a lesson in faith that I'd brought this whole thing down on myself?

I knew that was ridiculous. But I also knew that my faith was a factor in how this would affect me if I lived. If ever a time had come in my life to find my way closer to Jesus, it was here and now. Of course, there were no answers for those questions I was asking God. There was only faith. God was with me. It was up to me to find Him and open a door for Him into my soul. I kept my breathing deep and regular, and kept praying, letting my belief in God and the salvation offered by His Son calm me.

I found myself praying for Lorraine's safety at home. I'm not sure why I couldn't ask for help for myself, but for some reason, it seemed wrong. Lorraine's word *shallow* kept repeating itself over and over in my head. So I kept silently praying for my friends and for Lorraine. And I searched for God's love in the wilderness of my soul.

Finally Mike stood, stretched, and glanced in my direction.

"It's really late. We need to get a look at what's going on back in our camp. Maybe sneak in and grab some food and gear if they've left it unguarded."

"I'll go with you," Dave said, pushing himself to his feet.

Mike shook his head as Hollis snorted and came awake, muttering as he often did when someone woke him up.

"John and I will go," Mike said. "You stay here with Hollis. If we aren't back in two hours, work your way down the stream and try for the river."

I pushed myself to my feet and grabbed my shirt off the rock. It was surprisingly dry, considering it was the middle of the night in a cave. I wasn't too excited about the thought of trying to sneak back into our camp, but if Mike thought we should try it, I would follow him. We were going to get pretty hungry by noon tomorrow if we didn't get some food.

Mike tossed Dave his lighter and picked up the water bottle. He took a long drink, then handed it to me to finish. I did, then flipped it to Dave.

"How are you planning to get close to the camp?" Dave asked. "If I were you, I'd go down under the bridge again and try working your way along the road edge in the tree line."

"Actually," Mike said, "I was thinking about moving through the brush on this side of the road to that culvert about three hundred yards below the camp. I figure we can cross under the road there and come back upriver along the road. They won't be expecting us from that angle."

"We might not even have to cross the road," I said, remembering a rocklike bluff across from the campsite. "We might be able to see what's happening in the camp from the other side of the road."

"That's true," Dave said. "Be careful."

"We'll do the best we can, but the whole situation's a mess," Mike said. "If we're not back in two hours, don't wait here any longer. If they get us, they'll backtrack to here and find you guys as well."

"Wonderful," Hollis said, really awake now. "How about we all just sit tight, let them get tired of searching, and then make our break?"

"Because they have too much time to keep searching," Mike said patiently. "And we're going to get hungry."

"Three days before anyone even notices that we're missing," I said.

"Three days from now," Mike said, "we're going to be too weak to hike out of here. They can just wait us out, keep searching, and I bet they know it."

"And I'm not even sure that we can't be traced up that stream in the daylight," I said. "I'm sure we scraped a lot of moss and algae off those rocks under the water."

"I agree," Mike said. "We either have to make our escape or move again."

"Okay, I can see your point," Hollis said.

"Tell you what," Dave said. "While you two are gone, I'll

explore these tunnels. Who knows where they might come out? There's a pretty good breeze flowing through the one with the water."

Mike nodded. "Good idea. Don't get lost." Then he glanced at me. "Ready, John?"

"As I will ever be," I said.

"Good luck," Dave said.

"Yeah, good luck," Hollis said. "I hope the God you two are always talking about is with you. You're going to need Him."

"He's always with us," Mike said, his voice confident.

For once, Hollis didn't make some smart reply.

Then Mike and I headed slowly out of the cave and back toward the waterfall that hid its entrance.

"Stay against the wall to the left," Mike whispered. "You won't get as wet."

I let Mike lead, following him until we were standing on the rocks below the waterfall, looking out over the pool of water. The pounding from the crashing water was so loud that it seemed to make everything vibrate to some primal beat. Amazing how loud it was out here, in the open, and how quiet it was in the depths of the cave behind the falls.

The half moon was now directly overhead, the night clear, with what seemed like a million stars painting the black sky with a silvery glow. Under normal circumstances, I would have just stood and marveled at the beauty of this waterfall and the pool by moonlight. But tonight wasn't anything close to normal; that was for sure.

After a short time, my eyes adjusted and I could see fairly well. I could make out black shapes that were trees and thick darkness that was the jungle around the pond. It all looked frightening and dangerous.

I stood, pushing the fear back and working to get my bearings. Facing where the stream left the pond and then turned to the left, the road was directly below us, running right to left, with the small village of Pai to the right. I guessed we were a good three football fields in distance up the hillside from the road.

A few miles to the left, I knew that the river curved away from the road and turned inland. If I remembered my maps correctly, near there was an intersection of a few buildings called Tha Pai, where a secondary road left the main road and followed the river valley. I had no doubt the men who were after us would be guarding that intersection, figuring we would try for it and the few people who lived there. That had been the direction we had first headed. I was sure they figured we'd be there soon.

I was glad we planned to surprise them.

Mike pointed to the right and I nodded, letting him lead as we waded around the edge of the pond, then left the water, treading carefully on rocks to avoid leaving footprints. We veered right, dropping down into the jungle and moving toward the road.

Being under the trees in the thick foliage of the jungle cut off most of our light. We moved carefully, trying not to make any noise, which was almost impossible considering we couldn't see where we were stepping.

No wind stirred the jungle trees, and now that we were moving, the air felt hot and thick. Branches scratched at my legs and arms and face. I could feel a couple of the scrapes bleeding. Between the injuries and all the bug bites, I itched everywhere.

I tried to ignore it.

For what seemed like an eternity, we moved down the hill, angling all the time to the right. Somewhere in that period of time—one that I was sure I would have nightmares about for years to come—we must have crossed over a shallow ridge and gone down into another stream bed.

"This the stream for the culvert?" I whispered to Mike as we neared the sound of running water. I was fairly certain we hadn't gotten turned around and gone left, back toward the stream coming from the waterfall. Every time I had spotted the moon through the trees overhead, I had used it for a guide, and I figured Mike had done the same.

"It should be," Mike whispered back. "I don't remember another stream crossing under the road between our camp and the culvert I'm thinking of."

"Neither do I," I whispered.

It was amazing the information a simple walk along the road before dinner could give you. I was very glad Mike and I had taken that walk, with one of our guides pointing out different flowers and telling us the names of trees. I wondered if he'd been in on the kidnapping. I hoped not. I had really enjoyed his company.

Mike and I eased into the streambed, then, as silently as possible, we started working our way down the brush-filled valley. We often had to duck under low bushes and overhanging tree limbs. Twice I slipped on the rocks, bumping my knee hard on one fall. I knew it would hurt in the morning, if I lived to see the morning.

I glanced at my watch. We had left the cave around one thirty. It was now a few minutes past two. I had just spent an eternity in a half hour of creeping through the jungle. Amazing how time seemed to warp around what we were doing. We would have to pick up speed if we were going to get into camp, check things out, and then make it back to the cave before Dave and Hollis started for the river.

Finally the stream broke into the open and moved around the bluff face that I remembered being near the road directly across from the camp. The stream ran parallel with the road, more than likely running into another stream near the culvert.

The camp was just on the other side of the dirt road, but both banks of the road were steep and, in this area, impossible to climb without making far too much noise. I could tell we were within a stone's throw of where our tents were.

There were still lights glowing in the camp, but that didn't necessarily mean it was fully occupied. More than likely the glow was from the lanterns the guides had hung in the trees to illuminate the surrounding area.

Mike pointed up the bluff and I nodded, understanding that he meant we should leave the stream and make our way up the rocks through the brush until we could see across the road into our camp.

We started up, this time with me leading, picking my way over the rocks and through the trees and thick foliage as best I could in the moonlight. Every sound I made seemed to be extra loud to my ears. I was sure that if there was anyone in the camp, they could hear our every step, my every gasp. Twice I had to stop myself from holding my breath. The last thing I needed was to pass out while climbing.

We finally reached, from what I could tell, the top of the bluff. Climbing it at night, it didn't seem as tall as I remembered it looking from the road.

The top was almost flat and open in places, like a meadow. The wild sunflowers filled a good part of the open area on top of the bluff, running right to the edge of the trees farther up the ridgeline. The closed-up flowers looked strange in the moonlight, bright dots filling a black field. At least the field would offer us good escape cover if we were seen.

Mike led us around the top of the bluff and to a point where we could lean over a rock and look down. The road was a dark line cutting across under us, and the stream we had been in lay between the bluff and the road. The sounds of the river on the other side of the camp filled the night with low background noise.

Seemingly right below us, far closer than I had expected it to be, was the camp. We must have emerged from the stream right at the camp, hidden only by the banks on the road.

It became instantly clear that we weren't going back in there to get supplies or gear. Three men I didn't recognize, all carrying guns, sat near one fire and our four tents. They seemed to be talking, even arguing, but I couldn't hear anything they were saying over the background noise of the river beyond. They were dressed in black pants and shirts, and they would be almost impossible to see if they were in the dark jungle.

Down the road, between the camp and the bridge, another man with a gun stood on the road, watching carefully. If they had the manpower to spare to keep four guys here in camp, more than likely they had other men on the road in both directions.

Things had clearly settled down after our mad rush from the camp. These guys looked like they were firmly in "wait mode." There was no more gunfire coming from the jungle, at least that I could hear.

"Look to the left of your tent," Mike whispered.

It took a moment before I could make out what he was talking about. Then it suddenly became clear what I was seeing. Crystal clear, even from fifty yards away.

Three bodies, laid out side by side on the ground.

I could see the dark stains on the chests and clothes of two of the bodies. The gunmen hadn't even bothered to cover the corpses.

I wanted to turn away. But I forced myself to stay still beside Mike.

"Dear God," Mike said softly, starting to pray.

I prayed for the families who had lost their loved ones, all the time staring at those corpses, trying not to be sick.

One of the dead men was the guide who had walked the road with Mike and me, talking about the trees and flowers. I remembered him as a nice man. He had told us of his wife and two children in Chiang Mai.

I silently asked God to guard his wife and children, now that their father had been brutally killed.

I recognized another dead man as the company representative that Mike had been working with. He had been nice, friendly, and very smart. He had seemed to love rafting as much as Mike did. The two had talked a lot on the drive to this camp.

Beside me, Mike bowed his head and stared at the rock in front of him, clearly no longer wanting to look at the carnage.

The third dead man looked to be one of the van drivers. He looked young, not more than twenty. I knew nothing about him. I wished I had spent a few minutes with him to learn some details, any details, about his life. I hated it that he had died here and I didn't even know his name.

Mike raised his head, again looking at our camp. Then he whispered, "It seems that not everyone in the company was involved in our attempted kidnapping."

I nodded, not trusting myself to speak yet. But he was right. Either the kidnappers had planned on killing these three men all along, or our escape had somehow caused their deaths.

That thought made me gag. I barely kept the meager contents of my stomach in place.

We both stared at the camp.

"Dear God," Mike whispered finally, pushing himself back from the rock to leave. "Make us worthy of their sacrifice, bless their souls, and guard and help their families."

"Amen," I said softly. For the first time, I felt God's hand on me there in the jungle, felt it in a small thread of peace in my soul.

But I still hoped that no one would have to say the same words over me anytime soon.

When He came to the place, He said to them,
"Pray that you may not enter into temptation."
LUKE 22:40, NKJV

7:40 p.m., November 12
Bangkok, Thailand

JUST AS I EXPECTED, I FELT AS IF A BIG TRUCK HAD USED
me as a parking space by the time we climbed off the plane in
Bangkok. Three movies, two books, and a lot of sleeping to
cover the twenty hours. All the while, I kept coming back, over
and over again, to being excited at the idea of seeing northern
Thailand and the Pai River. I knew the river adventure would
be worth the long trip, if we could just get through the travel
adventure first.

In the seat beside me, Mike had talked at times like a kid. He was very excited about his dream from college finally coming true, even if it was well over a decade later. Though the plane flight was the longest I had ever taken, I had to admit, Dave's idea was a good one. I was excited to finally do this before we all got too old or set in our ways to make it possible.

However, I was beginning to doubt the sanity of flying so far on such a tight schedule. Even with only one day of rest in Bangkok, we were still going to be gone from home for over a week. Neither Dave nor Hollis could handle any more time than that away from their jobs. So that left us just enough time to rest after the flight, get to the river, spend three days on the river, travel back to the airport, and get home. Nothing else. Halfway around the world, and we hadn't even budgeted sufficient time for sightseeing in Bangkok.

And the trip home would be even more grueling, considering that we would be tired to start with after coming off the river. We were scheduled to spend our final half day on the river. After that, we would drive into Chiang Mai, catch a flight to Bangkok where we would have a three-hour layover, board a flight to Los Angeles where we would have another three-hour layover, and finally catch a flight to Portland. Very, very tight schedule. I knew that even the slightest misstep in our trip could set us adrift into a travel nightmare.

As we followed the crowds toward customs, I studied everything around me. The airport itself looked fairly new, with high, well-lit ceilings, sweeping grand architecture, and bright colors everywhere. The crowds were thick and ethnically mixed, with Western and native Thai dress being the two predominate styles. The noise level of this modern airport seemed very high, as thousands of people flowed and talked and laughed around us.

Somewhere, someone was cooking a wonderfully fragrant garlic dish, and that smell mixed with an incense smell in a very nice and subtle way I had never imagined possible.

The airport felt alive, the center of many things, as thousands and thousands of people's lives crossed paths. I wondered if all of Thailand would feel the same. I had a hunch it would.

I began to feel excitement and anticipation.

We made it through customs without a problem, then got our luggage and hiked to the check-in desks to confirm our return flight back to the States. You had to do that at least seventy-two hours ahead of your flight, and at seventy-two hours ahead of our return flight, we would be fighting whitewater on the Pai River. So we had decided to just do it as soon as we arrived.

After that, we trekked what seemed like three miles through the airport, dragging our luggage along with us, to find the domestic Thailand flights area of the giant terminal. We wanted to check in with Thai Airways International to make sure our flight to Chiang Mai in a day was still booked. It was.

So everything seemed set to go. Now, a day of rest loomed

ahead, and as far as I was concerned, I would crash and sleep through just about every moment of it. My poor jet-lagged body was deeply convinced it was the wee hours of the morning, despite the fact that it wasn't even eight at night according to local time.

We ended up hiking another half mile to find a shuttle to our hotel. If nothing else, this airport would get me into good shape just from all the exercise I got dragging our luggage through it. After sitting for most of twenty hours, the first mile I walked actually felt good. But I felt sorry for Hollis. Not only had he packed more than the rest of us, but he was in the worst shape to begin with.

As we stood waiting for the shuttle, I thought back over our very long trip. We'd spent two hours waiting in the Portland airport before our first flight, two-plus hours flying to Los Angeles, then another four hours waiting there, then twenty hours en route to Bangkok, two hours getting through the airport, then finally another shuttle ride to the hotel. After our day of rest in Bangkok, we still had an hour-and-a-half plane ride and a four-hour van ride to get to our hike-out point on the Pai River. I felt thankful we would be camping halfway through the four-hour drive on the first night.

I had tried to prepare myself for all this travel, but at the moment, as we crowded into the shuttle, I had been moving for almost thirty-two hours, and I could feel every minute of it. That kind of grind was almost impossible to prepare for. My body felt tired to the bone, and my mind had a foglike cloud over it. All I wanted was a good dinner and a warm bed.

How international travelers who did this all the time got used to it was beyond me. They had to be superhuman.

Dave and Mike looked to be in about the same shape I was in—functioning but exhausted. Hollis looked awful. He hadn't said much since we got off the plane, and he looked as beat as I had ever seen him look. None of us were young anymore, but clearly Hollis's weight and age were taking the worst toll on him.

Our hotel, the Comfort Suites Airport, was reasonably close to the airport in Bangkok terms. We had decided that it would be the best since our main purpose was rest, not sightseeing. And we had to be at the airport very early for our Chiang Mai flight. No point in fighting the city traffic in and then back out to the airport if we didn't have to. I felt bad about possibly not getting into Bangkok proper, but at the moment I was very glad Mike had gotten the hotel he had. Even though it was after eight in the evening, the roads I could see looked jammed with traffic.

Maybe the next day we could all take a trip into the center of the city and do a little sightseeing. Then I could get a sense of where Lorraine and I should stay, and what we could do on our own trip here.

The Comfort Suites was also cheap enough to allow us to all have our own rooms. Mike thought that was a good idea to speed up getting ready in the morning of the flight out, and to allow us all a little privacy before being close together in tents and on rafts for three days.

Walking into the hotel room made me feel as though I hadn't left the States. Except for a few local decorations, the room looked like most hotel rooms I had stayed in. It was fairly big, with a decent bathroom and shower, and it had satellite television. The sign on the small desk in my room also told me there was a pool and sauna on the main level. Maybe tomorrow morning those might come in handy. But right now, all I wanted was a quick shower and a good dinner. Perfect relief after that many hours on a plane.

We got checked in without problems, then decided to meet for dinner in thirty minutes. I thought about calling Lorraine as I got into the room, but decided I would call her after dinner, when I would have more time to talk, and it would probably coincide with her lunch break, giving her more time to talk as well.

The man at the front desk of the hotel recommended a restaurant called Scala Shark Fin. He said we had to try the Chinese soup delicacy, if nothing else.

Hollis looked like he was in much more jovial spirits after a shower and said, when asked about the choice of restaurant, "How often are we going to get to Bangkok? Let's go for it."

So we did.

On the way to the restaurant, I studied the surrounding area. It felt very suburban around the airport, with freeways and lit streets. The architecture was subtly different from the States, the terrain different, but the area near the airport could have been just about any Western city in Europe or North America.

The restaurant wasn't that far from the hotel. The cab driver dropped off the highway and twisted into an older neighborhood, something that must have been a village long before Bangkok grew around it. Suddenly the entire feel of the place changed. The streets got narrow and foot traffic heavy, with people walking both on the sidewalks and in the streets.

The restaurant was a quaint hole-in-the-wall place in what looked to be an older section of buildings. Shark fins filled all the windows along the street. The restaurant was small, with no more than ten tables lined up along one wall. A dozen people were seated, and they all stared at us as we came in, as if we had invaded some private place where we didn't belong.

I liked the shark fin soup but not enough to go out of my way for it again. Everything else was very close to what I got in a good Thai restaurant Lorraine and I visited all the time in Portland. Only in Bangkok, the portions were bigger. Far more than I could eat.

"How about we get a cab and see some of the sights on the way back to the room?" Hollis asked as we left the restaurant and started down the street toward a busy intersection. "At least take a drive through the city."

"Tomorrow," Mike said.

Dave and I agreed. Hollis didn't say anything, but he didn't look happy.

For some reason, that bothered me. Clearly, he had caught a second wind after eating and was eager to see some of the Bangkok nightlife. More power to him. All I wanted was a good night's sleep.

He shared a cab back to the hotel with us but then in the lobby told the rest of us to go ahead. He wanted to walk around a little. We set a time to meet for breakfast, a very early time, to keep us on schedule for the following morning, then headed for our rooms.

The last I saw of Hollis, he was striding toward the hotel bar.

A short time later, when I called home, I told Lorraine my concerns about Hollis and how they made me uncomfortable.

"Pray for him," she said. "If he decides to let loose, Bangkok will test him."

At breakfast the next morning, it became very clear she was right. He didn't show up.

9

Wisdom or money can get
you almost anything,
but it's important to know that
only wisdom can save your life.

ECCLESIASTES 7:12, NLT

2:21 a.m., November 15
Mae Hong Son Province, Northern Thailand

MIKE AND I MOVED AS SILENTLY AS WE COULD AWAY FROM
the bluff face and our old camp, through the field of wild sunflowers. We headed directly away from the road up the ridgeline. Neither of us said a word as we worked our way along in
the faint light from the half moon.

I was in a daze. I couldn't seem to clear my head. Between having the men shooting at us earlier as we ran and seeing those bodies lying there in our camp, I felt overwhelmed. I was more afraid than I had ever been at any other time in my life.

I kept coming back to the question of why this was happening to us. There just wasn't a good answer. Not that I could see, anyway.

After moving up the ridgeline for a least two football fields' worth of distance, we turned back to the left, moving down, crossing the water and then climbing back up the other shallow side of the valley until we reached the stream we had originally waded up from under the bridge. We eased into the water again and followed it up to the pond and waterfall, ducking behind the falls.

"It's us," Mike said after we got through the pounding water and into the front of the cave.

"Thank God," Hollis said.

As we entered, the smell of the campfire, the faint orange light, and the warmth of the cave felt welcoming. Too bad it wasn't a safe place to stay. I had no doubt that at first light, those men would be tracking us. And they were bound to find this cave. We had just left too much evidence in our trek through the jungle.

Hollis was sitting where we had left him, facing the barely burning log. He looked relieved to see us. I could only imagine how long the last hour must have seemed to him, sitting here alone, thinking someone might come and kill him at any moment.

"Dave's not here," he said. "He went down that tunnel right after you left and hasn't come back yet."

I glanced at my watch. We hadn't been gone a complete hour. Time warp again. We'd moved a lot faster than I thought we had, that was for sure.

"We'll give him a little while before we go looking for him," Mike said, slumping against a rock and facing the cave mouth. My best friend looked just about as tired and broken as I had ever seen him look.

I went back to where I had been sitting earlier against the cave wall and dropped to the dirt. I knew how Mike was feeling. The images of those dead men blotted out everything I looked at. It would be a sight I would never forget.

And I couldn't shake the feeling that we had been responsible for their deaths. Maybe, if we hadn't escaped, they would be alive now, held prisoner with us.

Of course, if those men had been killed so easily by our pursuers, there was no telling what would have happened if we hadn't made a break for it. Maybe they would be dead either way, regardless of what we did.

And maybe we would all be dead as well. I had watched enough of the news over the past few years to know that people who resorted to kidnapping for any reason were not usually compassionate to their captives. Maybe the whole point of the exercise was to just kill us all in the first place. Then our bodies would have been lying there on the ground beside the others. And our captors would be celebrating their success, instead of hunting us.

I bowed my head, closed my eyes, and tried to drive the image of those bodies from my mind. I had to stay calm and trust God. Panic would only get in my way. I needed to think, and think clearly, if we were going to get out of this cave, this jungle, alive. And I needed God's help to do that.

"So, did you get into the camp?" Hollis asked after we sat down.

Mike didn't answer him, so I eased my head up and looked at the man I called a friend, but I was fast running out of patience with him during the course of this trip. "Give us a moment. We'll tell you and Dave, when he gets back, all about it."

"I'm back," Dave said, appearing out of the tunnel. "Didn't expect you two to make it back ahead of me."

"Is there an opening that way?" Mike asked, looking up, beating me to the question by a half second.

"There is," Dave said. "The tunnel curves and winds for about five hundred or so paces past the spring. A couple of big rooms back in there as well. Real big."

"Any place good to hide?" Hollis asked.

Dave shook his head. "Nope. Nothing. The tunnel finally comes out into a big cavern with a large entrance leading out and into the jungle. The brush has grown up around the entrance, but there's a trail, and a number of people have been in the cave camping. From what I can see, some have been there fairly recently. I saw aluminum cans from some kind of local soda."

Mike nodded and didn't say anything.

I felt even more disappointed than I had before, if that was possible. Having a fairly well-known cave attached to this one was not a help to us. Now, for sure, they would find some part of the cave system. But at least it would give us a way to have our tracks come into here and not out again, beyond the tracks Mike and I made down toward the camp. That might be enough to help confuse whoever might track us in the morning.

It all depended on what we decided to do next. I had no real idea what plan would be best. We were a long way from civilization. We had purposely put ourselves here, for the thrill of it. Well, I was finding this all very thrilling. But not in a good way. For my next trip, I wasn't likely to go anywhere more thrilling than Orlando.

"So what happened in the camp?" Hollis asked again.

Mike glanced at me, clearly not wanting to tell them.

I decided to just blurt it out. "Three men with guns are in our camp. They don't look like they plan on leaving any time soon."

"Great," Hollis said, disgusted. "Just great."

If he thought that was bad, he really wasn't going to like the news I told him next.

"There was something else, wasn't there?" Dave asked, looking first at Mike, sitting with his head down, then at me.

I nodded. "Yeah. They had a guy guarding the road. He was new, too, and he looked like he knew what he was doing. We saw no signs of the men who came after us. They were probably still out there looking. Along with who knows how many more of their friends. But they'd left victims behind. The driver of the equipment van, the representative of the tour company, and one of our guides have been killed."

"Killed?" Hollis asked, his voice a shout that echoed in the cave.

"How do you know that?" Dave asked.

"Their bodies are lying beside our tents," I said, seeing the image as fresh in my mind as if I were back on that bluff again. "They were shot. We could see the wounds."

Dave dropped to the cave floor near the fire, shaken and clearly trying to wrap his mind around what I had been saying.

"We're going to die as well," Hollis said, the sound of panic ripping at the edges of his voice.

"Not necessarily. We're not dead yet," I said.

"We're hiding in a cave in a jungle. We don't know anything about jungles," Hollis said, almost spitting the words at me. "Those guys tracking us have all our gear. They know what they're doing and where they are. We're as good as dead."

"No!" Mike stood, his short and powerful frame seeming to dominate the cave as he took a step toward Hollis. His one word echoed around the cave. "We are far from dead. More than that, we have a responsibility here. Those men need to pay for what they did down there. They have to be stopped before they can hurt other innocent people. So we have to get out of here and report this."

Hollis started to open his mouth to say something, then looked at Mike and clearly thought better of it.

Mike stood there, glaring at Hollis.

"All right," Dave said. "So we know now, without a doubt, that these men are killers."

"That's right," I said. "And I'm pretty sure that they intend to kill us on sight. They don't dare let us live with the others dead. It's a long shot that they may want us alive for a little while, depending on what they had planned for us in the first place. But they're not going to let us go, not ever. Our escape either changed or sped up their plans, if they merely wanted to kidnap us for ransom."

"Great, just great," Hollis said.

I considered his words and his attitude. He'd not added one useful contribution to our efforts from the moment things went wrong. I prayed for patience.

Mike kept standing, staring at Hollis. Hollis had been wearing thin on me for years, and now, after Bangkok, I was tempted to let him just fade away into his own sordid and disgusting life. It looked like Mike was facing the same temptation. Not a Christlike attitude, but understandable under the circumstances. There are times when turning the other cheek gets hard to do.

But first, we had to make plans. If I was going to give in to my base desire to shun Hollis for the rest my life, I had to make sure we had lives to live.

"If we're going to make the river tonight," Dave said, "we had better get started now. But I can tell you this much, I'm not looking forward to going down that stream right through where they are looking for us. How about we pick another stream?"

Mike nodded, but didn't move.

Suddenly a plan of escape formed in my mind, complete and possibly even good enough to get us out of here alive.

"I think we should go through the cave," I said, "out the other side, and stay as close to the mountains as we can, working our way toward Pai, staying in the jungle."

"Doing that all the way to Pai?" Dave asked.

"Why not? We still have some time before sunrise. We could get some pretty decent distance between us and them if we start soon. It's going the one way they won't be expecting us to go, in a way they would never expect us to try."

Mike glanced at me, then sat back down on a rock. "It's a good twenty miles as the crow flies to Pai. That journey will be a lot longer, and a lot harder, if we stay in the hills and jungle."

"We rest a lot," I said. "We get farther away from here. Then, if we have to, we find a stream, head down it to the river and float the rest of the way."

"Won't they be watching the river for just that?" Dave asked. "I'd hate to be in that water in broad daylight with someone with a machine gun firing at me from the shoreline."

"We only float at night," Mike said. "And I agree with John. We only hit the water if we have to. It's exactly what they'd expect us to do."

I glanced at Hollis. "You think you can make the twenty-plus miles?"

"I can make it," Hollis said. "Beats sitting here in the dark waiting to get shot."

"That I agree with," Dave said.

Mike stood and moved toward the fire. "Let's get started, then."

Mike took the old fire log we hadn't used yet and knocked a bunch of the old charred surface from it as Hollis stood and backed away from the fire, watching Mike like he had gone insane.

I knew what Mike was doing. He was making sure that in our march through the jungle, we would have some dry firewood if we needed it to start a fire. The deadfalls in the jungle would probably be too wet to use for kindling. The log, after a little banging, turned out to be about the size of a rolled-up newspaper. He handed it to Dave. "This fit in that daypack of yours?"

Dave took it, nodding. "I even have some plastic to wrap it in. Good thinking."

"You got my lighter?" Mike asked.

Dave flipped it to him. "It's starting to get low on fuel, but there should be enough to get us through to the other cave."

"We need to stop and drink all we can on the way past the spring," I said. "Then fill up the water bottle."

"Everyone make sure you get all your stuff, and smooth out any footprints in the loose dirt," Mike said. "Then head for the tunnel. I'll go out last, clean up any signs we've been here, put out the fire, spread it around."

I grabbed my fanny pack, made sure the small bottles of antiseptic and DEET were still in it and that it was closed up tight, then strapped it onto my waist, turning it around so that it was out of the way in the small of my back.

Dave and Mike did the same with their packs. Then, with Dave leading, we eased our way into the tunnel as far as we could go with the faint light coming from the cave entrance and the fire.

"Ready?" Dave said, as Mike did a quick check of the cave and then went to the fire.

I stood just inside the tunnel entrance, watching him. Part of me didn't want to leave this cave and the false sense of safety it gave us. But another part of me, a much larger part, knew that right now I was starting the trip home to Lorraine. That's what I had to do. The key now was surviving the voyage home.

Mike dumped what was left of the water out of the bottle on the fire, then picked up the log by the unburned edge and tossed it behind a rock near the back of the cave. He spent a moment there, burying it under some dirt, then he went back to the fire ring.

He kicked the ashes around the cave, broke up the ring some, then smoothed out his boot prints. By the time he was finished, the cave was filled with smoke and dust, but in a few hours I knew it would be hard for most people to tell if campers had been there recently or long before.

Mike flicked on his lighter, and I turned and started into the dark tunnel. I took my first steps toward home, Lorraine, and the life I wanted to live with her.

And I would trust God to get me there.

10

No one who is born of God will continue
to sin, because God's seed remains
in him; he cannot go on sinning,
because he has been born of God.

1 JOHN 3:9

6:10 a.m., November 13
Bangkok, Thailand

AFTER TEN MINUTES OF WAITING AROUND IN THE LOBBY
of the hotel for Hollis to show up for breakfast, we decided to
just go on without him. We figured he was tired from the trip
and had overslept and that it wouldn't hurt to just let him sleep
for another few hours.

I didn't blame him, actually. I had gotten a good night's

sleep, but my mind still felt like it was tagging along about two steps behind my body. I was trying not to think about what time it really was back in Portland. The fifteen-hour time jump ahead made that hard to figure, and my head hurt when I tried.

I'd had a wonderful talk the previous night with Lorraine. I used my cell phone and didn't even mind the cost. I knew the twenty-minute call would be expensive, but the cost would be worth it. Just talking to her made me feel right, as if it didn't matter that I was halfway around the world; we were still together in mind and spirit and in God's eyes.

She told me a little about her day, just as she always did, and I told her a little about the flight and the shark fin soup. Then we talked for a while about how much fun it would be for the two of us, with lots of time, to make this trip, not for the rafting, but to see the wonderful sights and places this country had to offer.

"And swim at the beaches," she had said. "I hear there are some wonderful, white sand beaches there in the south that are open for business again after the tsunami. I'd love to sit on a beach with you."

"Well, it's certainly warm enough," I replied. "Imagine a hot summer day in Florida, then add some, and you have the temperature and humidity here."

"And this is the cool time of year where you are," she reminded me.

"We're not coming back in the hot time," I said, grinning. We had laughed, talked a little more. She told me that she'd been praying for me, and those simple words gave me comfort this time instead of worrying me. I told her that she had been in my prayers, too. We signed off with a mutual "I love you."

The moment I hung up the phone, I missed her again.

I had laid my head back on my pillow and the next thing I knew, my alarm was going off. I hadn't even bothered to get undressed beyond slipping off my shoes. I had been that tired.

For breakfast, we went over to the Asia Airport Hotel coffee shop, which turned out to be both similar to and different from any coffee shop I had ever been in. It had the feeling of a standard hotel coffee shop, with booths and tables with nice chairs. But I could order not only such standards as hash browns and eggs but also just about any Thai dish as well as a dozen Chinese and Japanese dishes, some of them quite exotic to my American eyes. Pickled duck feet, for example, were not what came to my mind when I thought of breakfast.

Frighteningly enough, all three of us settled for basic American food. I promised myself I would get more adventurous for lunch, and really try some new things at dinner. But for breakfast, to get my body caught up with the time shift and to feel at home here, I had oatmeal and raisins, an order of wheat toast, and a cup of regular coffee.

The breakfast was enjoyable, as was our conversation about the Pai River. The three of us studied a few maps of the better rapids, which Mike had brought along, then grabbed a cab back to our hotel, deciding that all three of us should roust out Hollis—get him up for a little trip into Bangkok proper. We had been told the ride into town on the hotel shuttle was at least an hour long in the middle of the day. So we planned to do a ride in, some sightseeing, lunch, a little more sightseeing, and then return to the hotel area for dinner and a good night's sleep.

I liked the idea of it all, right up to the point when Hollis answered his door after we pounded on it for a while, ignoring the Do Not Disturb sign.

"Sorry I overslept," Hollis said, standing behind the door with it cracked just enough so that he could look out. The room behind him was dark, the blinds pulled shut. His eyes were bloodshot, his hair not combed, and there was a smudge on the side of his cheek.

I could tell Hollis was upset. Actually, very upset.

"You all right?" Dave asked, clearly seeing the same thing I was seeing.

"Fine," Hollis said. "Tell you what, give me a half hour and I'll meet you all in the lobby." The door came open a few more inches as Hollis adjusted his stance.

"Half an hour it is," Dave said. We all started to turn away, when a woman's voice, speaking Thai, came from the room behind him.

We all froze in our tracks, staring at the red face of Hollis peeking out of his hotel room door. Behind him, we could now see the shape of a female form on the bed under the sheets. As we watched, she sat up and looked at us, her eyes wide.

"For heaven's sake, did you forget about Susan so quickly?" Mike said, the anger in his voice clear. "And look at her. She's young enough to be your daughter! What were you thinking?"

"Is it any of your business?" Hollis asked angrily.

"Yeah, it is. You are my friend, and I care about you and the state of your soul."

"Well, I was thinking about how good it would be to get away from my too-righteous friends," Hollis said.

Mike was too angry to speak any further. He spun away from Hollis and stomped down the hall.

I could not believe what I was hearing and seeing. It was almost too much for me to even imagine. I had come to accept that Hollis lived in sin with Susan because he had issues about marriage, issues that he'd grow out of with time and love. He clearly loved her and would eventually marry her, I figured.

But this was adultery. Or fornication. Or worse. Whatever it was, it was wrong. And Hollis wasn't willing to admit it.

I knew that God would forgive anything if the sinner came to Him in contrition asking for forgiveness, but it didn't look like Hollis was ready to even hear that, much less admit he needed to ask for forgiveness.

The woman spoke again from behind Hollis, and a light flicked on in the room. I got a clear look at her—and I would never forget her face.

Dave stood there, staring at Hollis. Finally he said, "You're an idiot, you know that?"

Then he turned and followed Mike.

Hollis looked at me.

"Deal with this. We'll talk when I can calm down," I told him. Then I, too, walked away before I could say something I might regret.

"Let's just go into town," Mike said to me as I reached the elevator area and waited for it to come. "Clearly Hollis is too busy."

"You're going to just leave him here at the hotel?" Dave said.

"I don't think he's ready to talk sense just yet," Mike said. "Can't preach to deaf ears. And I'm in no mood to preach, anyway. I'm angry, and I'll say the wrong thing. Speaking of that, what am I supposed to say to Susan the next time I run into her?"

I didn't say anything. Mike was doing just fine expressing my feelings at the entire situation.

"Come on." I touched Mike's arm gently. "Let's go into the city and get some lunch and think about what to do next after we calm down."

"Yeah," Dave said, "Hollis is an idiot, but that doesn't mean we should let him spoil this trip for the rest of us."

"You don't understand," Mike said, facing Dave. The level of his voice was low and intense. "The very essence of my belief, everything about the person I am, tells me to stay away from people like Hollis, people who would even *consider* doing what he did last night in God's presence, let alone actually doing it. But I know that it's my job to minister to him. And I'm too angry to even try right now."

"You've known who he was for years," Dave said.

"True," Mike said, shaking his head. "And that was my mistake. I've been closing my eyes to his lack of faith, his poking fun sideways at my God, because we've been friends for a long time. I should have seen how weak he was. And done something about it. I should have seen this coming."

"It's not your fault," Dave said as the elevator doors opened and all three of us stepped on board. "You're not your brother's keeper."

"Oh, but I am. Remember what God said to Cain when he said he was not his brother's keeper? And remember Galatians 6? 'Brothers, if someone is caught in a sin, you who are spiritual should restore him gently. But watch yourself, or you also may be tempted. Carry each other's burdens, and in this way you will fulfill the law of Christ.' Right now I'm finding it hard to forgive myself, much less Hollis. Of course, it's not my place to forgive him. It is God's."

"And it's God's duty to judge him too," Dave said, surprising me. Dave rarely talked about his faith or his knowledge of God, yet I had always had a hunch he lived a faithful, God-filled life.

I could see that Mike was slowly getting angry, not at

Dave, but at himself. But I saw that the anger was going to come out at Dave if I didn't stop it.

"Maybe this is the opportunity you've been waiting for," I said. "Maybe we should reach out to Hollis, help him see the error of his ways."

"He won't listen," Mike said. "And I'm in no shape to do it right now."

Mike's words shocked me. Jesus said we should love and forgive all sinners. Although, He also showed us there was a time for anger. After all, He'd been angry when He threw the money-changers out of the temple.

Was this the test Lorraine had known was coming? She had always been polite to Hollis, but she'd kept her distance from him. Had she always seen him for who he was? Why hadn't she told me?

"Let's just play it by ear," Dave said.

I put my hand on Mike's shoulder before he could say anything. "Let's head into the city, find an interesting-looking, but not dangerous, place for lunch, and talk about it there."

Mike glanced up at me, then nodded his head. "After we've all calmed down, right?"

"All three of us," I said, glancing at Dave.

Dave, who didn't usually show strong emotion, was clearly as upset as Mike and I were. He nodded, then said, "John, always the peacemaker."

"At this moment," I said, "that's a good thing."

We stood in silence as the elevator moved toward the ground floor.

I felt the same way as Mike, but clearly Mike was taking the actions of Hollis much more personally than I seemed to be doing.

I was disgusted and angry at Hollis. Yes.

And my faith and beliefs would never allow me to do what Hollis had done, even if I were here alone, even without Lorraine waiting for me at home. I never would have even considered it. Or even thought about it.

What kind of person could do such a thing?

I was furious with Hollis for putting us through this, almost as furious as I was that he'd gone looking for temptation last night. And had given in to it. I was finding it hard to forgive.

But there had to be a way to deal with this situation that would bring us all, even Hollis, closer to God. I silently asked the Lord to help me find the new path, one that would bring us closer to salvation.

11

For I the LORD thy God
will hold thy right hand,
saying unto thee,
Fear not; I will help thee.

ISAIAH 41:13, KJV

2:35 a.m., November 15
Mae Hong Son Province, Northern Thailand

I GAVE A SHORT PRAYER FOR OUR SECURITY AS WE
stepped out of the cave mouth and into the jungle, turning
right, heading in the general direction of the distant village
of Pai.

The moon was still high in the sky, the stars bright. Except
when we were under trees and in deep brush, they gave us
enough light to see by.

Mike was in the lead, moving carefully, picking the best trail he could, trying to walk on places where our footsteps wouldn't show. Dave was behind him, then Hollis, then me. We walked in a line, single file, to keep the size of the trail we left to a minimum.

In the cave entrance, we had stopped for a moment and adjusted our plan a little. We had decided to go through the jungle a mile or so, then work down a stream toward the road. I had suggested that change because I was afraid we might find ourselves heading up the wrong valley, working our way more toward the northern border than toward Pai. As long as we kept the road and the Pai River close, we were both in danger and on the right track. So we had decided to use the road as a guide, checking it every mile or so, then going back into the jungle and continuing on foot.

Within a half mile, Hollis was breathing hard, and we decided to stop and rest, sitting on some rocks. We had gone down into one streambed, back up over a ridge, then down into a second. We were resting on the top of another ridgeline. The going was hard and slow, but at least we were moving, trying to save ourselves instead of sitting and waiting for them to find us.

No one said a word. At this point, there wasn't much to be said.

When we stopped, we passed around the bottle of water, finishing it off. At the next stream, Mike said he would check for bacteria, and we would drink again and fill the water bottle if the stream was safe enough. I had a hunch that most of these streams we were crossing were spring fed by the mountains above us and were clean enough. And if we couldn't find a safe stream, eventually, if enough time went by, we would just have to drink and take our chances.

I had seen rafters airlifted off of rivers to emergency rooms after not listening to their guides' instructions to filter their water or otherwise make sure it was safe before they drank it. Modern humans just don't have the right immune defenses for the bacteria that lived in streams and rivers these days. Compared to our ancient ancestors, we were pitiful weaklings. After drinking safe, pure water for a few generations, a single sip of unfiltered river water with the right bugs in it could knock a healthy American flat on his back in less than twelve hours and could kill him if he wasn't able to get medical help fast enough.

We didn't dare take that chance. We were better off going thirsty for a day or so, because someone on his hands and knees loudly retching his guts out made a very easy target for men with machine guns.

I glanced at my watch as we started again: 3:10 a.m. We still had a few hours until sunrise, and we needed to make the most of those hours.

We finished our rest break, then went over the hill and down to a small stream cutting through the jungle. With the flame of his lighter blocked by all four of our bodies huddled around it, he tested the water and found it good. We all drank as much as we dared, washed off our faces and arms, refilled the bottle, and kept going.

As we moved through the jungle, climbing up the next ridge, I tried to take my mind off of the scratches and bug bites and humid night air by wondering what Lorraine might be doing. It was three in the morning here, so fifteen hours behind would be noon in Portland the day before. More than likely, Lorraine was leaving her office, going with another legal secretary down Hawthorne Street to a small café there that she loved.

I had eaten so many lunches with her in that café, I could visualize her sitting there at the small, wooden table, smiling, laughing, working on her salad, always with the Ranch dressing on the side. Sometimes she had a Diet 7-Up with her salad; other times she just drank water.

I was so far away in my mind, so into seeing Lorraine's face, that I hadn't realized Hollis had stopped in front of me, right at a place where the path Mike was following emerged from the jungle along the top of the ridge. I ran smack into the back of Hollis, getting his sweat on my arms and chin.

"Careful," he whispered, motioning for me to get down.

We both did, then crawled out to hide behind a couple of larger boulders. From what I could tell in the dark, it looked like there was the front edge of a steep cliff ahead, with just some small plants and rocks between me and the edge. Beyond the cliffs, the stars were blocked by a very tall mountainside that loomed over us like a dark monster. We sure weren't climbing over that.

The sound of the river was fairly strong here and seemed to be coming from just over the edge of the cliff. Had we somehow gotten mixed up and headed toward the road? Or had the valley just closed down toward the river and the road?

Mike and Dave were dark figures ahead of me. Both were crawling slowly toward the cliff edge.

I forced myself to not hold my breath as they reached the edge and peered over. I had no idea what had startled Mike, but it had to be something important for him to be so careful.

I could barely hear him whisper something to Dave, then, after another long minute, the two of them slowly backed away from the edge, coming to rest beside Hollis and me. As he reached us, Mike dropped onto a rock, shaking his head. I had seen him discouraged before, but not so far tonight. This had me worried. Very worried.

"Go take a look," he whispered. "And be very quiet."

"I'll stay right here," Hollis whispered, glancing at the edge of the rock cliff. I had forgotten he was afraid of heights. He hadn't told us that until one day on a trail a hundred feet up overlooking some class-four rapids we were scouting—not exactly the best time to find it out. It had taken us a good hour to ease him back off the trail on that day.

I nodded to Mike and crept as silently as I could toward the edge. The minute I looked over it, I saw why he was so discouraged. And at the same time, I knew exactly where we were.

The valley had closed down, and as we followed along the mountainside, we had just eased our way back to the road and the river.

The road was now right below me, maybe two hundred feet down. On the way in, I remembered having Mike point out some class-three-minus rapids, just a mile or so below where we ended up camping. I had forgotten all about them until now, yet there they were in front of me, filling the night with their constant roar.

Staring through the van window at the rapids, I hadn't noticed that the road and the river were in a steep-walled rock canyon at the time. Now that canyon was like a cut in the darkness ahead. And unless we were willing to scale a few thousand feet up some very steep rock faces, we weren't going to be going around this area.

But the landscape wasn't the biggest problem.

Right below me sat a man with a gun strapped over his shoulder. He was situated in the middle of a bridge spanning a stream that entered the river along the cliff face. He seemed relaxed, sitting in a folding chair like he had no cares in the world, like he owned the entire road. His back was to me, and he was perfectly positioned right at the opening into the canyon. Even in the faint light of the half moon and stars, he could see everything floating on the river, and coming up or down the road for a half mile in either direction.

There would be no getting by him.

Whoever these men who wanted us were, they had thought things through and picked the perfect camping spot just in case we got away. We had no way to go up the river and no way to go down the river.

And they had lots of time to find us before anyone missed us.

No wonder Mike looked defeated.

For a second, I felt defeated too.

But there had to be some way past this guy.

I studied the brush along the road near him. It cleared out, becoming just rocks and open ground as it entered the canyon.

The other side of the river looked to be the same, although with more brush. In the darkness, I couldn't tell if the brush on the other side was enough to give us cover or not. And I didn't much like the idea of crossing that river above those rapids. To do so, we would have to backtrack toward the camp a good distance and then get lucky on the swim across the river so that no one saw or heard us. It wasn't something I really wanted to try.

I studied what I could see for a few moments longer, then backed away from the edge.

"Let's move up the ridgeline," Mike whispered as I rejoined the others, "as far as we can away from the road."

Dave and I both nodded. Hollis glanced at the edge of the

cliff, then fell in behind Dave as we moved as silently as possible up the ridge.

We were lucky in a way. The ridge was a gentle climb as we moved toward the dark mountains blocking out the stars in front of us. I figured we had gone at least four hundred paces, maybe more, when Dave stopped Mike and pointed to the left.

The cliff had long since become just a steep slope down to the stream. For a moment I couldn't see what Dave was pointing at, then I did. It looked like another opening, an entrance into a cave tucked in the rocks almost directly across from us.

We didn't have much farther to go up the ridge before we would be rock climbing, so I figured the cave was as good a spot to retreat to for the moment as we were going to find. I was about to say something to Mike, but he must have agreed with my thinking, because without a word he turned and headed down to the stream, then across it and up the rocks toward the cave entrance.

From the stream, the cave's entrance was hidden, or at least I couldn't tell where it was up ahead. Plus, it didn't look like there was any sort of trail leading up to it. To get there, we had to climb carefully from one boulder to another. If it was much higher, I knew that Hollis wouldn't make it, but he didn't seem to be hesitating so far.

There were so many caves in these mountains that only the best ones were used as tourist stops. This clearly wasn't going to be one of the best. I just hoped it was deep enough for us to hide for a short time and decide what to do next.

I had no idea how we were going to get past that guard on the road, or around him. But I knew that we'd think of something, even if was simply outlasting him, if we could just find a way to survive the coming day.

I glanced at my watch as I waited for Hollis to follow Dave up over the edge of a large boulder. It was a few minutes after four in the morning. We didn't have much darkness left. We were either going to have to make some sort of workable plan quickly or take a chance on moving in the daylight, hoping they didn't have someone standing lookout from a high point in the hills around us.

Or we were going to have to hole up during the light and hope the men following us, men used to these hills, weren't good enough trackers to find us after the sun went down.

It didn't feel like much of an option.

But we were running out of time, and escape plans. Something would have to change, and change fast, if I was ever going to get to see Lorraine's smiling face again. I listened for God's still small voice. It was silent, but I began to wonder if it had led us right to that cave.

12

The path of the upright leads away from evil;

whoever follows that path is safe.

PROVERBS 16:17, NLT

10:32 a.m., November 13
Bangkok, Thailand

BY MUTUAL CONSENT, WE DIDN'T TALK ABOUT HOLLIS ON
the shuttle ride from the hotel into downtown Bangkok. I
could tell it was a wound festering just below the surface for all
three of us, especially Mike, but we didn't talk about it. I tried
to calm down and just let myself enjoy the sights going into
one of the most interesting cities on the planet.

The traffic was bad, but the shuttle driver in the big van
didn't seem to notice as he sometimes missed other cars by

fractions of an inch. I tried not to pay attention to his driving, but instead looked at the passing buildings and people. I felt a profound sense of relief when he dropped us off.

I knew Lorraine would ask me what I thought of Bangkok when we talked later tonight, so I tried to make myself pay attention to my feelings about the city and not let my worry over Hollis get in the way. Besides amazement at the traffic jams seemingly everywhere, the feeling I had was disappointment. Downtown Bangkok was very modern, full of the same types of buildings found in any city. For some reason, I expected Bangkok to be more Asian in feel and nature. Maybe the area where we were dropped off wasn't a good example of the real Bangkok. From what I could see around us, there were mostly banks, shopping malls, and large hotels.

Even a large majority of the people in the streets in this area wore business suits.

But Bangkok had a fairly distinctive smell: part river, part earth, part incense, all mixed with a large sprinkling of garlic. With the thick, hot air and very little breeze, the odor was an overwhelming aspect of the city's atmosphere, and I found myself liking it.

It was already very hot and humid, and all the cars and people around us seemed to make it even worse. We were going to have to find bottles of water fairly soon. We ducked into an out-of-the-way alcove near the front of a hotel to huddle around our map of Bangkok. The city was so big, there was no chance we were going to see even a tiny part of it in a few hours. There seemed to be hundreds of temples, called wats, many, many museums, and who knew how many tourist areas of interest. Just the idea of taking a boat ride on the river interested me. But there wouldn't be time.

The van driver had pointed out one of the terminals for the sky train, a mass transit system that soared over all the traffic. The new subway system was also open, but we figured if we were going to do any mass transit, the sky train would give us a better feel of the city in the short time we had. We decided to take a ride toward the Chao Phraya River, get off there, do some walking, and find a place to eat.

I went to a sky-train vending machine near the turnstile and bought all three of our tickets, costing me sixty baht— about two bucks. The car we chose was clean and had large windows that allowed us to take in the beautiful day and all the sights. Even for the middle of the day, the sky train was surprisingly empty. But I had a hunch that near either rush hour, the cars would be jammed solid with human cargo.

My anger at Hollis was draining as my attention focused on the teeming crowds I could see as the sky train moved among the buildings downtown above congested roads, a thousand restaurants and markets, and swarms of people in brightly colored clothing, all seemingly intent on getting somewhere. Lorraine would love this, and it would be fun exploring it with her.

The moment I realized that, I was finished exploring for

the day. I didn't want to have my experience here colored anymore by my wrestling with Hollis's actions and how to influence his spiritual growth. Lorraine and I could spend time in this wonderful city and make it ours. I hoped we would get the chance to do that with many of the world's major cities.

We got off at the terminal near the river, then Mike pointed in a direction and Dave and I followed. After a few blocks of working my way through crowds, more intent on not getting hit or losing Mike in the crowds than I was on looking around, I was stunned when we stepped into an open area with the famous Oriental, Bangkok Hotel, across the street. We were in what was called the Farang Quarter, the old diplomatic enclave. Inside The Oriental was the Authors' Lounge, which I'd read about, where such writers as Noel Coward, Joseph Conrad, and Graham Greene used to sit and drink.

This area felt more like what I had been expecting all of Bangkok to look like. Everything around us seemed to be filled with lush green plants or bright flowers or people. And the architecture of most of the buildings was right out of turn-of-the-century France or was Buddhist in nature.

"See anyplace interesting for lunch?" Mike asked, smiling.

There had to be a good ten restaurants within sight from the corner we stood on, not counting the restaurants I knew were in the hotel.

Dave pointed to one directly across the street from The Oriental, and Mike nodded and headed there.

We went through the door and into a long, fairly narrow room, with booths down one side and a counter filled with food down the middle separating us from a grill area. It reminded me a great deal of a New York deli, only the smell wasn't that of corned beef, but of Pad Thai and curry.

The place was pleasantly cooler than the street by a good twenty degrees. An ancient air conditioner in the window at the back actually seemed to be working.

Mike picked a spot in the middle of the restaurant, at a table for four, and almost instantly a waiter was standing over us talking fast in Thai.

Mike shook his head, said a few words back that I didn't understand, and the waiter immediately switched to English, showing us the menus, taking our drink orders, and bringing the bottles of water we had ordered faster than we could get settled.

"I wonder how many languages he speaks?" Dave said after the man left to give us a few minutes to decide what to eat.

"More than likely five or six, maybe more," Mike said. "Certainly Thai, Chinese, Japanese, English, and French. In this kind of tourist area, you'd almost have to speak all of them, plus a few more of the regional dialects."

The waiter showed up again, and I settled on a noodle dish that the waiter claimed wasn't too spicy and was the specialty of the house. It turned out to be wonderful, with a sprinkling of shrimp and ground-up chicken over the noodles.

We were halfway through the meal when Mike finally addressed what we had all been avoiding. "All right, what do you two want to do about Hollis? And the rest of the trip?"

I glanced at Dave and he looked at me.

"Go on with it," Dave, said. "Hollis's life is a mess, his morals are nonexistent, and he clearly has not accepted Jesus into his life. Most of that we've known for years. We just didn't think about it too hard. It's our job to do something about it."

"I agree," I said, finding myself surprised that I had said that. "We're here, and the four of us came here together to float that river. That's exactly what I think we should do."

"So you're forgiving him?" Mike asked.

"No," I said. "Not exactly. I'm too disappointed in him to grapple with that just yet. But it's not my place to forgive him, it's God's place. It's my place to be understanding of my fellow man and live the best life I can live. And in the process, if I can help Hollis find the path to Jesus, then I will."

"I agree," Dave said. "We make it clear to Hollis that his actions have jeopardized our friendships, and then we talk to him. If he values our friendship at all, he might actually listen."

"And if he doesn't, we're stuck on a raft with an angry and resentful man for three days," Mike said.

"We've been on rafts with worse company," Dave said. "You want me to start naming a few names?"

Mike shook his head. "No need." He laughed. "I probably can name them for you."

I had a hunch which trips and people Dave was talking about, and I was glad he didn't start recounting tales of people I would rather forget.

"I'm just angry at myself for allowing this to happen," Mike said.

"What? You don't control Hollis," Dave said a moment before I could say the same thing.

"I don't want to control him," Mike said. "But I have been getting more and more uncomfortable being around Hollis over the last few years, especially since he moved in with Susan. By coming on this trip, we gave Hollis a golden opportunity to play around. I shouldn't have let him go off by himself."

"You're not alone in the guilt. This trip was my idea," Dave said. "Remember?"

"Hang on," I said. "We're getting off point here. We're not responsible for Hollis's actions, only our own."

"So what *is* the point?" Mike asked.

I stared at my best friend. "Do we want to let Hollis continue down the path he's chosen? Or do we want to take this chance to help save him? It's not like he can ignore us in a raft on a river for a week. Right?"

"You've got a point." Mike put some money on the table, more than enough to cover our bill, then stood. "Let's get going. It's gonna be a long and difficult trip."

If only we'd known how right he was.

13

Let us examine our ways and test them,

and let us return to the LORD.

LAMENTATIONS 3:40

4:21 a.m., November 15
Mae Hong Son Province, Northern Thailand

MIKE HELPED HOLLIS, THEN ME, UP THE FINAL FEW FEET
to a ledge in front of the cave mouth. The hole in the rock we'd
seen was actually more of an illusion made by a few boulders
casting dark shadows. During the day, I was sure the illusion
would vanish completely.

But there actually was a cave behind one of the boulders.
We were going to have to crawl on our hands and knees to get
back into it, though, from the looks of the opening.

Dave had taken Mike's lighter and gone in. The three of us waited for him to reappear. I was glad Dave wasn't afraid of tight spaces and the things that might live in them. Never in a million years would I have been able to do what Dave was doing right now. My fear of insects and spiders and the things that my imagination conjured up was just too strong.

I stared down the valley toward the river and the bridge with the man sitting on it. I couldn't see him or the bridge from the cave ledge, and I could barely hear the rumble of the river. But I knew they were both there, impossible to get past. Yet for our very survival I knew that, somehow, we had to try. Our only alternatives were to hide until we starved or to go back in the other direction, back toward the camp and those bodies and the men with guns.

That direction wasn't a good option either. We had no good options, it seemed to me.

Around us, the jungle seemed deathly silent at this early hour of the morning. I looked to the east, trying see if there was even a hint of the sunrise to come, but couldn't see a thing, not even a faint pink tinge to the mountains in that direction.

Dave popped back out of the small hole in the rock.

"Amazing place," he said, keeping his voice low. "You have to crawl on your stomach for about ten feet, then walk hunched over for another twenty paces, but then it opens up into a huge cave, far bigger than the last one we were in. I can hear the sounds of a stream somewhere in the back, and there are some sort of drawings on one wall made with charcoal and burnt ocher. Doesn't look like anyone has been in there since the Stone Age."

"Is there a breeze?" Mike asked.

"A good one, coming from the entrance here and moving to the back."

"Great," Mike said. "Let's go inside, get a fire started. Try to figure out what we're going to do next."

I had noticed some wood, bleached white by the sun and scattered among the rocks below us like bones. Clearly, the wood had been left there by high water floods years before.

I pointed down. "Let me gather some more wood from down there, see if I can find anything dry enough to burn easily."

"Good idea," Mike said, glancing in the direction I had pointed. "I'll go with you. Dave, use that dry wood in your backpack to get that fire started so we can save as much of the fluid in the lighter as we can."

"Got it," Dave said.

"What can I do to help?" Hollis asked.

"Stick with Dave," Mike said. "Help him build a fire ring, then after he gets the fire started, check the cave for any wood that might burn, or anything else we can use."

Hollis nodded, clearly relieved that Mike was giving him something to do. In the trek from the last cave, Hollis hadn't complained at all, even though I could tell all the climbing and hiking was wearing on him.

It had worn on me, and I was in much better shape. I wondered if recent events had opened his heart to change.

Mike and I found lots more dry wood in the rock field than we could use in one night and day. So we tossed all we could onto the ledge before climbing back up. We stacked it out of sight behind a rock, then took a few pieces each and crawled into the cave.

Dave was right, you did have to crawl for a short distance on your stomach. And since I didn't have a lighter, I was crawling in absolute darkness, pushing the wood ahead of me. I kept my mind focused on going forward. After a short distance, I was asking God for help to keep from panicking.

I hated slithering on my stomach through the dark. Hated thinking about the tons of rock above me, pressing on my back. Hated the very idea that I was forced to do this.

I could feel myself slowly losing control. It was as if I could actually feel the tons of rock above me, pushing downward, ready to crush me at any moment. I stopped, took a deep breath, and tried to make myself calm down.

Mike shoved a piece of wood against my heels. "Sorry," he said. "You all right?"

His voice coming in the dark from behind me sounded strange and muffled, but it calmed me. God was clearly watching out for me. He'd just sent Mike to me at exactly the right moment.

"Sorry, just resting. I hate this."

"Not fond of it either," Mike said.

I focused on the space ahead of me, not thinking of what was over me, and kept crawling. Shortly, the ceiling got a little higher, and I was able to get to my hands and knees and crawl. Maybe I could've walked stooped over, but I could see the light coming from the fire Dave was starting, and I just increased my pace.

A moment later I was walking upright into a massive chamber, lit by the faint, flickering light from Dave's fire. A sense of relief flooded over me as though I had just survived a near-death experience. Sweat poured off me like I'd just run a good hundred yards at full sprint.

"Thank You, Lord," I whispered.

"Amen," Mike said, moving up beside me.

I took my wood over to the fire and dropped it beside Dave, then went to look around. The floor of the cave was fairly smooth, covered in a fine sand. The walls were steep and rough, with what looked like other caves or tunnels leading off from the main cavern in different directions at different heights.

The place was huge, far deeper than the fire could push back the shadows. And the ceiling seemed to get even higher the deeper it went into the mountain. Hundreds of people could live in here, in just what I could see, with a few ladders to get to some of the other caves in the walls.

On one large wall on the left side of the entrance, I could see what Dave had mentioned about drawings. If we got out of

FRED STOEKER AND DEAN WESLEY SMITH

this alive, we were going to need to report these cave drawings to the right people. Who knew if they had ever been seen by modern men? Who would go looking for caves at all out here in the remote jungle?

Desperate people like us. That's who.

The crackling of the fire didn't overwhelm the sound of running water from deeper in the cave. It sounded more like a stream than a spring.

"I'll go find the water and test it," Mike said as he dropped his armload of wood on top of the pile I had brought in.

Dave flipped Mike his lighter and then added more wood to the fire, bringing even more light to the cave after the piece caught. Luckily, the tunnel to the outside world curved just enough to block any firelight from observers in the jungle. And the small entrance to the tunnel was behind a boulder. No one would see the light.

I looked around, studying everything I could see in the flickering yellow glow. This actually might be a safe-enough place for us to try to remain for the daylight hours. I doubt they could track us up that ridge and over those rocks to this one spot.

Clearly, God was watching over us, and had been all along. From the instant when things went wrong, in fact. For example, if Mike hadn't overheard those men talking in a language he knew, we'd never have escaped.

If we hadn't dead-ended at just the right spot on that cliff, we'd never have found this cave. Some people called that luck. I knew it was God answering our prayers.

We'd chosen to test ourselves in the wilderness. We'd bitten off more than we could chew. He had chosen to use our situation to bring us closer to Him. Of that, I had no doubt.

I could see Hollis moving like a shadow figure along one wall, searching among the rocks a good fifty paces deep in the cave. I thought, if we had decided in that restaurant not to go on with the trip, if we had gone home, we would be fine right now. Bored, sitting in the airport, or on a plane, but not here, in this cave, fighting for our lives. And Hollis might have been lost forever. I was seeing changes in Hollis that amazed me. Amazing how God twists and turns our decisions to work to His good.

After a few minutes, Hollis returned, shaking his head. "Not much in here. A few pieces of old pottery, but nothing that will burn, or that we can use in any way."

At about that point, Mike appeared like a ghost from the back of the cave and strode across the flat floor toward us.

"There's an even bigger cave back there," he said. "And a nice-sized stream that flows down through a series of caverns toward the river. I tested the water and it's safe to drink."

"You think there might be a way down to the river through there?" Dave asked. "We're a good half mile or more above the river here."

"Anything is possible," Mike said. "And we should check it

out. But I doubt it. More than likely the stream just drops into a crack and comes out through a cliff face near the river. We'd drown if that happens and we tried to ride the water. But this cave goes really, really deep. And there are more drawings back there."

"And a pretty good breeze going somewhere," I said, indicating how the smoke went up and turned inward. "There might be another entrance to this place higher in the mountains." *That entrance might help us, if we can just find it*, I thought.

And if we don't get lost forever in a labyrinth of cave passages in the process.

I sat on the smooth, sandy floor of the cave and looked at the other three men. Under normal circumstances, I would be thrilled that we had found a place with such historical value, a place that more than likely hadn't been seen in decades, if not eons. Only experts would be able to tell us how old these drawings, and the pottery shards that Hollis had found, really were. But they looked ancient to me.

"Let's take stock," Dave said. "See which way we want to put our money."

Hollis sat on a rock just back from the fire. Dave sat on the ground on the other side of the fire from me.

Mike just paced.

"Our most logical way out is blocked by the river and that guard on the road," Mike said. "I really don't want to try to free-float those rapids if I can avoid it. And without knocking out the guard, we can't get down that canyon on either side of the river without being seen."

"So what other direction can we go to get help?" Dave asked. "Back the other direction along the road seems to be out of the question. If I remember the map right, it goes deep into the mountains before looping around. Plus, we'd have to get past at least seven or eight armed men. And we don't know what the terrain is like in that direction either."

"What's over these mountains?" I asked, trying to remember the maps we had looked at, and our exact location on those maps.

"More mountains," Mike said. "Due west, you would run into the road again as it loops back south. Also, the town of Mae Hong Son. But I don't think any of us are up for a rugged hike through way too many miles of wilderness and mountains to get there."

"Especially without food," Hollis said.

"Yeah, especially without food," Mike echoed.

That was the first moment I actually noticed I was slightly hungry. More water would keep some of that hunger at bay for a time, but I had a hunch we were going to get very, very hungry before this was over.

"How about across the road and river, headed north?" Hollis asked.

"Even worse mountains," Mike said, "and in about fifty

miles, the border with Myanmar, the old Burma. Remember the Burma Road from World War II? Really nasty terrain. Very sparsely populated. If we go over the river and head due east, we would eventually hit the main highway coming out of Chiang Mai, but that's a good long hike as well."

"South is a good two hundred miles of the same stuff," Dave said. "We really are in the middle of nowhere here."

"That's what we wanted for our challenge, remember?" I said. "One of the most remote rivers in the world."

"Yeah," Dave said. "I remember."

"Well, we got it, that's for sure," Hollis said.

"Yeah," I said. "Let's see what we learn from it."

14

A rebuke goes deeper into
a man of understanding
than a hundred blows into a fool.

PROVERBS 17:10, RSV

2:52 p.m., November 13
Bangkok, Thailand

BY THE TIME THE CAB HAD DROPPED US OFF IN FRONT OF
our hotel, I hoped to never experience the terror of a ride like
that again. Clearly, the driver knew what he was doing, but sitting in the front seat beside him in the small green cab simply
gave me far, far too good a spectator's view of the traffic of
Bangkok and what it took to get anywhere in the city. And at
the speed the cab driver liked, which was a whole lot faster

than I'd have chosen to drive through the scrum. It had been like a wild amusement park ride gone terribly wrong. I was sure he'd hit at least five different bumpers, sometimes on the expressway at over fifty miles per hour. But we actually hadn't. From my fingernail-biting position, it just *looked* as if we had.

I thanked God wholeheartedly for a safe return to the hotel. Now all I wanted was something cold to drink and a cold shower to wash off the sweat.

"I'll go to my room and call Hollis," Mike said. "How about we meet in the lobby in a hour, and I'll let you know what he says?"

Dave and I both agreed, I paid the cab driver, and we headed in through the sliding front doors of the hotel.

As we entered the cool lobby, Hollis stood up from where he'd been seated on a couch near the front desk. Clearly, he had been sitting there waiting for some time. There were two empty bottles of water on the coffee table in front of him and enough empty candy bar wrappers to form a small pile.

"Guys," he said. "Can I talk to you?"

Mike indicated that we should join Hollis in the lobby area where there were a number of chairs and couches, all arranged in seating groups. I picked a group in a corner, with four chairs, all facing each other across a small coffee table. The big lobby windows on two sides of the chairs looked out over a well-tended flower garden and a parking area beyond.

After we all sat down, I said directly to Hollis, "Okay, go ahead."

Hollis looked just about as pained and embarrassed as I had ever seen him look. He nodded, looking down.

We waited for him to gather himself. As we sat there for those long seconds, I realized I was willing to listen, but that was about all. Right now, I didn't much like Hollis or myself. I was a Christian. I should be willing to reach out and help Hollis find a way to God. But right now, I just wanted to run back to my room and shut the door behind me.

Finally he looked up at us, glancing at all three of us in the eyes, then started to talk, his words coming out in a rush, "I'm sorry. I'm not really sure what got into me. I have no excuse for my behavior, even though I've been trying for hours to come up with one. I know how angry you three must be with me, and you have every right to be. I'm just very sorry."

With that, he looked down at his feet again.

"How well do you know the three of us?" Mike asked, his voice surprisingly calm.

"Pretty well," Hollis said. "I know that none of you would ever consider doing what I ended up doing last night. And that all three of you find it morally reprehensible."

I nodded. Dave did as well.

"That's right," Mike said, anger now creeping into his voice. "You know that, yet last night you decided it was worth risking more than a decade of our friendship to do what you wanted to do."

Hollis shook his head and kept looking at his feet. "I don't know what I was thinking, or why. I'm just an idiot."

"Because we happened to find out? Or because of what you did?" I asked.

"Because of what I did," Hollis said. "When I saw that girl when I woke up this morning, I was sick at heart. I sobered up this morning and realized what a jerk I was. I struggled to think of ways to talk to you, John, about what I had done, to tell you about it, maybe to ask for help, I don't know. I didn't know how I could have done it, and I didn't know what to do next. I love Susan more than anything. Even I can't believe I could betray her like this. What was I thinking?"

He kept looking at his feet, shaking his head.

"Look, Hollis," Dave said, leaning forward. "You have nothing to guide you, nothing that gives you a path to follow like the three of us do. Unlike Mike and John here, I seldom speak of my faith. But I live it, I feel it, and I follow it, just like they do, with the same passion and belief that if I follow God's Word, He will enable me to lead a life pleasing to Him."

Hollis said nothing, just kept staring at his feet and shaking his head.

"I have no idea how you are going to find a path for yourself," Dave said, going on, "but that's what you're going to have to do. You need to let Him into your heart and ask for His forgiveness. You need to find the Lord, find a way to get centered, find a way to step into faith and to let Him guide you."

Hollis still didn't look up. I couldn't tell how he was taking Dave's words, but it didn't look to me like he was hearing them in any real fashion.

"We've decided that we're going on with the trip," Mike said. "All of us. Unless you'd like to go back alone, we want you with us."

Hollis's head snapped up with that. "You'll forgive me?"

"Hollis, look," I said. "There is much you don't understand about faith and the level at which the three of us hold our faith in our lives. God tells us, in many ways and in many places in His teachings, to avoid the sinners and the unfaithful. But He also tells us to minister to those who have strayed from the path. You see, we're all sinners. But He gives us mercy through the gift of Jesus. You're going to have to listen to us discuss that with you if you want to continue on with us."

"I thought He told you to forgive the sinner," Hollis said, rather desperately. "Even if you hate the sin."

"If the sinner is truly contrite," I said.

"I am," Hollis said.

"That's between you and God," I said. "And only God can judge how really sorry you are. But we've got issues too. Maybe we aren't strong enough in our faith, but we're really angry and upset at you for what you did. It's going to be impossible for us to go on with you as if nothing ever happened here. And we'll be talking to you about it. Are you going to get angry about that?"

"I won't," Hollis said.

"You always do," Mike said. "The Lord teaches us to understand a man by his actions, not his words. Your words are often right. Your actions are another story."

Hollis glanced at Dave, then at Mike, then at me. "You're serious, aren't you?"

"Very," Mike said. He pushed himself to his feet.

"Hang on, Mike," Hollis said. "I'll go home. You three keep going. I should be paying the price for what I did."

"Hollis," I said, "that's what you don't understand about faith. We all pay the price when someone sins against God."

"But you did nothing," Hollis said.

"We associated with you," Mike said, his words blunt and no longer hiding his anger. "We've known you for years, and we haven't tried to set you on the right path. That's over with now."

"I see. I'm not sure I can go on with you. Just go on with the trip," Hollis said. "I'll get a flight home, try to make my peace with Susan if she can find it in her heart to forgive me."

"You need to ask God for forgiveness first," Dave said.

"I've been trying to do that since you three left," Hollis said, staring at Dave. "I honestly do believe in God. I just don't know how to ask for forgiveness for an act as stupid and sinful as this. I don't know how I could have done this, to be honest."

Hollis's words stunned me a little. Throughout the years, I

had heard him question us about our beliefs, cynically at times. I had just assumed he had no faith, or very little. And the fact that he was living with Susan seemed to back up that opinion. But all along, had he actually been struggling with his faith, trying to understand it? Like me?

Dave looked at Hollis for a moment, then glanced at where Mike stood before looking at me. "Would you two excuse us? I would like to talk to Hollis about his faith in private, in my room."

I nodded, instantly understanding what Dave was going to do. Between Dave and Mike, only Dave could find out just how sincere and believing Hollis really was. And if he really was a man who was struggling to find his faith, even enough faith to ask God for forgiveness from a terrible sin, could we convince him to come along with us? Could we reach out to him?

Mike nodded. "I'll check out the flight options, but I won't change anything until we meet for dinner." He glanced at his watch. "It's three thirty now. Be back here by six."

With that, he turned and moved toward the elevators.

I stood as well, nodded to Dave, and followed Mike. There was nothing more I could say to Hollis. If he truly was searching for his faith, I would do what I could to help him.

I would trust Dave's judgment on this one. Dave knew Hollis better than I did.

I stopped and got a large bottle of water from the gift shop, then went to my room. Twenty minutes later, I had finished my shower and was dressed, wondering if a nap might be the right thing to do.

Instead, I picked up my cell phone and called Lorraine. It would be eleven in the evening there, and I hoped she was just getting ready to go to bed.

She answered on the second ring, and the happiness in her voice after she heard it was me lifted my heart.

"So, to what do I owe the honor of this early call?" she asked, laughing. "I hope you'll still call me later, before you go to bed."

"Of course I will," I said. "It's just been a rough day here, and I wanted to get some grounding is all."

"Using me, huh?" she said, then laughed. "Well, use away. What happened?"

I told her about how we had found Hollis after breakfast. Her only comment to that was, "Oh my."

I told her about our short venture into Bangkok proper and Hollis's decision to head for home.

"I'm so sorry," she said. "I know how much this trip means to you."

I then told her about our conversation with Hollis, what he said, and what Dave was doing right at that moment.

"If Hollis is struggling to find faith," she said after I finished, "no matter what Dave says, can you find it in your heart to forgive him enough to help him find that faith, and continue on with the trip and be with him?"

"I honestly don't know," I said. "I hope I can. I will pray that I can."

There was a pause on the other end of the phone, then Lorraine said softly, "John, you are a wonderful person, and I love you more than you can know. Trust yourself and your God. You will make the right decision. You can do this."

"Thank you," I said, feeling better than I had felt all day. "And thank you for believing in me."

"God believes in you," she said, laughing. "I'm just the lucky one who gets to marry you."

15

Say to the righteous that it
will go well with them,
For they will eat the fruit of their actions.
ISAIAH 3:10, NASB

5:01 a.m., November 15
Mae Hong Son Province, Northern Thailand

WE HAD TO MOVE SLOWLY TO KEEP OUR WOODEN TORCHES
lit. I had decided that Hollis and I would be the ones to see if
there was a back to this cave complex, to follow the draft of air
as best we could. Mike and Dave were going to try to follow
the water, to see if it actually might be a way out and around
the guard. None of us gave either direction much of a hope,

but we had to find out for sure before we could try anything else. And with the sun coming up outside, we had the time. We certainly weren't leaving the cave until it got dark again.

Dave and Mike had gone back through the front tunnel and brought in the rest of the wood that Mike and I had gathered. They also moved a rock over in front of the opening of the cave, making it even less likely to be spotted.

But there was still a chance the men might track us to the cave, still a chance they might come inside and find us. And that chance kept all four of us moving, looking for another way out.

Mike said he almost got stuck in the narrow opening trying to turn around after putting the rock in place. Even in the light of the fire, I could tell that had bothered him a great deal. He ended up pushing himself backward through the opening tunnel. I doubt if I could have done that. Until I'd wound up in this cave, I hadn't realized just how claustrophobic I was.

Hollis and I didn't have the lighter, so we were very, very careful about the makeshift wooden torches that we were using for light, making sure that we kept both long sticks burning at all times. I carried a few more sticks of wood with me, just in case we had to go a long distance and needed more to burn.

Having to keep the dry wood burning caused us to move slowly. The wind in a narrow area in one cave had once caused both torches to go out at the same time, but there were enough embers in the wood that we were able to shelter them and get them burning again with a little help from a ripped-off corner of my shirt.

Luckily, my cotton shirt had long tails, and I still had my T-shirt under it, so I had a lot of kindling on me.

The caverns around us were massive in height, reminding me of churches I had toured in Europe. In some places, the rocks seemed smooth, as if cut by human hands. There were stalactites and stalagmites throughout, forming all sorts of fantastic shapes that we had to climb and move around. I just wished I could enjoy the beauty all around me more. Maybe on a future trip, if we survived this one.

The second cave had drawings on the walls much like those in the first cavern, mostly around the location where the water went down into another chamber. Not only was there a breeze blowing from the cavern where we had made our fire, but there was a breeze coming up from the cavern with the water. We found that promising.

I knew that this steady wind had to be going somewhere. If we could find out where that exit was, we might be able to use it to get around the guards. I prayed that we would find it, that it would be passable, and that it would help us.

"I had no idea this area had so many caves," Hollis said as we entered still another cavern. I counted it as our fourth main cavern. So far there had only been one exit in and out of the caverns we'd explored, so I wasn't too worried about getting lost. I was more worried about losing our light.

"If I remember right," I said, "we're not that far from Tham Lot National Park, an entire park dedicated to a massive cave. I read about it in one of the guidebooks."

"Bigger than this one?"

"A lot bigger, at least from what we've seen so far," I said. "The book says it takes boats and guides to get around in that one. These limestone hills are just conducive to the formation of caves, especially with so much rainfall every year in this region."

"Makes sense," Hollis said. "Right now, I'm very glad they're here."

"So am I."

Six caverns into the massive cave, we had to climb up a rock slope to get to a clear opening at the top of the pile where the wind was going. We stopped at the bottom to rest and look around.

Underground, my sense of direction was likely to be off, but for some reason, I thought we had been heading slightly south, toward the river and road. I hoped that was right. Otherwise, we were just going farther and farther underground.

Hollis looked at the rock slope and shook his head. He was clearly getting exhausted. Not only was he the most out of shape, but his last few nights had been far from restful. His sense of guilt had been very wearing on him. And climbing over and around in these caverns wasn't easy work. It had me tired out as well.

"You stay here," I said. "Sit down, rest, and keep that torch burning. Let me climb up there and see if it's worth going on."

"Thanks," he said, easing himself down onto a flat rock with a sigh of relief.

I worked my way to the top. The climbing was easy and the rocks held firmly in place when I stepped on them, as if the rock slide had been there for a long, long time. The climb was a good four stories, and by the time I reached the top, I was breathing hard.

On the other side, the slide went back down about half the distance to another arched cave entrance. I glanced up at the ceiling right over my head. The pile of rocks wasn't so much a slide but an ancient cave-in of the ceiling and one wall that had filled a large part of this cavern.

"It's going to take me a bit to see what we're dealing with up here. Stay put," I said back to Hollis at the bottom of the cave-in slope. "I'll climb down the other side and take a look, give you a shout if I find anything."

"I'll come looking for you if you aren't back in fifteen minutes," Hollis said.

"Good."

I sheltered my stick from the wind for a moment, allowing it to burn a little deeper into the wood before I started down the slope. At the bottom, the floor of the cave became smooth, and the archlike tunnel ahead of me seemed dark and frightening. Clearly, from the marks on the walls, a lot of water had flowed through here at one time in the past.

At least I could walk upright in the tunnel. The breeze was blowing firmly at my back, pushing me into the darkness.

Keeping the flame of the stick I was carrying low and sheltered so it would stay burning and I could see ahead, I headed into the tunnel.

It turned to the left and got narrower, then turned back to the right and opened up into a massive arched cavern, with cave paintings stretching high into the air on two of the walls. One massive stalactite hung from the ceiling, almost touching the cave floor. Even in the faint light from my torch, I could tell the colors in this cavern were bright and vivid.

"Wow," I said softly, stepping to one side of the tunnel and out of the main wind so that the wood I was carrying would burn brighter.

There was another stream flowing through this cavern, forming a pool right in the center that looked nice enough to bathe in. And beyond the pool, I caught a glimpse of something faint, as if there was a light ahead of me.

I braced my burning stick between two rocks near one wall and moved toward the middle of the cavern, letting my eyes adjust. Finally I realized exactly what I was seeing. Outside, the sun must've been coming up. There was light coming through a tunnel ahead. I had found the exit for the wind. The question was, where did it come out?

I eased forward, making sure I stayed on hard rocks so that I wouldn't leave any sign I had been here. The tunnel turned to the right and opened up into the light of dawn. The tunnel mouth was covered with brush, and two large trees grew on the right side. The mouth itself didn't open directly outward, but was hidden by coming out sideways toward the two trees.

I eased my way out and onto a rock so that I could see through the brush. I was on a cliff face.

A very steep cliff face.

The river was a good two hundred feet below me. The cliff below me was so steep I couldn't see the road under me at all, even though I knew it was there and could see it on either side of me.

Below and a few hundred paces to the right, I could see where water poured from the cliff and ran down the rocks and through a culvert under the road. More than likely that was the stream I had just found in the cavern behind me. I couldn't see where the stream Mike and Dave were following came out.

Back to my left was the bridge where we earlier had seen the man with the gun. He and another guard were now sitting in lawn chairs under a tree to one side of the bridge. Guns rested across their laps as they stared into the river.

They were keeping us from using the road and at the same

time making sure we didn't try going down the river. If we did, we'd be easy targets; that was for sure.

I looked at those rapids in front of the two men. There was no free floating those rapids unless we were very desperate. I didn't want to try it even at the best of times. Running the rapids while dodging bullets was a losing proposition if I'd ever heard of one.

I eased to my right, keeping rocks and brush between me and the guards to make sure they didn't see me. I was looking for any way off this cliff face, some sort of animal trail down or hill tribe trail up from this opening that we could follow out. There was nothing but two hundred feet almost straight down to the road and a cliff face as far as I could see above me.

Leaning out as far as I could without being seen, I looked away from the men. I could see what looked like a faint trail, which led across a rock ledge, on the other side of the tree trunks. I couldn't make out where it went, or if it actually was a trail. It seemed so narrow, I sure didn't want to even think of trying it unless there was no other option. One slip and gravity would save those gunmen the cost of a bullet.

I eased back into the tunnel and returned to the cavern, stopping for a moment to let my eyes adjust before using my barely burning stick of wood. I had found another exit to this cave. But I doubted it would be one we would want to try to use.

But maybe we could use it to distract the guards so that one of us could escape and get help. But that would mean tackling those rapids in free float. That also might be deadly to whoever tried it.

Everything just kept coming back to no good options.

"Lord," I said to the silence in my head, "I'm listening."

16

When I had lost all hope,

I turned my thoughts once more to the LORD.

JONAH 2:7, NLT

5:50 p.m., November 13
Bangkok, Thailand

AFTER GETTING OFF THE PHONE WITH LORRAINE, I ASKED
the Lord for guidance on the decision we were about to make.
I didn't want to abandon someone searching for his faith right
in the middle of his most testing moment, when he needed all
the help he could get.

But was he willing to listen to us without coming unglued?
That would be a bad thing in a raft on a roaring river.

I would have to trust in Dave to come to that judgment. I liked Dave a great deal, admired his life at times, and knew he could get to the truth with Hollis. I was slowly absorbing what Lorraine meant by my faith being shallow. I thought Mike had the strongest faith in the group, but I was starting to understand that Dave's faith ran so deep and so strong, that it was often silent on the surface. Every detail of his life was based out of his faith, without question, without thought. Lorraine was the same way.

I sometimes questioned things too much, doubting God's wisdom, even though I didn't mean to. God was giving me the understanding slowly, but I didn't yet see the path there. Watching both Mike and Dave was giving me part of that path. And Lorraine, in her calm wisdom, was helping guide me.

How had I become so blessed to have such wonderful people around me? It had to be God's way of helping me through my uncertainty.

As I rode the elevator down to the lobby a few minutes before six, I found my stomach twisted, worrying about the decision ahead. Could I accept Hollis and his actions if Dave told me Hollis needed us to help him into his faith? I didn't know the answer, but I was trusting God to give it to me at the right time.

Dave and Mike both stood in the lobby, talking. There was no sign of Hollis.

Mike saw me coming and pointed to the restaurant down a hallway in the hotel. "Eating here tonight all right with you?"

"Anything to keep me out of that traffic is great with me." I had no desire to replicate my hair-raising ride back from the city in that cab, even if it was for just a short distance.

We didn't say anything more until the three of us were seated in the nicely-laid-out dining room. The lighting was low, with plants covering most of the walls and planter areas between booths, which gave each booth area the feel of being in its own little jungle clearing.

The menu was pretty standard Thai food, with some European dishes, Japanese dishes, and steaks added in. I ordered one of my favorite dishes that I ate in Portland, wondering how different it would taste here.

"So how'd the talk go?" Mike asked.

"Surprising, actually," Dave said. "Did either of you know that Hollis was raised in the church, right up to the time he went off to college and met us?"

I didn't know that. And that fact surprised me.

Dave went on. "His father was the pastor of the Presbyterian church in the town he grew up in. Hollis knows his Bible, maybe better than I do."

"Knowing is one thing," Mike said, clearly interested in what Dave was telling us. "Living it is another."

"I agree," I said. "Are you saying that the Hollis we met in college was rebelling against his father and his church upbringing?"

"That's what it seems like to me," Dave said. "And once Hollis established that college image, he says he just sort of maintained it, even though he says it felt more and more wrong as time went by. He said he felt he was living a lie and was embarrassed to tell us."

"Now that would be like Hollis," Mike said, shaking his head. "Always worried about what everyone else would think of him instead of just living his own life."

I had seen that pattern in Hollis so much, I just took it for granted. I knew I also acted slightly different with these guys than I did with my other friends or with Lorraine's friends.

"Exactly," Dave said. "He even told me he was relieved when he moved to Hood River because he could be himself there. Over the last three years, he and Susan have been attending services in a Christian church there. He's actually been helping build a new addition on the church in his free time, offering his labor and sometimes supplying materials."

"He never said anything about that, either," I said, now really surprised.

"Of course he didn't," Dave said. "For some twisted reason that he had locked in his head, he felt he had to maintain his college image with us. The wild, crazy, cynical, care-about-nothing kind of guy."

"Even with us being so vocal about our beliefs?" I asked.

"Think about what you're saying. That's only really become evident in the last five years," Dave said. "Other than trips, he hasn't been around us much in that time."

"True," I said. "And we didn't talk about God much with him, figuring he wouldn't be interested."

"All that doesn't excuse or explain his actions and his lack of faith here, of course," Mike said.

"Of course it doesn't," Dave said. "And Hollis didn't tell me all this to try to do that. Most of this I pried out of him, got him talking like none of us have ever heard Hollis talk before. He's a very closed-up man inside."

"And a confused one," I said.

"Very," Dave said, nodding.

Mike sighed. "So what happened last night? Did he tell you?"

Dave nodded. "Hollis said he was restless when we got to the hotel."

"That much was very obvious," I said, "but I was so tired, I didn't care."

"Yeah, me too," Mike said.

Dave went on. "Hollis said he roamed around, then went into the bar to have a drink before going to bed."

"Let me guess," I said. "One drink led to another."

"That's what he told me. He said he got talking to the bartender, a nice guy who knew the northern area and had rafted the upper parts of the Pai River. Hollis said he kept drinking, they kept talking, and after a while this woman who was a friend of the bartender joined them."

"Was she a prostitute?" Mike asked, the disgust clear in his voice.

"More than likely," Dave said. "He doesn't remember her name, but he remembers that she was from the south somewhere. The three of them, still talking about rafting and the area in the north, closed the bar and went to Hollis's room with a few more beers. Eventually the bartender left. Hollis said he was so drunk that what happened after that all seems like a bad nightmare."

"Couldn't stop himself, huh?" I said. "Is that his defense?"

"Not defense so much as explanation, I guess," Dave said. "He claims he was very, very drunk and tired."

"I hope he at least took precautions," Mike said, shaking his head. "Who knows how many diseases a hooker in Bangkok would have?"

"That's a bit more than I was prepared to ask," Dave said.

That thought made me shudder. If he hadn't, Hollis might not only have made a mistake of the soul, but a fatal mistake in life as well. I sure hoped that wasn't the case.

"When Hollis told me all this," Dave said, "he broke down completely. He said he's been asking God for forgiveness all day. He doesn't know why he backslid now. He felt like he had been making such great progress."

Dave shook his head and stared at the bottle of water in his hands. "Watching a friend like Hollis cry like a baby is not something I ever want to do again. I ended up praying for forgiveness with him before I left."

I sat back. So what we imagined had happened when we went to Hollis's room this morning, actually had happened. It made me angry at Hollis, and disgusted with myself for not being able to rise above that anger. Jesus taught me that I should help sinners who were asking for help, who were trying to find their path to the Lord. Why was I finding it so hard?

We sat there in silence, thinking.

The waiter finally came and took our dinner orders, which broke the period of silent meditation over what to do next, now that we had the truth in front of us.

"So," I said, "do you believe he is actually asking for forgiveness?"

"I do," Dave said. "He's having a very dark night of the soul. This might very well be the event that changes his life completely, if he can come out of this."

"So he's an idiot, just like he said he was earlier," Mike said. "But he's a contrite idiot."

"Luckily, he didn't get robbed. He didn't, did he? He still has his passport, wallet, and credit cards?"

Dave shrugged. "I think so. He didn't say anything other than that she demanded some of his money when she left, and he gave it to her, which leads me to think she was a professional, not an amateur. Right now, his dignity and pride are hurt. He's a man in a lot of pain over his own sins."

"Is this really causing a crisis in faith for him?" Mike asked. "Is he really trying to get to the Lord, and is this just a horrible backslide while he's struggling?"

Again Dave shrugged. "From what he told me about his background, what he and Susan have been doing, his life with his father before college, and his life now in Hood River, I would say yes. He is trying. I think we should ask him to come with us. He needs help. Lots of help."

"And do you think we can help him?" I asked. "Is he ready to accept our help in finding the Lord?"

"I think so. I'm going to try," Dave said. "He listens to me, and he really does believe in a higher path to God. He just has a lot of baggage with his father's badgering and his college days to overcome. I think he can do it, but it's going to take some time. And now he somehow has to get past what he's done here."

"He might never get past it," I said.

"That's true," Dave said. "And that would be a shame."

I agreed with Dave on that.

"Some of this is what I expected," Mike said, shaking his head, trying to understand. "Some of this isn't. I didn't know about his background, and I'm not sure why I didn't."

"None of us ever asked," I said. "I know I didn't."

I had to admit, some of this wasn't what I had expected,

either. Over the last number of years, I had become less and less charitable with Hollis, less understanding, and I had to admit, I looked at him less, saw him less. I had let a friend go adrift, and for that, I suddenly felt very, very embarrassed as well. Maybe if I had paid more attention to him, brought him into more discussions about my faith and the Lord, I might have been able to help him find more strength. Maybe last night's failure would never have happened.

"He really is an idiot," Mike said. "I just can't believe how much so. Now the question is, what are we going to do?"

"I think we should go on and make him come with us," Dave said. "If he's going to be sitting around, I would rather he be on a raft on the Pai River with us than at the airport alone."

"So would I," Mike said.

"I'll agree with that," I said. "But that doesn't solve the problem of Hollis getting upset with us when we try to share our faith."

"I think we give him the option to join us in the morning," Dave said. "Right now, he's in a lot of emotional pain. He's asking God for forgiveness. I think it would be a step in the right direction for him if we offered forgiveness to him and asked him to join us tomorrow for the rest of the trip. It might start him on the right track."

"I'm willing to do that," Mike said, "if he promises to try to come to the Lord. If he promises to let us try to help him. If he is actually willing to work at his faith."

"So am I," I said, remembering Lorraine's words. I felt offering this to him was the right thing, and I needed to trust that feeling.

"At this point," Dave said, "from what I saw this afternoon, I think that would be an easy promise for him to make. But I'm still not certain he'll join us."

"It would take tremendous courage to face us tomorrow morning," I said, trying to imagine how Hollis would feel. "And for the rest of the trip."

"That it would," Dave said.

Mike nodded. "All right. After dinner, if you wouldn't mind, Dave, tell Hollis what time the shuttle to the airport leaves in the morning. Tell him we'll be waiting for him."

"I'll do that," Dave said.

The waiter picked that moment to bring the food.

I dug into my wonderful-smelling steak, trying to decide which way I hoped Hollis would decide to proceed tomorrow morning. I knew the answer the moment I thought of the question. I hoped he would have the courage to show up and step into facing what he had done and finding the road to God. If he did that, I would do what I could to help him as a friend.

As Ephesians says, we should be kind and compassionate to one another, forgiving each other, just as in Christ, God forgave us.

17

Where there is no guidance the people fall,
But in abundance of counselors there is victory.

PROVERBS 11:14, NASB

6:47 a.m., November 15
Mae Hong Son Province, Northern Thailand

ON OUR WAY BACK TO THE FIRE AND THE OTHER ENTRANCE,
I told Hollis what I had found. By the time we got back, we
had burned through our original sticks and had to start two of
the extras I had been carrying just so we had enough light to
make it back.

Mike and Dave hadn't returned yet, which worried me
a little. Could the cave tunnel have been that long in the

direction of the stream as well? If so, I found it hard to imagine how big this cavern complex was.

"If they're not back in an hour," I said to Hollis, "we have to go looking for them."

"I agree," he said, tossing what was left of his torch wood into the fire ring. Then he sat down, his back against the smooth surface of a stalagmite to one side of the cavern.

I went and sat close enough to him to talk without shouting across the large space. From there, we could both see the entrance, and be able to either run or get into position to attack whoever was coming through. I just hoped that they couldn't track us up those rocks and to the hidden entrance of this cave.

"You all right?" I asked.

"Exhausted, beat up by the jungle, emotionally drained, and scared witless, but, yeah, I'm all right."

I laughed. "Describes how I'm feeling exactly."

"So why is this happening to us?" he asked, after a moment of silence. "I keep coming back to that question."

"I think God is using our hubris in coming here to bring us closer to Him," I said. "We chose to be here. Now we have to choose what we do next. Everything in life is a test, in one fashion or another. This is, without a doubt, a nasty exam."

"I noticed. I've been praying with almost every breath I take that we get out of this," Hollis said. "I feel like I can't do anything right. I feel like I'm being torn apart."

"Pray for guidance," I said. "Pray for help making decisions. He will help us get out if that is His plan, and if we are smart enough to understand His plan."

Hollis nodded, staring down at his feet. Then he said, "I'm really sorry, John."

"I know you are," I said.

"Do you think God is punishing me, all of us, for what I did?"

I stared at him for a moment. He really didn't understand his own faith, that much was clear.

"No," I said. "We have free will. We choose our actions. God gave us that gift. And we have forgiveness for our sins through Christ's gift to us. It's up to us to find God's presence in our lives, no matter what we've done. This isn't your fault," I said. "Just keep praying for forgiveness and guidance on decisions. Trust in Him."

"I'm trying," he said. "I'm so sorry, John. So sorry."

"I know."

At that moment, before I could say another word, Mike and Dave appeared through the tunnel leading to the next cavern and the stream. Only Dave had a burning stick for light, and it was almost out. He tossed it in the fire as Hollis had done.

"No way out that way," Dave said.

"But one amazing and beautiful underground lake down there," Mike said. "Never seen anything like it."

"And the good news is we found a pretty good hiding spot that I think we should move our camp to," Dave said. "Two caverns down the stream path, we accidentally found a side cavern so hidden that even if there was a fire going in it, you wouldn't be able to see it from the main cavern. And there is a crack in the ceiling with a draft going out that would take the smoke directly up and out."

"What's wrong with right here?" I asked, not sure I actually wanted to move deeper into the cave.

"We're exposed if someone comes through there," Mike said, pointing to the entrance. "We would have to fight them, stop them somehow, and once they knew we were in here, a few well-placed explosives would make sure we wouldn't get out."

I nodded. The idea of someone tossing explosives through the opening hadn't occurred to me. And it scared me. The idea of getting shot frightened me beyond words, but my worst nightmare was being buried alive under rock. With no hope of rescue. Mike was right, if they found us in here, we had to be away from that opening.

"So," Mike asked, looking at me. "Any luck your way?"

"Found the back entrance," I said.

"You're kidding?" Dave said, his voice suddenly very interested.

"Nope. It's there. It's a nice-sized tunnel opening onto a cliff face about two hundred feet right above the road. The tunnel opens sideways to the hill and is covered by brush and trees. More than likely, it can't be seen from below."

"But no way down?" Dave asked.

"I'm not sure. Not that I could see in the dawn's light," I said. "There might just be a game trail down to the right, but I didn't want to take a chance of being seen by the guards on the bridge."

"Guards?" Mike asked.

I nodded. "Two of them. Both sitting beside the road, staring at the river, as if they are expecting us to try escaping that way."

That brought silence to the cave. Only the faint crackling of the fire broke the tomblike stillness.

I had no idea what we were going to do next. Not one clue. And neither did anyone else, it seemed.

Mike eased to the ground, his back against the cave wall. Dave sat cross-legged on a smooth area of the cave floor, his back to the fire.

Finally Hollis spoke. "It seems we're in a real standoff at the moment. They want us dead, but they don't know where we are. We know where they are, and we want to escape but can't. They win in the long run because we're going to starve to death eventually."

"So one side or the other has to break the stalemate," Dave said. "They find us, or we make a break for it."

"Information helps break deadlocks," I said, suddenly knowing what we needed to do next. "We should set up a new camp near the back entrance, watching their patterns, watching how many of them there are down there. What they are doing from hour to hour."

"Great thinking," Mike said. "We could also find out what the traffic is like on the road, and if any of them go down the canyon toward Pai at any point."

"Perfect," Dave said. "Who knows, they might give us an opening. If we're watching them, we'll be in a better position to do something about it if they do."

Mike nodded. "Okay, then, let's move our camp closer to the back entrance, take turns on lookout through the day. We don't dare go out of here anyway while the sun is up."

"If they leave the bridge for a minute," I said, "we might be able to get far enough out to see if there's a way off that cliff from that back entrance as well. In the daylight. If I'm right, it's a climb I'd hate to try for the first time in the dark."

"We can only hope," Dave said.

I felt like I suddenly had more energy. We were doing something at least, not just running and cowering in caves.

We decided we needed to move all the remaining wood first and get a person set up on guard duty. I suggested that we wouldn't need a fire at the other end until it got dark because of the light coming in through the entrance into that cavern, but Mike figured it was better to keep a small fire burning in the area near the cave-in just to make sure we had light to move around if his lighter died.

I concurred. It wouldn't be fun to be trapped in this cave without light, that much I knew for a fact.

"Do we need to drink on the way there?" Dave asked.

I told them about the stream and pool near the cliff entrance, in the big room with the stalactite.

"Deep enough to take a bath in?" Hollis asked. "I'd love to wash off about six layers of sweat and jungle grime."

"More than deep enough," I said. "And from the odors in this cave, I think it might not be a bad idea for all of us to do that. Keep them from tracking us by sense of smell."

"Funny," Mike said, shaking his head as he gathered up an armful of wood. "But still a good idea."

We found a place for a fire right at the base of the cave-in, where there was no chance of anyone seeing the light through the back entrance. Dave took the first guard-duty shift, and Hollis took the first bath, while Mike and I went back to grab the last bits of wood and to erase as many of the signs of our presence in the front chamber as possible.

We put out the fire, scattered the fire ring, swept the dirt around, and then slowly brushed off our footprints as we backed out of the cave. I had no doubt that anyone with any tracking skills would know we had been there, but if someone just crawled in and looked around with a torch, they would think no one was in here and leave.

I could hope.

Mike and I took a drink from the stream in the second chamber, then headed on.

"We might want to set up one more guard," I said as we crossed into the third chamber.

"Top of the rock slide in the next chamber," Mike said.

"You read my mind," I said. "We'd see anyone coming in after us with enough time to at least try to get off the cliff out the entrance, or try to fight anyone who came through the tunnel into the last chamber."

"Also," Mike said, "it would give us something more to do while we wait for dark. We need to rest and keep our minds occupied."

"What's going to happen at dark?" I asked.

"I don't know," Mike said. "But something has to happen. We're going to have to take action. Hollis is right. We can't just sit here and starve."

18

There are "friends" who destroy each other,
but a real friend sticks closer than a brother.

PROVERBS 18:24, NLT

4:48 a.m., November 14
Bangkok, Thailand

THE SUN WAS A LONG WAY FROM COMING UP, A LONG,
long way. But through the windows of the hotel lobby, that
was hard to see since there were so many lights in the parking
areas and the surrounding city. I could see that the nearby
highway was already jammed with cars. Or maybe it had
remained jammed all night. That wouldn't have surprised me.

I had brought my luggage down to the lobby and then
managed to pour myself a cup of the blackest coffee I had ever

seen. From the looks of it, the pot must have been sitting there all night. It tasted as strong as it looked, but it was exactly what I needed.

"Sorry, the doughnuts aren't here yet," the man behind the front desk said as I turned around from the small coffee and service area.

"This is fine," I said, holding up the cup. "Thanks."

I dropped onto a couch near the front door, hoping that the rest of the guys wouldn't be too long. Otherwise, they were going to find me sound asleep in the lobby, and I would catch all sorts of ribbing about that for days.

I sipped the harsh taste of my coffee and fought to stay awake.

I had talked to Lorraine after dinner the night before, waking her up in the middle of her night. She hadn't seemed to care that I'd disturbed her, and she sounded interested in what had happened. But first she'd asked me what I had eaten for dinner. When I told her it was a steak, she just laughed and said it figured. I *would* go to a country halfway around the world and eat the same thing I could get in Portland.

"Comfort food," I said. "Who knows what we're going to eat up on the river?"

She had just laughed. I could almost see her shaking her head at me in fond amusement. I would hear about this for years, I knew it.

I then told her what Dave had found out from Hollis, and what decision the three of us had come to in the restaurant.

"Sounds like a good path to follow," she said. "But I wouldn't count on Hollis being there."

"Why not?"

"Making the promise to his friends and God will be hard, forgiving himself even harder. But if it's the Hollis I have seen when you guys interact, he won't be able to face you three again. If he does show, it will be to tell you three to go on without him."

"I hope you're wrong," I said.

"I hope I am as well," she said. "If he shows up, it will mean he values all of your friendships, and really wants to try. Be gentle and forgiving with him if he does show up. He's going to need your friendship, not your scorn."

"I'll do my best," I said.

"I know you will," she said.

There was a pause. I said, "I'm going to miss you. Miss talking to you, miss talking about everything in our lives."

"I will be right here," she said. "You can always count on that."

"I know."

The conversation had been exactly what I needed to get me balanced and allow me to get some sleep. But now, at ten minutes before five in the morning, it felt like I hadn't gotten any.

Dave was the next person out of the elevator, carrying his backpack and pulling a bag. He looked surprisingly wide awake.

"Good morning," he said, smiling at me.

"Morning is still a few hours away," I said. "I'm sure of it."

He laughed as Mike came out of the second elevator, looking much more like I felt. His hair was still wet from his shower, and he hadn't gotten his shirt tucked in quite right.

He dropped his luggage beside mine and, without a word, went to the coffee machine.

"It's ugly black and nail-dissolving strong," I said.

"Perfect," he rasped.

Dave moved up to the front counter and talked to a clerk there, then turned. "You want me to check you both out?"

"Please," I said.

Mike nodded and went over to help him.

I eased back on the couch and closed my eyes. No Hollis yet. No surprise. If he didn't show up this morning, that would be the end of things.

After a few minutes, which seemed like just an instant in nap time, Mike and Dave came back to me. Dave handed me my checkout receipt and I stuffed it in my fanny pack, making sure that my passport was still where it belonged as well.

"Van leaves in eight minutes for the airport," Mike said, sipping on his coffee. "It's only an hour flight to Chiang Mai."

I took another sip of my coffee, managing to get some of it into my stomach. After we checked in at the airport, I would need food to soak up some of this acid I was drinking. I managed to push myself to my feet. "Better get this luggage in the van then."

The next moment the elevator dinged and Hollis emerged, pulling his bag. If Mike and I looked as though we'd had a short night, Hollis looked as if he hadn't slept a wink. I hadn't seen such large circles under eyes since I'd fallen off a raft and banged into a log nose-first. My eyes had turned bright shades of blue and had deep, dark rings under them. Hollis looked just about as bad now as I had looked then. I didn't really want to think about the night he must have just had.

"Glad you could make it," Mike said, nodding to Hollis.

Dave put his hand on Hollis's shoulder, but said nothing.

I just nodded to Hollis and put out my hand. He shook it. I was surprised he was here. Very surprised, actually. And impressed. As the time for the van to leave had approached, I figured he didn't have the courage to show, not even to say good-bye.

The four of us stood there in the brightly lit lobby, the moment slowly growing more uncomfortable with each tick of the clock. Finally Hollis let go of my hand and started to say something, his mouth opening and closing like a trout out of water.

Dave waved him off. "It will save until later. We have a plane to catch."

"And a new city to see," Mike said, acting far more jovial than he had looked just a minute before. He clearly was doing his best to help Hollis through this.

"And a river to ride," I said, doing my part in easing out of the uncomfortable moment. I grabbed my bag and headed for the front door and the airport shuttle van beyond.

"Guys, wait," Hollis said.

I turned and looked at him. It seemed Lorraine would be right. He had just come down to say he wasn't going.

"I have to say something," he said.

Dave nodded that he should go ahead. Mike and I just stood there, waiting.

Hollis took a deep breath, and I hoped he wasn't going to pass out. He looked that bad. Finally, after a few open-mouthed false starts, he blurted out, "I am very sorry for what I did. I have been asking God for forgiveness, and I expect I will be doing so for some time to come."

None of us said a word, letting him just go on.

He took another deep breath again and looked directly at Dave, then at Mike, then at me. "I need to say this as clearly as I can to you three. I am sorry for what I did. I am just beginning to understand how my actions have an impact on everything in my life, everything between the four of us. I know I can't change the past, but I hope to become a better person because of it, with your help."

"God's help," Mike said.

Hollis nodded. "God's help. And your help. I understand that better now. Last night, I finally came to realize one important thing, got it through my thick skull. God works in this world through people and events."

"Exactly," Mike said, nodding.

I was surprised those words had come out of Hollis's mouth. Maybe this really would be the event that set him on the right course.

"Life tested me and I failed," Hollis said, going on. "But God has given me friends to help me back on my path to Him. Coming down here to the lobby, deciding to go on with the trip, was the hardest thing I have ever done, but I knew God would want me to be here, to go with you three, where I have support as I try to live my life the way it's supposed to be lived."

I nodded, surprised. Hollis seemed to be here for the right reason. He had put away his pride and stepped onto the path. I was impressed.

"So, for being my friends, thank you."

All of us nodded, not sure what was the best thing to say.

Finally Dave slapped Hollis on the back. "How about we go find a river? We have lots and lots of time to talk."

Hollis nodded, a mist in his eyes. "I would love that. But any chance we can get some breakfast along the way? I'm starved."

I laughed. It felt as if a huge weight had lifted from my shoulders, a weight I didn't even know I had been carrying. It was nice to have the guys all together, both in life and in God.

19

Thorns and snares are in
the way of the obstinate
and willful; he who guards himself
will be far from them.

PROVERBS 22:5, AMP

1:56 p.m., November 15
Mae Hong Son Province, Northern Thailand

WE HAD SPENT THE MORNING TAKING TURNS ON GUARD
duty and napping. One person would sit at the top of the rock
slide, watching back into the darkness. Another would lie on
his stomach, watching the men on the road below. The other
two would try to rest.

Mike had figured it would be good to change every hour,

giving the people who were resting enough time to nap. But after the first hour, it became clear that the person in the sun in the mouth of the cave could not bear the entire hour, and neither could the person on the rock pile deal with staring into the dark for an hour. So we changed the shifts to thirty minutes, and it worked fine. One guard duty, half hour off, another guard duty, another half hour off.

On one of my rest periods, I stripped down to my underwear and took a bath in the lower end of the pool. The water was amazingly cold, but it felt wonderful. Getting the layers of dirt and sweat off me helped my mood a great deal.

I put more antiseptic on my cuts and scrapes after I got out, then covered my arms and face with DEET to keep the bugs away. I hated putting my filthy clothes back on, but I had no choice in the matter. It was wear my filthy clothes or go naked. I hadn't dared grab a change of clothes as we left the camp just ahead of the machine gun fire.

Feeling refreshed from the bath and several large mouthfuls of water, I very much wished I had something to eat. Having more than enough clear, clean water was helping keep some of the hunger away, but not much. I mostly tried not to think about it, and that worked part of the time.

Besides resting, napping, and taking baths on my breaks, I spent my guard duty asking God for guidance in finding a way out of this or thinking of Lorraine and praying that she was safe. I knew that tonight, after the sun went down, we would have to try to escape. In one way or another, we would have to leave the comfort and illusionary safety of the cave and make some sort of move to find help.

We hadn't talked about a plan yet, but I knew we were all thinking about it. Every moment spent looking out of our cave made it clearer that we were going to have to get back to civilization under our own steam.

For a major road, and the only real road in a vast part of the country, there had been surprisingly little traffic. So far, between us all, we had counted fewer than twenty vans, trucks, and cars going past us in either direction. The two men just sat and watched all the ones coming from Pai go past. Then one of them would talk into a walkie-talkie, to tell someone else what had just passed.

That led me to think they knew they had us trapped in a certain area. I vaguely remember there was a canyon on the other side of where we had camped. I hadn't paid much attention as we came through it because we had gone through so many just like it in those last few hours. I just hoped no one could see the entrance to this cave complex, or track us to it.

A couple of times the two men sitting beside the road had waved casually at a truck driving past, as if it was standard to have men with weapons in this area. Either that or they were friends of the gunmen coming to help search for us. That thought had depressed me for an hour or so.

At a little after two, in the middle of Mike's shift on the

ledge, he suddenly scooted back and motioned that Hollis and I should come and look. Dave was back on the rock slide standing guard.

I crawled up beside him, making sure that I had nothing shiny that would reflect the sun and catch anyone's eye down on the road. Hollis moved in silently beside me.

Below, on the narrow road, not only were the two men there, but another five had joined them. All had what Mike said earlier were AK-47s slung over their shoulders on straps.

My stomach clamped up at the sight. Seven of them with high-powered weapons. And, more than likely, there were more men back in the camp as well, and still more guarding the road on the other side of the river.

Clearly, the attempt to kidnap us had been a well-organized operation orchestrated by some group, more than likely a large group. Whoever was responsible, they clearly thought nothing of killing anybody in the way if they needed to. Those bodies back in the camp made that clear. And their continuing pursuit of us made it clear that they didn't give up easily.

Again, I kept coming back to the question, why us? Why now? What did we have that they wanted? Or were we just supposed to be easy targets to give the world a lesson in their bloodthirstiness?

"Whoa, look at that. That's the bartender," Hollis whispered beside me.

For a moment, I didn't understand what he said. I turned

my head slowly and looked at him. His eyes were wide, like he was seeing a ghost.

"What?" Mike whispered.

"Third man on the left," Hollis whispered. "Tall guy, dark hair, mustache. He's the bartender from the hotel."

"Are you sure?" I asked, staring at the guy. We were a good two hundred feet up and a few hundred paces along the road. It might be possible the guy just looked like the bartender.

"I'm sure," Hollis whispered. "Trust me, I'm never wrong about a face." He looked like he was going into shock.

Mike nodded and all three of us went back to watching the men below.

My thoughts were swirling, and I could only imagine what Hollis was feeling. Had this happened to us because Hollis had told the bartender something? Or was the bartender just a plant there in the hotel, looking for suckers like us to rob or to use as some kind of political bait?

From the looks of the numbers of men involved, I would bet this wasn't about money. For one thing, we didn't have that much of it. We were Americans, sure, but we were middle-class Joes, not Rockefellers or Hiltons. For another, there were too many hands down there to split the take with. We didn't have enough money between us to make robbery worth the effort for that many men. I was betting we were supposed to be tools to help them make some political statement. More than likely, we were just in the wrong place at the wrong time, and some faction of a fringe group decided we would be easy targets after seeing us in the hotel.

The men on the road seemed to be having a spirited discussion. One pointed back in the hills, another pointed to the river. Every so often a word or phrase drifted up to us.

"Can you understand any of what they are saying?" I whispered to Mike.

He shook his head and said nothing.

We watched as the bartender said something. They all laughed, then another pointed back up the road and five of them headed that way, back toward our camp. At least they weren't coming up the stream toward the cave entrance.

I let out a slow breath, then scooted back into the cave.

After a moment, Hollis joined me, shaking. He was clearly upset and trying to get himself back in control.

He moved to the pool where he splashed water on his face and took a drink. I kneeled down beside him and did the same, letting the cool water on my face and neck calm me a little.

"You're sure it's the bartender?" I asked.

"I'm sure," Hollis said, his voice low.

"You told Dave that you and he talked about rafting up here. Did he seem to know the river?"

Hollis nodded. "Very well. He knew everything about this area, including the fact that there are a lot of caves here. And he knew some of the people who worked for the guide company Mike had hired. I remember him saying that as well."

"Well, we've just seen the evidence of that," I said. "Under the circumstances, that doesn't come as much of a shock."

Hollis looked at me like he was a lost boy about to be punished. "Is this all my fault?"

"What? Are we back to that again? Of course not," I said, relieved that somewhere in the last few terrible hours God had finally given me the grace I'd been searching for. I'd lost all need to blame Hollis for his actions. "We were just in the wrong place at the wrong time. It happens. Do you honestly believe that in one night you got the bartender so unhappy, he got ten of his closest friends to kill three people and try to kidnap or kill us?" I shook my head. "Of course this isn't your fault. Stop thinking like that."

He sighed. "Hard not to."

"I suppose I would think the same way in your position," I said. "But it has to be a coincidence that you met him in the bar. This whole deal had to be set up earlier than when we spent that night in Bangkok. It was probably put in play from the moment we made our reservations. They were looking for marks. And they'd have found us, even if you hadn't decided to spend the night on the town. I'm sure of it."

"I'm not," Hollis said, staring into the dark waters of the pool in the cave. "He seemed to be really interested in what we were doing. He wanted to know how many of us there were, that sort of thing. And like a fool, I told him everything, thinking he was just being friendly to a tourist."

"And how could you have known any different?" I asked. "The world is a dangerous place. We aren't back home, where we know the rules pretty well. We're way out of our comfort zone. We knew that; we figured coming here to such an out-of-the-way place was a part of what we were bargaining for. Adventure. Well, we got it. But we weren't alone. Lots of rafters go on this river, otherwise there wouldn't be a bunch of guide services bringing rafters in here. If we did anything wrong, we picked the wrong guide service. And we couldn't have known that coming in. Mike said the service was the best in the area—highly recommended."

He nodded, but I could tell I wasn't getting through to him.

"Hollis, look at me."

He did.

"This is not your fault. We were in the wrong place at the wrong time. When we made our decision to come here, we sealed our fate. Not when you sampled the high life in Bangkok. You need to forgive yourself, just as God forgave your sins when you asked Him to. And just as I have forgiven you. This has nothing to do with God punishing us. We just put ourselves in the way to be easy targets."

He nodded, then gave a thin smile. "We weren't as easy as they expected."

"You're right. They underestimated us, and they are going

to pay dearly for that, as soon as we get out of here and report them to the authorities. They have to be stopped. And we'll stop them."

"Assuming they don't find us first," Hollis said.

"Yes, assuming that."

I took another handful of water and splashed it on my face. Hollis did the same, then we both stood.

"I have one more question for you," Hollis said, his face twisted in worry.

"Go ahead," I said.

"If I die out here, am I going to hell?"

"I don't know," I said. "That's between you and God. Only you know if you have truly let Him into your heart. But I do know God is not punishing us. He's got a plan for our lives, one we can only accept, not predict. We chose to come here. Now we get to deal with the consequences. We must pray for His guidance to get out of here, accept Him more fully into our actions and lives, and let Him guide our steps. He has promised us forgiveness of our sins. I believe in His promises. He has asked us to pick up the cross and follow Him. That's all we can do. Even here. No matter what happens, we are assured of one thing. God's love."

Hollis nodded. "I have been praying for His forgiveness and for His guidance."

"As have I," I said.

"So have I," Mike said, coming in from the exit and joining us. He went directly to the pool to wash the sweat off his face and arms.

Hollis and I stood, watching him until he was finished. It was my turn to stand guard over the road, but I was hesitant to go out there just yet.

After Mike stood up, his face red from the cold water, he looked directly at Hollis. "I don't want to hear one more word, not even one more thought, from you about this being your fault. You're forgiven. By God and by us. Understand?"

"Yeah." Hollis smiled. "Too late."

"Water under the bridge, old friend." Mike just shook his head. "Look at us. Soft, old, easy American targets. My guess is we were like ripe fruit for the picking for some whacked-out group with a political statement that they feel needs shouting to the whole world."

"Yep. But now they're finding it a little tough to get us into the fruit basket," I said.

"Yeah, that we are," Mike said, then added, "so far."

He put his hand on Hollis's shoulder. "Listen to me. This has nothing to do with your night in the bar. We must have been being scouted by the members of the group working in the rafting agency. The rafting tour agency set that hotel up for us."

"I didn't know that," I said.

"They said that was the best hotel for our purposes, it had the friendliest staff. They furnished the van drivers as well. More than likely, this group had people not only in the bar, but in the restaurant and on the cleaning staff to look for targets."

"And there I sat," Hollis said, shaking his head, "drinking and making sure they picked us."

"No," Mike said. "You don't know that. And it doesn't matter anyway. What's done is done. We face forward, and we figure a way, with God's help, to get out of here."

"Yeah," I said, smiling at Hollis, trying to get him out of the defeatist way he was thinking. "Let it go now. There will be plenty of time for us to get even for all this at the next party at my house."

"Exactly," Mike said, grinning. "You're buying the pizza. But right now, you're relieving Dave on the rocks. Remember?"

"Got it," he said, clearly relieved to be rid of the guilt he'd been carrying. He turned and headed deeper into the cave, toward where the fire was still burning.

After he left, Mike turned to me. "How're you feeling?" he said.

"Better. I think all that praying is beginning to pay off."

"Me too."

I took another quick drink from the pool, splashed water on my face, and then headed toward the ledge overlooking the road. Thirty minutes spent in the sun staring at men who wanted to kill me wasn't my idea of a good time. But we had to have the information on their movements if we were going to have any hope of getting out alive.

More than anything, I wanted to hug Lorraine, to hear her wonderful voice again, to listen to her laugh. I had a lot to live for. And I planned on doing just that.

20

His heart is secure, he will have no fear;
in the end he will look in triumph on his foes.

PSALM 112:8

11:10 a.m., November 14
Chiang Mai, Thailand

THE SMALL COMMUTER JET BUMPED THROUGH THE ROUGH
air on its descent into Chiang Mai. Only about half of the
thirty-six seats were occupied. We all ended up with window
seats for the one-hour-plus flight from Bangkok, and I was
glad, because it gave me a chance to really see some of Thailand, albeit from a bird's-eye view.

The plane leveled out momentarily at about twenty

thousand feet, and everything below us on this beautiful, sunny day was clear. We flew over dozens of lush valleys with row after row of trees in groves and over square fields that seemed to stretch as far as the eye could see. Incredible mountain ranges divided the valleys, with more rivers, streams, and small lakes than I could ever count. Deep forests covered the mountains, the shades of green varying from the faintest tinge of spring leaf to greens so rich that they seemed almost black.

Chiang Mai filled the very center of one of the greenest, most beautiful valleys I had ever seen. The mountains around the city seemed to tower far above the level of the plane as we came in. From one guidebook, I knew the massive towering wall of a mountain on the west side of the city was Doi Suthep. A fantastic-looking temple had been built right at the base of the almost-sheer wall, where it could look out over the entire city. I could see that one of the city's major roads led up toward the temple.

The landing pattern took us almost completely around the city. I tried to ignore the rough air and just stared out the window at a place that seemed a lot bigger than I had imagined it would be.

The Ping River, tucked along one side of the city, wound through the valley like a beautiful blue and brown snake. Hundreds of small boats dotted the river, and even more were moored along its banks. Everywhere I looked, I could see wats and other historical temples, their tall, sharp spires towering over the other structures like needles trying to reach for the sky.

I wished we had the time to visit just one wat. Maybe on the way out, if we left the river a little early. Today we didn't even plan to get into Chiang Mai at all.

I could see the faint outline of the Old Walled City, as the center of Chiang Mai was called. The moat that protected the old wall still existed, framing the entire area in what looked like a square cut right out of the center of the city. The Walled City had once been the capital of the immense independent kingdom of Lanna.

The more we neared the ground, the more I knew that I wanted to come back here with Lorraine. I wanted time, maybe days and days, to explore this fantastic-looking city full of history. Not to mention the beautiful valley around it.

We landed on the southwest side of the city and taxied to what looked to be a fairly modern airport. A man by the name of Katid met us as we came off the plane. He was the smiling, talkative representative of the tour company that Mike had hired to supply and take care of all our equipment and get us to and from the river. He looked to be in his midthirties and he spoke almost perfect English.

He helped us get our bags and then led us outside the terminal to two waiting vans. We put our luggage in the back one, piling it on top of a mound of tents, rafts, and boxes of food. We then climbed into the lead van with Katid and a driver named Wasin.

I was surprised at how much cooler it was here in Chiang Mai than in Bangkok. I wasn't instantly sweating the moment I stepped out of the building. I mentioned that fact to Katid and he laughed. "This is the cold season," he said. "The rainy season is just over. It will remain this temperature for a few more months, then get warmer."

"How cold does it get here?" Hollis asked.

"In Fahrenheit degrees, forty-five at night in the hills," Katid said. "Warmer in the day. But this week it is hotter, sunny all day, so fifty-five at night in the hills."

"Perfect," Hollis said.

I had to agree, it sure sounded perfect.

Katid took the backseat of the van, pushing aside still more supplies. Mike took the front seat. Dave, Hollis, and I got the benchlike second seat. I purposely sat in the middle so I could see the road clearly through the front window and what we were passing out the side windows.

Wasin also spoke perfect English, and between him and Katid, they gave us a running commentary of the sights as we went directly north from the airport and got on Highway 11, also known as the Super Highway, which ringed the city. It swung to the west as houses, temples, and the Chiang Mai University Art Museum flashed past. The traffic was heavy but nothing like getting in and out of Bangkok.

"This is Highway 107," Wasin said, turning off of the Super Highway. "It is the northern connector from Chiang Mai to the Mae Hong Son Loop."

The six-lane road quickly turned to four lanes, then as it neared the edge of the valley outside of the city, dropped to two lanes. Small farms, square fields, and groves of trees covered everything on both sides of the highway. The homes looked more like shacks than anything else, and there were oxen everywhere, with a number in fields pulling old plows. It was as if we had stepped back more than a hundred years in time and farming methods. The landscape looked like ancient Oriental paintings.

The road climbed out of Chiang Mai, twisting up a narrow canyon, then switching back a few times before going up over a ridge and starting down into another valley. I silently thanked the Lord that I had decided to sit in the middle so I could see the road. It was so twisty that if I hadn't, I might have been carsick in a half hour.

Twice, on the first hill, we had to pull almost off the road to let a wide bus go by. Another time, a smoke-belching truck pulled over to let us pass. But the farther we got from Chiang Mai, the fewer cars and trucks we saw.

We went through two more valleys, each as beautiful as the other, both separated by a harrowing climb up and over a ridgeline. Finally, in the third valley, we neared what looked to be a fairly-good-sized town.

"Mae Mai," Wasin said. "We stop for fuel and lunch."

"Oh, thank heavens," Hollis said.

"This is the place where we leave the highway and turn west," Katid said from behind me. "The road gets much worse."

"Much worse?" I asked, glancing back at him.

Beside me, I heard Hollis moan softly.

"Very narrow, very rough," Wasin said, nodding. "Mae Hong Son Loop. But only about seventy kilometers until we reach camp."

"Seventy?" Hollis asked. "How long will that take?"

"Two hours," Katid said as Wasin pulled the van in to what looked to be a combination roadside café and fuel stop. "If we are lucky. Or maybe more. Not to worry. We will reach camp and have a wonderful dinner there. Lunch now."

Wasin laughed as he shut off the van. "He is right, no problem today. But it is the road tomorrow, after we leave the Loop, that will really challenge my driving. I always look forward to it."

I had no doubt that Wasin was very, very serious about the level of challenge. The road we had already traveled would be equivalent to a rarely used country road in the western part of the United States. If the next seventy kilometers were going to be even worse, I had visions of the worst logging roads I'd ever seen. Or perhaps even worse than that. Logging roads in the States were at least wide enough for trucks.

With lunch—a bowl of soup and a Diet Coke—I took a

couple of Dramamine pills to make sure my motion sickness didn't arrive anytime soon. I offered them to everyone else, and the guys took me up on my offer, including Mike. I'd noticed that even in the front seat, he didn't say much during the trip, and he looked a little white faced.

Well, we wanted remote. We were getting remote. Primo remote, in fact. It just wasn't a picnic getting there.

21

Prepare plans by consultation,
And make war by wise guidance.

PROVERBS 20:18, NASB

5:51 p.m., November 15
Mae Hong Son Province, Northern Thailand

THE SUN HAD DROPPED BEYOND THE MOUNTAINS IN THE
west, and the valley below had grown dark and noticeably
cooler. The night was going to be much, much colder than last
night. I wasn't certain if that would help us, or hinder us, in
whatever we decided to do.

I couldn't believe we had been in this valley for only one
day. It had been about this time last night when we had arrived
at the camp, full of excitement over the coming rafting trip

and at the chance to see the unspoiled landscape of the Thai mountains.

Well, we'd had our share of excitement. And we'd seen plenty of unspoiled scenery up close and personal.

But our plans hadn't shaken out the way we'd anticipated.

Speaking of planning, I had spent all day trying to come up with any sort of escape plan from this deadly place. And I just couldn't think of anything beyond one of us trying to climb over the mountains above this cave, somehow keep on track, somehow not fall, and somehow come down near enough to the road to make the twenty-mile hike into Pai to get help.

I wasn't enthusiastic about the plan's success.

At night, the climb out of this valley would be nearly suicidal; during the day, we risked the chance of being seen. If it could even be done.

"Down to one guard on the bridge again," Mike said, moving back in from the ledge over the road. "And pretty soon we're not going to be able to see much from out there until the moon comes up."

"Traffic?" I asked.

"None in the last half hour."

I could understand why. If the road to Pai was in the same shape as the road we had come in on, I wouldn't want to try driving it after dark. It had been frightening enough during daylight hours.

I turned to Hollis, who was sitting with his back against a rock. "Let's get Dave and see what we can come up with."

All three of us headed into the tunnel toward the fire at the base of the cave-in. Hollis put a few more sticks into the flames as Dave came down to join us. We sat around the fire so we could see one another's faces in the flickering yellow light.

"One good thing," Mike said. "The daylight went by and they didn't track us into here. I'm betting they still think we're hiding on the other side of the camp. Or up by that pool with the waterfall and cave."

"So we're safe until we starve to death," Dave said.

"Anything we might try to find out there in the jungle to eat?" Hollis asked.

I glanced at Mike. If anyone knew what might be out there that was safe to eat, it would be him. It hadn't occurred to me even to read an article about it. I hadn't thought I would need it. But he spent most of the spring, summer, and early fall on rivers in different parts of the world. He might know.

"Maybe if we get really desperate. But until then, no. We'd have to hunt and trap animals, which would be more likely to bring those killers down on us than to result in dinner. And we shouldn't risk eating any wild fruits," he said. "I don't think I can trust myself to recognize any of the plants in this area, and more than likely, we'd find something that would be poisonous."

"I agree," Dave said.

"I was just hoping," Hollis said.

"So that means hiding out here until someone misses us isn't an option," I said.

"No, I don't think waiting even another night is an option," Mike said. "We're going to start getting weaker from the hunger. We need to make our move tonight, while we still have our strength."

"Speak for yourself," Hollis said. "I'm so hungry, those sticks for the fire are starting to look good."

I knew what he meant. We all did.

The faint crackling of the fire was the only sound in the cave. Over the years I had sat around a lot of campfires with these three men but never one that felt like this. Or one that had been so life-and-death important.

Finally Dave asked, "Anyone have *any* ideas?"

"We wait until first light," I said, "and I try climbing over the mountains above this cave. Go for help."

All three of them shook their heads at that idea.

"Why not?" I asked.

"You'd get caught, and they'd torture you until you told them where we are," Mike said.

I didn't much like the sound of that, but I had to agree with him—more than likely they could get me to talk. I wasn't a professional spy or soldier. I wasn't trained to endure something like that.

"Or you'd get hurt in a fall, and we'd starve waiting here for you to come back," Dave said.

"Happy bunch," Hollis said. "But I agree. We all go to-gether. And I honestly don't think I can climb what I saw of this mountain from our camp that first night."

"I'm not sure any of us can," Mike said.

"Well," I said, almost glad that they hadn't liked my idea, "that means we go down the river or down the road, which means getting past that guard somehow."

Now Mike and Dave were both nodding. Clearly they had been thinking along those lines as well.

"I think the road is our best option. How about this? Two of us set up a diversion, and we get the guard off the bridge," Mike said, "and the other two wait in hiding and knock him out, tie him up, take his gun, and then we all make good time down the road. We hide at first light."

"Sounds simple," Dave said.

I didn't think it sounded so simple. But neither did my idea of climbing mountains.

"What happens if he gets off a shot, warns the others?" Hollis said.

"We run as fast as we can," Dave said, "and hope we can stay ahead of them until we find another bolt-hole."

"If you guys don't like that idea, maybe we can get into the river below the rapids," Mike said, "and let the river take us. The road isn't that close to the river in most places between here and Pai, if I remember my map right."

Again, we were back to silence.

I didn't much like that idea, but I sure didn't have anything better. We had to get down that road below us, somehow get past that guard and that canyon.

The image of those three bodies beside our tents flashed back into my mind. Wasin had been a nice guy, a decent driver. He'd said he had a family in Chiang Pai. He shouldn't have died like that. No one should have. This was all so stupid.

"So, how do we sneak up on the guard?" Hollis asked after we had all sat with our own thoughts for a few minutes.

"I've been studying that," Mike said.

"We all were," I said.

"There's a bunch of brush on the other side of the stream, uphill from the bridge," Mike said. "You can't see it from the ledge, but I remember it from last night."

I remembered it as well.

"Dave," Mike said, "you and Hollis could work your way down the stream as silently as you can to that spot. John and I will circle out wide and come in near where the guard would have to leave the bridge to get closer to that brush. You make some noise when we get into place. When he comes off the bridge, we'll knock him out with some rocks, tie him up with his own clothing, and hide him under the bridge."

"And what happens if he just starts firing into the brush when he hears the noise?" Hollis asked.

Mike narrowed his eyes in thought. "Good point. Stay uphill and lob some rocks into the brush. He won't know if it's us or some animal coming to the river to drink. He shouldn't shoot right off. If he does open fire, we'll retreat back here to the cave because I'm sure the others will be coming toward him at a dead run."

"I like it," Dave said, nodding.

I had a really bad feeling about this, but it sounded like the best plan we had. As far as I could see, it was the one that had a real chance of working.

"It's not perfect, but it's the best I've been able to come up with. Let's take some time and think about this," Mike said. "We need to let the moon come up before we try it. Too dark otherwise."

"Let's pray for guidance on this," Dave said.

I had been doing that all day. Lorraine's voice kept coming back to me.

Listen for the still small voice. Trust it.

Right now I couldn't tell if it was God's voice saying this was a bad idea or the voice of my own fear. But doing nothing seemed just as bad. The still small voice in my head didn't like that option at all.

Two long hours later, Dave came back to the fire from the ledge over the road. "Still one guard, sitting in the middle of the bridge watching the water. Moon is above the ridgeline."

"All right," Mike said, glancing at all of us. "Everyone ready?"

"Anyone have any better idea?" I asked.

No one said a word.

"Then I'm ready," I said, picking up my fanny pack and strapping it on.

"Ready," Dave said.

"Ready," Hollis said. "Just wish I wasn't."

Each of us carried a burning stick plus an extra piece of wood as we headed back to the front of the cave through the caverns. We had decided that we would build a fire near the entrance before we left, just in case we had to come back fairly quickly.

The closer we got to that tiny hole of an entrance, the more I didn't want to crawl in the dark again. Just the thought of it had me sweating. Maybe I should just suggest that I try to find that wisp of a trail on the cliff face and go out that way. At least there, I would be in the open instead of feeling crushed by tons of rock.

We built the new fire, then Mike turned and said, "I'd like to pray for guidance for a moment."

"So would I," Dave said.

I couldn't have agreed more.

All four of us stood silently around the fire. I kept my eyes open, staring into the fire, asking the Lord for the safety of my friends. And asking the Lord for guidance in this very difficult situation.

Lorraine's words came back to me clearly. I listened in the silence, not really knowing if I would recognize the voice. I hoped I would. I asked for guidance to help me hear what I needed to hear.

"Stay right on my heels going out," Mike said. "I'm going to move fast, all right?"

I nodded. "Thanks. Fast is better."

"I know," Mike said. He patted my arm. "You'll make it."

I took a deep breath as Mike moved to the opening and ducked down.

I stood directly behind him, trying to ignore my sweating palms and fast heart. I had never been this claustrophobic before. I had no idea why I was having such trouble now just thinking about going into that tunnel.

I pictured Lorraine's smiling face, imagined her laugh. There were so many things about her that I needed, that I loved. And I thought about what my Lord expected of me. He would want me to make an effort to live. Right now, my faith, my trust in God, and the desire to build a life with Lorraine were all that I had to keep me going.

Mike ducked down into the tunnel and started out.

I stayed right behind him, trying to keep Lorraine's face in my head instead of thinking of the crushing rock right over my back.

Millions and millions of tons of rock. Impossible not to think about it.

The cave got smaller. Tighter, more confining. I was on my

stomach, crawling as fast as I could behind Mike, bumping into his heels. The rock above pressed down on my back, hit my sides, felt impossibly hard against my chest and stomach.

The complete blackness was like nothing I had ever imagined. Thousand of tons of rock right over my back. No light. Only the sounds of my own breathing in my ears.

I could feel myself start to panic. I had to get out of this hole and do it quickly. I jammed myself forward and bumped hard into the bottoms of Mike's feet.

He had stopped. Was he trapped?

I was trapped with him. My blood pressure skyrocketed, and I could feel sweat beading up on my skin.

His muffled voice came back to me. "Moving the rock we rolled in front of the hole."

Hollis bumped into my feet. I felt pressed in from all sides. *Calm,* I told myself. *Stay calm.* It wasn't working. *Breathe slowly.* I exhaled carefully, trying to get on top of the panic.

Everything around me was pressing in, closing down tighter and tighter. The rock pushed the breath out of my lungs. Sweat poured into my eyes.

Suddenly Mike moved.

Hollis bumped into my feet again.

Somehow I made myself go with Mike, forward, fighting like a drowning man to reach the surface.

A breath of cool night air caught me in the face. I hit my

head as I moved too fast, trying to stand and run. The pain startled me.

Then, like a hand reaching underwater to grab a drowning man, Mike grabbed me under the arm and pulled me into the moonlight and the wonderful open sky.

Cool air swirled around me as the stars overhead spread out in front of me.

I staggered to a rock and sat down, forcing myself to breathe deep and slowly. My heart felt as though it would break right out of my chest.

"You all right?" Mike whispered as he helped Hollis out of the tunnel.

"I think I'll let them just shoot me rather than go back in there in the dark," I said.

Mike grinned. "I figured as much."

He didn't know I was serious.

22

The wise man's eyes are in his head,
but the fool walks in darkness.

ECCLESIASTES 2:14, NASB

4:15 p.m., November 14
Camp near Pai River, Northern Thailand

WHILE WE WERE EATING LUNCH IN MAE MAI, THE OTHER
van had gone ahead to set up camp. After lunch, we turned
west, off the so-called main highway and onto Highway 1095.
It became a one-lane excuse for a road, dropping down into
lush valleys, winding along streams and rivers, then climbing
up steep mountains in switchback after switchback.

Wasin often slid the van into the narrow corners, sending
up clouds of dust behind us. In places, the road was paved; in

other spots, it was rutted from rain flowing across it. I thought he drove about ten miles per hour too fast all the time, but he seemed to know what he was doing, and he clearly knew the road.

The traffic became light, something I was very thankful for. Twice we had to back up to a wide area in the road to let a truck pass. I saw far more oxen-pulled farmers' carts on the road than cars, especially as we wound our way through the valleys.

After one rest stop and three hours of some of the most intense driving I had ever experienced, we finally pulled off the rough road and stopped where four men were setting up tents and another was working over a fire.

As I climbed out of the van, the first thing I noticed was the sound of a river close by. Its rumbling filled the air and made me excited at the idea that tomorrow we would be on that same river. One of the most remote places on the planet and we had gotten here. I didn't even want to think about how far I was from home.

And Lorraine. I would miss calling her tonight, talking to her like I always did before I went to bed.

"Look at those mountains," Mike said, pointing across the road at the ring of peaks that seemed to encircle our camp. "I don't think even mountain goats would be happy on those things."

I couldn't agree more. Across the road the trees and the thick jungle slanted up into some of the most rugged mountains I had seen. Far rougher than the Alaska or the western Canada ranges. It was no wonder this area was so remote from the rest of Thailand. And after that drive in, it made even more sense to me that few people ever came here.

A rich dirt smell filled the air, along with the wonderful smell of burning wood from the campfire. There was something about getting into the mountains on the first day of a trip, something that relaxed me, that made me feel I belonged there. I really wasn't anywhere near as much a mountain person as Mike was, and I hated sleeping on a thin pad over rough ground. But still, every time I reached our first camp on any trip, it was as if I had found some natural drug that made me feel at one with God's wonderful world.

And from what I could see around me in the lush, green jungle, the fantastic brown mountains, the pinks and oranges of the sunset, God had spared nothing in making this place fantastically beautiful.

The four of us unloaded our suitcases and took them to our tents. Tonight we would transfer the clothes we needed into raft packs, and the tour company would take our suitcases and meet us with them after we came off the river.

Food furnished, travel furnished, rafts furnished. It doesn't get much better than this, I thought.

Two hours later, after a walk up the road and a wonderful dinner of fresh fish cooked over an open fire and served on a bed of rice, Mike came to my tent.

I was feeling about as tired as I could remember feeling on the first night of a camping trip, and was looking forward to falling into my sleeping bag early. We planned on waking before sunrise to get breakfast, and then we'd head on up yet another side road to our hike-out point. From there, we would hike another ten miles in before camping one more night, then putting into the upper river the next morning. One of the guides had told us the rainy season had just finished and the upper river had a lot of water in it, with the best rafting he'd seen in a long time.

The sun had long ago dropped behind the tall peaks, and the valley was dark, with most of the light in the camp coming from the two fires the guides kept going. The night was warm, warmer than Katid told us was normal at this time of the year. I had a lantern in my tent and was using it to make sure I had moved everything into my raft pack that I would need in the next few days on the river.

"We have a problem," Mike whispered, crouching in the opening of my small tent.

I started to respond, but he shook his head and indicated I should keep quiet as one of the guides walked by outside.

"What?" I whispered, moving up closer to him.

I figured that Hollis had done something stupid again or

was having some kind of guilt crisis or that Mike was having second thoughts about dragging Hollis down the river in his current state. They hadn't talked at all on the ride from Chiang Mai. Actually, Hollis hadn't talked to anyone much and twice had fallen asleep on the winding mountain roads. At dinner he had looked worn out and pale.

Mike checked to make sure no one was around. "I overheard two of the guides talking. They didn't know I understood some of what they were saying."

I nodded, waiting for him to go on. He glanced around again, clearly afraid of something. Then he said, "They are planning on kidnapping the four of us tonight. They were talking about the timing."

I stared at Mike in the dim light, trying to see if he was joking or not. He didn't look like he was. He kept looking around in all directions. He looked more frightened than I had ever seen him look before.

"Are you sure?" I whispered. It was the only question I could think to ask. What he had said wasn't sinking into my tired brain.

"Yeah, I'm sure," Mike said. "They've decided that they'll move on us at midnight. They figure we'll be asleep by then."

I glanced at my watch, making sure I was reading it right for local time: eight twenty.

"Why? Why would they do that?"

"I don't know," Mike whispered. "I don't know."

His voice sounded as if he was in the middle of some sort of complete panic. In all my years with Mike, I had never heard that tone from him before, and I didn't like it at all.

The newscasts over the past several years had been full of Westerners being kidnapped by different groups around the world. Some survived; some were killed; many were never heard from again. It had become so commonplace on the news that I had stopped paying attention, adopting the attitude that it always happened to someone else. It could never happen to me.

So much for that attitude.

"Any idea what we should do?" I asked. "Can we call for help?"

"My cell phone is as dead as week-old road kill. No reception up here."

"So we're on our own. Can we trust any of the guides?"

"Maybe, but I wouldn't know which ones," Mike whispered. "They might all be in on it."

"So what do we do?" I was desperately trying to wrap my mind around this entire idea. I couldn't seem to do it.

"I think we should all just sort of stroll off toward where they set up the privy area. Two at a time, around eleven. From there, we duck into the jungle toward the river and hide, waiting until they make their move."

"And if you're wrong about all this?"

"We look silly and laugh about it in the morning," Mike whispered. "Tell the guides we ate something funny at the rest stop and spent all night in the latrine. Whatever. But I'm not wrong. I know what I heard."

"All right. I believe you. Do we tell Dave and Hollis?"

Mike shook his head. "No. Not yet. If they get any advance notice, they'll panic. Especially Hollis. He's already unsettled. We just wake them up and get them to go with us. I'll take Dave; you get Hollis."

I nodded, my stomach twisting into a tight knot at the possibility that Mike was right. If they did want us, for who knew what reason, and they got us, our chances of survival were very low. None of us were rich enough to pay any ransom, and our government sure didn't bargain with people who would do this sort of evil thing.

"You get to Hollis's tent at ten before eleven," Mike whispered. "I'll get Dave after you two are out of the camp. Act as natural as you can while leaving. They won't suspect that we have any idea what's happening. Make sure Hollis has his shoes on."

"Got it," I said. I looked at Mike one more time. "This isn't a joke?"

"No joke," he said.

With that, he stood and headed toward his tent.

I sat there for what must have been ten minutes, just trying to get my heart and breathing back under control.

Mike was serious, I was sure of that. He thought he had heard some of the guides talking about kidnapping us. We didn't dare stick around to see if what he heard was true. If it wasn't, we could always come back into camp.

If it was, Mike's skill with languages might have just saved our lives, assuming, of course, we could escape.

I went back to packing my rafting bag. After a short time, I realized it would be far too heavy to haul through the jungle at speed, so instead I got out my fanny pack and put in it what I thought I might need. The little thing didn't carry much, that was sure. Even my flashlight was too big to fit.

Then I tried my cell phone. No reception at all.

I shut off my flashlight and lay on my sleeping bag, clothes still on, staring at the ceiling and checking my watch every ten minutes.

I kept asking the Lord for guidance in this situation. I had never faced anything like this before, and if Mike was right, this would be a test of my ingenuity like none other. We'd gotten ourselves out here into the middle of nowhere with the best of intentions. Now it looked like we'd managed to get ourselves in over our heads.

Around nine I got another idea. I got up, pretended to stretch, then went for a casual stroll past the two vans, checking to see if either of them had a key in it.

Neither did. And both were locked up tight.

So much for the idea of taking a van and making a break for it. I went back to my tent and to the waiting and praying.

The minutes dragged past.

The guides, cook, and two drivers gathered near the far fire, away from our tents. Every so often I could hear them laughing about something. Under the circumstances, it sent chills down my spine. But mostly I just heard the sounds of a few birds and the low rumbling of the river.

That, and my own very loud thoughts. Thoughts of Lorraine. Thoughts of the Lord's strength. Thoughts of who would do what Mike was suggesting. Thoughts of what we would do in the jungle, how we would escape. The jumbled ideas and thinking twisted my stomach into a tight knot, and sweat beaded on my forehead.

Finally, at fifteen minutes until eleven, I crawled out of my tent and moved over to Hollis's tent, figuring it would take me five minutes to get him going. No guide or driver was close by, but I was so scared, my stomach felt like I was about to lose my fish dinner.

I eased inside the small tent and shook Hollis hard on the shoulder.

He sat up, startled. "What?"

I put my hand over his mouth and whispered, "Quiet."

He brushed my hand aside, then whispered back, "What are you doing?"

"Get dressed. Quickly. Quietly."

"I am dressed. Why?"

"Get your shoes and socks on. I'll explain in a minute."

He pushed me away and put on his shoes. "This better not be a joke."

"No joke," I whispered. "Now, we're going to walk naturally, as if we're having a discussion, toward the privy area. Follow my lead."

"Is this payback for the trouble back in Bangkok?"

"No. I forgave you for that. We all did. You know that. Don't ask questions. Just come with me."

"You're nuts, you know that," he said.

"Trust me, Hollis. Please," I said. "Come on. In God's name, just trust me. It's important."

He stared at me and must have seen something on my face and in my eyes that made him reconsider, because I certainly wasn't trying to hide my feelings. I doubted I could at that moment.

He nodded and followed me out of the tent, standing and stretching.

"Lead on," he whispered.

A laugh came from the guides seated at the fire, but no one seemed to be looking in our direction. Hollis got ahead of me, and we walked as if we were out for a nightly stroll down the path toward where the rafting company had set up a few logs for a privy.

Once we got there, I motioned for Hollis to be silent, and we went right on past, off the trail, and out into the jungle. I did my best to not make much noise, but to my ears in the still night, Hollis and I sounded like a herd of elephants pushing down trees.

I ducked behind some brush so that I could see the trail from the camp and motioned for Hollis to join me.

"Now, you want to tell me what's happening?" Hollis whispered. "You're starting to scare me."

"In a minute," I whispered back. "Mike and Dave should be right behind us. I'll explain when they get here."

I glanced at my watch. It was almost eleven.

Hollis shook his head. "This had better not be a joke."

"I hope it is, actually," I whispered. "I really hope it is. Meantime, keep it down."

A few moments later, Mike followed Dave toward us. I stepped out of our hiding place and motioned to him.

"Head toward the river," Mike whispered. "Quickly. Stay under cover. I think we might have been seen."

"I sure wish someone would tell me what's going on," Hollis said as he dropped in behind Dave and Mike.

"Hush," Mike said. "Move it."

I brought up the rear, right behind Hollis, as the four of us worked our way through the dark jungle as best we could. The bright stars and the faint moonlight helped, but not much. I kept tripping over rocks and tree roots, getting slapped and scraped by branches and bitten by bugs. I sounded more like a one-man band than a stealthy woodsman.

All at once we heard a chorus of yells from the direction of the camp.

"That tears it. They've discovered we're gone," Mike said. "Hurry, follow me."

He cut to his left, moving in a direction I figured was up the river and slanting toward it. But I couldn't be sure. I just knew that there was a lot of shouting—angry shouting—from the camp.

They weren't happy back there.

Then came the gunfire. Shots through the jungle like a death knell. Never in my entire life had I been more frightened than I was at that moment.

More firing. More angry shouting.

We moved faster.

"What's happening?" Hollis demanded, his voice harsh as he followed Mike.

"They were going to kidnap us," I said. "Stay down, hush up, and keep following Mike."

"Kidnap?" Hollis whispered, glancing back at me, his eyes wide.

"Yeah. Kidnap," I whispered back. "Keep moving or they might do it yet."

The nightmare was real. Mike had been right. I had so hoped he was wrong.

Bursts of gunfire echoing through the jungle made it clear he hadn't been.

23

O my God, I am too ashamed and disgraced
to lift up my face to you, my God,
because our sins are higher than our heads
and our guilt has reached to the heavens.

EZRA 9:6

8:37 p.m., November 15
A bridge southeast of Pai, Thailand

THE FOUR OF US STAYED TOGETHER, WORKING OUR WAY AS
quietly as we could down the streambed until we got within a
football field's length of the road. The moon seemed much
brighter tonight than last night. Either that, or I was getting
used to creeping around in the jungle in the dark.

"Give us five minutes to get into position," Mike whispered

to Dave and Hollis. "Then move up to a place where you can hit that clump of brush off the bridge with a decent-sized rock."

Dave nodded. "We'll make some noise. I promise."

Hollis just looked pale, even in the faint light.

My stomach was so twisted in knots that I was having a hard time breathing. And even though the night air was cool, much colder than last night, I was sweating. I didn't much like this plan of trying to ambush a man armed with an AK-47. I wouldn't like it even if he didn't have a gun. I had never attacked another human in my life, and I had hoped to go through the rest of my time on Earth missing that experience. Lorraine called me the ultimate pacifist, and I was comfortable with that label.

"Let's go," Mike whispered.

I nodded and then followed him up the shallow bank out of the streambed and into the jungle that covered the top of the ridge. Once in the trees, Mike headed toward the left side of the bridge.

In my imagination, every crack of a twig under my foot sounded like a firecracker going off. Every swish of grass against my leg sounded like a car scraping against a curb. Every rustle of leaves as I moved a branch aside sounded like rain against a tin roof. I couldn't believe the guy couldn't hear us coming. I hoped the sound of the rapids in the river was covering our noise, but I couldn't imagine how it could.

We reached an open area in the jungle where we could see

the bridge. In the faint light, the man sitting in the lawn chair was no more than a dark outline, like a child's paper-doll cutout. But this was no child's toy. If this didn't work, that paper cutout of a figure might kill us all.

We pushed on through the jungle underbrush, moving as slowly and as carefully as we could. It seemed to take us an eternity to reach the path coming off the west end of the bridge. I kept talking to God, asking Him for help on just about everything as we moved, including finding the trail. I was beginning to give up hope that we would ever find it when we broke out of the jungle, and the path from the road was right in front of us.

The worn rock trail went down to the streambed and under the bridge, more than likely made by the men who had worked on the structure at some point in the last half year.

Mike indicated by pointing that I should hide behind a tree ten feet from the bridge on the left side. He crept over to, and then into, a large clump of bushes on the other side of the path from me. Then he picked up a fist-sized rock and indicated that I should do the same.

I found one quickly, holding it in my sweating hands, not believing that I intended to hit a man on the head with that very rock. I asked God for guidance, asked for His forgiveness for what I was about to do, asked for His help in my blow. I wanted to knock the guy out without hurting him too much, yet put him out sufficiently to allow us to escape.

As I crouched, my legs shook from nerves, and I had to

keep shifting to stop them from quivering for fear the motion would draw attention to me.

I took as silent a deep breath as I could, made sure I was in a position that I could move from easily, then waited. Every second seemed to tick past in an agonizingly slow way, like watching for a faucet to drip that you are not sure is leaking.

The sound of the rapids was loud. Very loud, echoing down the canyon just below the bridge.

It felt as if the waiting went on forever. Had something happened to Dave and Hollis?

Even though I was expecting the sound, waiting for it, the rock thrown by Dave into the brush below the bridge startled me, causing me to jerk and almost drop my rock weapon.

The guy on the bridge stood instantly, spinning around, gun ready, surveying the area of the streambed and the brush behind him.

He walked to the other side of the bridge and looked down. I waited. Then he walked back to our side. The roar of the rapids covered the sounds of his footsteps, so it looked like he was moving without noise in the faint light. Very surreal.

Then he clicked on a flashlight and started to scan the area of the streambed and the surrounding jungle and trees. I just hoped that Dave and Hollis were well hidden. The light seemed fantastically bright to me after the time spent wandering around in the dim moonlight.

The beam of the flashlight swept past my hiding place once. Then I could hear the guy coming toward Mike and me. As he got closer, I could finally hear his footsteps crunching on the bridge surface. The bright beam of light continued to jerk back and forth over the stream and jungle.

I didn't want to look for fear of exposing myself, showing him where I was, so I just kept my face hidden behind the dark bark of the tree, my eyes down so that they wouldn't reflect light.

I could see Mike, his head down as well, frozen in place, waiting.

The man's boots sounded impossibly loud on the dirt as he stepped off the bridge and onto the path ten feet in front of me. I couldn't see him, but I could imagine his gun aimed at me and ready to fire.

Ready to kill all of us.

He moved slower than I had expected, clearly studying the area in front of him and the brush around the trail. Then he directed the beam of his flashlight across the streambed onto the opposite bank of the creek, checking to see if any of us were trying to sneak past him that way.

Then he moved another few steps closer to me and checked part of the area under the bridge.

My heart threatened to pound out of my chest. I managed to keep breathing in shallow breaths.

I again asked God for guidance, for help, for forgiveness for what I was about to do.

The images of the three bodies lying beside our tents came clearly back to my mind. I didn't want Mike's body there too.

Or Dave's.

Or Hollis's.

Or mine.

I had to do this. This had to work.

We hadn't asked for this situation. We'd been selected as victims, possibly even by the man now stalking us with a gun in his hand. With God's help, we were going to work to get out of it.

That thought calmed me just a little. My mind seemed to clear, as if a fog of confusion that had been covering me had lifted.

I took a deep breath as the man appeared on the trail between Mike and me. He took one step past us. Mike moved. It seemed like slow motion as Mike came up and caught the guy with a glancing blow across the side of the head.

The guy spun away just as I moved, trying to turn his gun on Mike while I came at him from behind.

Mike stepped right into the guy's arms, missing with a second blow of the rock. The two were suddenly clutching each other in a strange life-and-death dance. Mike was fighting with the guy with desperate strength, the gun trapped between them.

Mike managed to get his arm over the guy's mouth so he couldn't yell for help.

I tried to hit the guy on the back of the head with my rock, but he moved at the last instant, and I hit him hard on the shoulder. The blow knocked the rock from my hand. But the force of my rush shoved the man over on top of Mike, and all three of us hit the ground hard with me on top.

I heard a muffled explosion under me. He had fired the gun. I was still alive. Was Mike?

I thought in a flash, *Did the other kidnappers hear that?*

But I had worse things to worry about now. The guy fought like a maniac, twisting and turning between us, struggling to escape the hold that Mike and I had on him.

He smelled of garlic, and his grunts sounded animal-like.

I got my hands around his neck, pushing down hard on him, trying to get him to stop moving. His skin felt slick, covered in sweat.

He wouldn't stop thrashing, twisting, pushing back at me.

Mike seemed to be holding on as tightly as I was. Now he had the guy's arms, pinning them to his side.

The guy thrashed, kicking back at me. The heel of one of his boots hit me in the back of my right leg. It hurt like crazy, but it wasn't enough to knock me off of him.

Suddenly he feinted to the right, then rolled to the left and off of Mike.

Mike and I both went with him, me riding his back like a cowboy hanging onto a bull. I kept all my weight, all the pressure I could, on the back of his neck, trying to hold on to him and trying not to let him roll over and shoot me.

As he moved off Mike, I shoved the guy's head down hard, hoping to pin him against the ground and still be on his back. The last thing I needed was an angry, armed terrorist running around loose among my friends and me.

Mike yanked hard at the man's shirt. That action, combined with my shoving him from behind, forced his head and face directly into the rocks and dirt of the trail.

Our captive jammed one arm under his body and shoved back, trying to lift himself off the dirt. I shoved him back down with all my might.

I heard a loud crack.

Under my hands something changed position in his neck. I could feel the guy's bones and neck muscles slide into a position that felt unnatural and very wrong.

Instantly he stopped struggling.

I kept up my pressure, kept his face forced into the dirt, fearing he was faking and waiting for me to release him. The guy didn't move. His body felt heavy and limp.

Mike scrambled away from the guy, twisted around, and came back to grab the gunman hard, helping me hold him down. But the guy didn't struggle.

I did my best to try to catch my breath.

Still no movement under me.

Mike nodded to me, indicating he had the guy in a lock. I slowly eased the pressure off the man's neck and head as Mike rested on him with a knee in his back. The gun was sticking out from under the man, aiming down the trail at the stream.

Finally I let go, wiping the man's sweat off my hands on my pants. The feeling of his slick skin, the bones moving under my fingers, the sudden crack of abused bone and flesh, would be with me for the rest of my life. I had no doubt I would have nightmares about that feeling.

I had hurt him and hurt him bad, I was sure of that.

Mike carefully pulled the gun out from under the guy, not letting up from the pressure he was holding on him. The guy still didn't move.

"Is he out?" I asked.

Mike nodded, grimacing in pain. He reached into his pocket and grabbed some strips of cloth we had cut off our shirts earlier, then yanked the man's hands behind his back, tying them quickly and tightly.

Then, keeping the gun in his hands, Mike slid off the man's back to the ground. His face screwed up in pain. I could see he was hurting, but in the faint light, I couldn't see why.

The man's flashlight had rolled under a bush and turned off. I grabbed it and came back to Mike.

"You all right?" I asked, then sheltered the flashlight against my body and clicked on the light. I knew at once he wasn't. There was blood all over his hands, and one leg looked almost black with blood.

"Shot me," Mike said, his voice breathless. "In the leg."

"Hold this," I said, handing him the flashlight. I ripped back his pants leg. There was a bullet hole in one side of his leg, right below his knee. I couldn't see an exit wound.

"Give me some more of that ripped cloth," I said.

He did, and I wrapped a tourniquet around his leg just above his knee, then found a piece of wood, put that in the tie, and twisted the cloth tight as Mike bit his lip but didn't cry out in pain.

"We're going to have to remember to loosen that every little bit," I said.

He merely nodded.

Then I got out the bottle of hydrogen peroxide from my fanny pack and poured some onto the wound.

Mike grimaced and gripped my shirt but said nothing.

I used some more cloth to tie off the hole lightly, hoping to slow down some of the bleeding. It didn't seem like it was bleeding that bad, which was good. If it had been bleeding worse, Mike wouldn't last long. As it was, he would need medical help very, very soon.

"I think I got it," I said.

"Thanks," he said between gritted teeth.

Clearly, the pain was bad. Very bad.

Early on in our camping trips, all four of us had taken a basic first aid course, just in case someone got hurt. Bullet wound care hadn't been covered in that course, but cuts had. I was doing the best I could to keep my best friend from bleeding to death.

"I think the bullet hit a bone," he said, his voice barely containing the pain. "Leg feels broken."

I glanced around for some branches that would work as splints. We wouldn't be able to move him until we got his leg supported in some way or another. And we were going to have to move quickly in case anybody back at the camp heard that shot. Or worse, if the shot had been heard by a friend of the gunman who happened to be close by.

I was hoping we would be spared that. The sound of the shot had been muffled between Mike and the man with the gun. I'd been right there when it went off, and it hadn't sounded that loud to me. But that wasn't in my control. Fixing up Mike was. I couldn't see any splint material close by. I would need help on this.

I grabbed a rock off the trail and tossed it in the direction of the brush. Then I followed it three seconds later with another rock. That was the signal to Dave and Hollis that the coast was clear, at least for the moment.

"Better check him," Mike whispered, pointing at the gunman on the trail. "Don't need more trouble." The pain clearly was terrible, robbing the energy out of his voice.

"Good point," I said. The guy was still down, still unmoving. He was as limp as I had ever seen anyone be.

I tried to find a pulse on his neck, but couldn't.

Carefully I rolled him over onto his back.

The moment I did that, the man's head rolled like there was only skin holding it onto his body. His eyes were open and blank, staring up into the night sky.

Dead.

Oh no.

The thought sent me scooting back along the ground away from him like he was after me.

I had killed a man.

Dear Lord, what have I done?

24

Nothing in all creation can hide from him.

Everything is naked and exposed before his eyes.

This is the God to whom we must

explain all that we have done.

HEBREWS 4:13, NLT

9:12 p.m., November 15
A bridge southeast of Pai, Thailand

I SAT STARING AT THE MAN I HAD KILLED AS DAVE AND Hollis splashed across the stream and scrambled up the bank to our position.

It felt as if a dark cloud had descended over my eyes, as if the night and the moon had gone away. There was nothing for me but that body, that man whose life I had taken with my bare hands.

My world had narrowed down to just him, the feeling of him dying under my hands, his blank eyes staring up into the night sky.

I had done the worst act possible in God's eyes. I was a killer. Could God ever forgive me? Could I forgive myself?

How could I have done such a thing?

I was shocked speechless.

"Are you two all right?" Dave asked, reaching us ten steps ahead of Hollis.

"No. I got shot," Mike said. "In the leg. John's got it taken care of, but I'm going to need a splint to move."

Dave kneeled down over Mike's leg as Hollis reached the trail. Mike shined the flashlight on his leg and let Dave inspect it.

"It's not bleeding anymore," Dave said. "But we've got to get you out of here. You're going to need serious medical attention fairly soon on this one. First aid's not going to do it."

"I know," Mike said.

"Dear God," Hollis said, kneeling beside Mike and staring like a kid who had never seen blood before.

"Did you hear the shot?" Mike asked.

"No," Dave said. "Just a lot of scuffling and then silence."

"Good," Mike said. "Guess our bodies muffled the noise. So maybe the bad guys aren't all running in this direction. But someone might come along at any moment. We have to get moving."

"Your opponent doesn't look any the better for the fight," Dave said, indicating the man I had killed.

"He's dead," Mike said. "Broken neck."

Hollis rotated on his knees like he was being confronted by a ghost. He stared at the dead gunman, his mouth wide open in surprise and horror.

"Oh," Dave said. "John, are you all right?"

I couldn't make myself answer him. I just kept staring at the dead man's open eyes, remembering the slick feel of his skin in my hands, the moment his neck broke under my fingers.

Suddenly I needed to be sick.

I turned and heaved, but there was nothing but water in my stomach. It felt as if I were turning my entire self, every cell in my body, inside out. I stayed on my hands and knees, shaking, facing the ground, wishing I had been the one to die.

How could I have killed a man? Even when I had gone hunting with my father and friends, if I saw a deer, I shot over the thing's back to scare it away. I hadn't killed anything larger than a spider in my entire life.

Until now.

Now I had killed a man, committed God's ultimate sin. *Thou shalt not kill.* The words were engraved on my brain from my earliest memories. I'd never expected to break that commandment. I was too ashamed to even ask Him for forgiveness. I wanted to die myself.

Even though I wasn't looking at the gunman, the image of the dead man's eyes stared back at me in my memory. I tried to heave my guts out again. Those empty eyes of his would haunt me through the rest of my life.

I had killed a man. How could I go on? How could I live with myself?

Dave put a hand gently on my shoulder, and I moved into a sitting position, wiping off my mouth.

"We need to get moving," Mike said. "I need splints."

Dave patted me on my shoulder and then stood.

"Hollis, help me," Dave said. He pulled Hollis to his feet and together they went into the jungle.

Mike lay there on the trail. I could see the blood staining his bandage.

My best friend would die if I didn't make myself move as well. I pushed myself to my feet and stared down at the man I had killed. His neck was at an odd angle, his arms still tied by the torn strips from our shirts.

His eyes, those dark orbs that would haunt my every nightmare, stared up at me.

I had to do something about those eyes. I moved over to him and, using both hands, closed his eyes. I hated to touch him, hated the feel of his still-warm flesh under my fingers. I wanted to be sick again, but I couldn't let myself.

Mike needs my help.

I repeated that thought.

Mike needs my help.

A small voice in my head kept saying that same sentence over and over again.

Suddenly the image of the bodies laid out beside the tent came back to me. Had this man been one of the killers who'd ended those three innocent lives? It didn't justify what I had done, but the thought calmed my stomach a little.

"Look. It was an accident," Mike said. "We did not mean to kill him."

"You didn't kill him," I said. "My hands broke his neck."

"And by doing so, you saved my life." Mike pointed at his leg. "And Dave's. And Hollis's. He shot me, remember? He was trying to finish me off. He would have killed us all. We did what we had to do."

I said nothing. There was nothing I could say to myself that would justify what I had done.

"John," Mike said, his voice low and comforting, "you saved my life in that fight. Now I need your help even more. We have to get moving down the road, away from here. We've got to get some distance between us and them before they discover what has happened."

Suddenly the black fog over my mind lifted.

Mike needs my help. He isn't going to make it unless I can pull myself together.

"Right," I said. I didn't have the time to think about this now.

I stared at the dead man for a moment more, then turned and looked at Mike. I knew what had to be done. It had come to me all at once, like some vision. I knew that now there was only one chance of us getting out of this alive. And that chance depended on me completely.

"No," I said.

"No, what?" Mike asked.

"We can't hike out of here. Not with your leg like this. We can't move fast enough with you along. So you have to stay here, in the cave, and wait. Sorry, buddy."

"What do you mean? We won't survive out here for much longer."

"I know," I said. "I'm in the best shape. I can move fastest if I'm alone. I'm going for help. Dave and Hollis are going to take you back up to the cave. You all can walk up the stream-bed so you won't leave a blood trail."

"Is that so?" Dave asked as he and Hollis came back in with two sticks that would serve as splints on Mike's leg.

I nodded, answering Dave. "That bone is shattered. Mike won't make it through twenty miles of this terrain. Blood loss and shock will kill him before we've gone a mile. And that's if we aren't killed first. Moving through the wilderness carrying Mike isn't exactly going to be a quiet process. But alone I can do the distance in six or seven hours, maybe even make Pai before sunrise if I don't have to do too much hiding. I'll get help and come back."

"They'll be coming after you," Mike said.

"Yeah," I said. "In fact, I plan to make sure of it. I can hide alone far easier than all four of us. And make better time. One way or another, this plan will work. Even if I'm not back by tomorrow night, I doubt they will have this bridge guarded anymore."

Dave nodded. "You're right. They'll think we've gotten out of this area. They'll be looking for us on the road past the bridge. We can try to move then, if we have to."

I knelt beside Mike's leg.

No one said another word as Dave and I braced the leg with splints and tied them on. Mike was in so much pain that for a moment I thought he might pass out.

"John, I'll go with you," Hollis said after we had finished getting Mike's leg splinted.

"No," I said, turning to face Hollis. "I'm sorry, but I can move faster without you. And it's going to take both of you to get Mike back into that cave."

"Take this," Mike said, reaching for the AK-47 that lay on the ground beside him.

"No," I said again, feeling ill again at just the thought of taking it. "I'll be a moving target. You guys won't. It will do you more good. With it, you can defend yourselves in the cave if they find you."

Mike and Dave both nodded.

I turned and moved back to the man I had killed. I was pretty sure he had extra ammunition clips in his jacket. I had felt one or two press into my skin as we fought with him.

I dug around in his pockets, pulling out the clips, then a lighter, then two candy bars. I added the flashlight the guy had been shining when he was trying to find us.

This bounty of things we needed seemed so strange in my hand that I couldn't believe I was holding them. I finally held them up for Dave to see, and he shook his head, saying, "The Lord provides in strange ways."

I didn't reply, but I didn't feel that God had anything to do with that killing. That was all adrenaline, fear, and anger. But I wasn't turning my back on these spoils of war, either.

I broke off half of one of the two candy bars and stuck it in my pocket. My stomach was too upset to eat it now, but I would need some energy along the way.

Then I handed the rest of the bars, the ammunition clips, and the flashlight to Dave, along with the man's lighter.

For some reason, I felt as though I was thinking clearer than I had ever thought before. I knew exactly what had to be done next. Later, though, when I looked back, it seemed more likely that at that moment I was in deep shock.

"Help me," I said to Dave.

Dave put the clips on the ground beside Mike and the gun, stuffed the candy bars into his pockets, then joined me. I moved around to the man's shoulders; Dave took up a position at his feet.

"What are you going to do?" Hollis asked.

"Buy us a little more time," I said.

Dave nodded, and together we picked up the dead man. He felt far, far heavier than he looked, and his head rolled against one of my arms, looking like it might just twist off at any moment.

I wanted to be sick again, but I somehow swallowed the bile and kept moving down the bank.

The gunman smelled far worse than he had before, as if he had soiled his pants as he died. I had heard that people did that, but I hadn't thought about it until now, when the stench of it was filling my nose.

Together, Dave and I stumbled down the bank on the trail toward the stream where it ran under the bridge. Dave dropped the man's legs once, but somehow I managed to hold onto him all the way.

We laid the body in the cold water in the fastest part of the stream.

"I hope the Lord sends this man to the hell he belongs in," Dave said. "And lets his soul burn forever there."

I looked at Dave. "I'd rather pray to God for His mercy than for His justice. My hands took this man's life."

He had been a man. He had been a sinner. But we were all sinners.

I had killed him.

I was no better than he was or than Hollis was for his fornication. I was worse, as far as I was concerned. Far worse.

I knew better than to kill. I knew God's Word. I had promised to follow it.

"You did what you had to do," Dave said.

I didn't say anything, just watched as the body floated off. It got caught on a rock about twenty feet beyond the bridge, and I stood there, numb, trying not to think, as Dave splashed down the edge of the stream and got the body floating in the current again.

A moment later the body of the man I had killed vanished into the rapids heading toward the river. It would wash up on the riverbank downstream somewhere. But maybe his friends wouldn't find him, certainly not anytime soon. And that might buy me just a little extra time as they looked for him.

I rinsed the feel of the man's skin off my hands in the stream, then we both climbed back up the bank.

Mike had moved off the trail and was leaning with his back against a tree. Hollis was busy spreading dirt and rocks and plant matter over the bloody areas. Mike's wound had left the ground black with blood in the moonlight.

"Help me up," Mike said.

Dave and I moved to Mike's side and helped him stand. For a moment, I thought the pain would knock him out.

Then Mike took a deep breath and nodded. "You're right, John. I wouldn't make it."

"But I will," I said, hoping I sounded a lot more confident than I felt. "I'll be back with help soon."

I picked up the gun and handed it to Dave. He slung it over his shoulder. Hollis pocketed the flashlight. I gave Hollis my fanny pack with the hydrogen peroxide and Advil in it, and Hollis strapped the pack around his middle. Then Dave handed me the water bottle. It was three-quarters full. More than enough for the time being.

"Get going," Mike said to me.

Hollis took my spot under Mike's arm, and the three of them looked at me.

"I will be back with help. Wait in the cave at least until dark tomorrow."

"May God be with you," Mike said.

I said nothing at first. I knew God could forgive anything. But I wasn't sure I could call on God right now, feeling the way I felt. I was a killer. I suddenly had an inkling of how Hollis had felt, back in that hotel lobby. I wondered how he'd found the inner strength to face us, to go on. I wanted to run away from myself, from my hands that had felt a life end under them. I wanted to turn time back, make everything come out differently.

But that wasn't going to help us now. Or ever.

Time to get moving.

"See you tomorrow," I said finally.

The three of them turned and started down the bank toward the stream. They would stay in the water all the way to the spot below the cave, then try to go directly up without leaving too much of a trail. I sure hoped Mike would make it that far. I had no doubt that if Dave had to, he would carry him. And from the way Mike looked, it just might come to that.

Things were that desperate.

I knew if I didn't get back here with help very quickly, Mike would die. I couldn't let that happen.

I took one more look around to make sure that we had left nothing behind, that no sign of a fight showed in the trail's dirt and rocks, that no blood stains were visible. Hollis had done a good job.

Then I turned and went up on the bridge. I felt almost naked up there in the open, on the road, over the stream.

Below me, in the stream, I could see Mike and Dave and Hollis, the three closest friends of my youth and adulthood, working their way slowly up into the dark of the hillside jungle.

It was now up to me to save their lives. I had never felt more afraid in my life.

I would have time later to deal with what I had done, to come to terms with my sins, to seek the forgiveness I knew God promised me for my sins, no matter how terrible they were. I didn't deserve it.

But right now my friends needed me to focus, stay on the task at hand, and get back here with some kind of help.

At a jog, I ran past the lawn chair sitting alone on the bridge. It had belonged to the man I killed.

It was empty.

As empty and alone as I felt.

25

Though you already know all this, I want
to remind you that the Lord delivered his
people out of Egypt, but later destroyed
those who did not believe.

JUDE 1:5

9:42 p.m., November 15
Highway 1095, southeast of Pai, Thailand

I HALF JOGGED, HALF WALKED ALONG THE ROAD AWAY
from the bridge, maintaining the best pace I could. My boots
weren't cut out for running, and not having eaten or slept in
a day didn't help my energy level. But the thought of Mike
dying kept forcing me into a jog, made me try to move faster.

Besides, I wanted to put as much distance as I could between me and the men who were after us.

They weren't going to be happy when they discovered their bridge guard was missing.

The sliver of a moon gave me enough light to see, and thankfully, the temperature was much cooler than the night before.

The road stayed with the river through the canyon, then started upward, winding its way back and forth up a mountainside, following the natural terrain of the land as it climbed. The roaring of the river faded away in the distance until my footsteps on the hard gravel surface became the loudest noise.

I stayed to the right side of the road, ready at a moment's notice to drop into the jungle or trees or rocks beside the road if I saw anyone, or if a car or truck came along. I didn't think the would-be kidnappers had another guard on the road on this side of the bridge, but I wasn't completely sure of it. I knew I shouldn't take a chance on it, yet I had no choice but to stay out in the open on the road if I hoped to make the journey fast enough to save Mike's life.

I just prayed that if there *was* another guard posted along the road, that I would see him before he saw me.

The road got steeper as it climbed away from the valley floor. Any attempt I made at running fell back to fast walking after twenty or thirty steps. Even fast walking seemed difficult. I found myself sweating and panting as I climbed, and twice I almost stopped, only pushing on because I couldn't handle the thought of Mike dying because I'd failed him.

I had enough blood on my conscience as it was.

After what I guessed was two miles, I finally reached the top of a ridge. The road wound along a cliff top. There was a rock wall on my right, a long drop into darkness on my left. I felt trapped on this part of the road. If someone came along, I had nowhere to hide except a shallow ditch between the road and the cliff face.

I ran along the top of the ridge, relieved when the road finally crested and started back down through the jungle. There, I slowed to a normal walk to catch my breath. I downed half the bottle of water, then forced myself to eat a part of the candy bar. I tried not to think about where I got the bar from. I just ate it. It wouldn't do Mike any good if I passed out from hunger halfway to Pai.

The nuts and caramel of the candy tasted better than I had ever thought anything could taste. I chewed on it slowly, letting the sense that I was eating reach my mind and stomach.

Then I took another sip of water.

The road in front of me slanted downward through the jungle, with trees spreading over the narrow lane to block the light. I suddenly felt as if I were walking into a dark tunnel, and for a moment my claustrophobia returned. But then I caught a glimpse of some stars and the moon through the branches, and that fear cleared away. *Thank You, God.*

The eyes of the man I had killed seemed to float in front of me in the pitch darkness of the descending road. *Dear God, what have I done? Why did I push so hard on his neck? Why didn't I just grab another rock and hit him with it to knock him out? Why did I put myself into this situation? Why did I want to test myself against the wilderness?*

I felt disgusted at my anger at Hollis for his actions in Bangkok. I'd wondered then how he could have given in to temptation so easily. Now I knew. I'd killed a man. Without meaning to, I had committed a mortal sin. I knew now that I wasn't fit to stand in judgment over anyone. I understood exactly what Christ meant when he stopped the people from stoning a woman. He had said, "He that is without sin among you, let him first cast a stone at her."

No one is blameless. We are all sinners. Judgment is the Lord's, and it is our mission in life to find a measure of God's grace in our hearts for others when they repent. As it says in Luke, "If your brother sins, rebuke him, and if he repents, forgive him."

Like Hollis.

Now I was glad that I'd found the inner strength to forgive Hollis and that I'd helped him reach for the Lord. I had told him that the Lord offered forgiveness of sins, no matter how heavy, if a sinner asked for it. I'd need to learn that lesson. Because now I need God's infinite forgiveness for myself.

And I felt afraid to even talk to God.

Lorraine's face appeared like a vision in front of me on the dark road. I kept walking toward her, trying to get to her. Then her eyes became the eyes of the dead man, and I pushed them both away, focusing on the faint edge of the road and nothing more.

Nothing.

How could I ever again face the woman I loved? How could I ever tell her of my sin? Would she ever be able to forgive me?

A low rumbling caught my attention and I stopped, trying to hold my breath and listen. The darkness seemed even more intense, with no moon or stars showing through the branches over my head. The edge of the road was only a very faint line between one shade of dark and another.

For a moment, I thought the rumbling was that of a truck. Then it became clear I was hearing a stream. Or maybe the river. I had descended a long way in the dark. Maybe the road went back near the river? Mike had said, from his memory of the map, that he thought it didn't, but nothing was certain. He might not have paid that much attention to our route farther away from the camp. I knew I hadn't.

I kept walking, alternating between thinking the sound was that of a truck coming and knowing it was a waterfall. It was amazing what tricks the mind can play with perception in almost complete darkness.

I really was in the wilderness.

We had picked this river for its remoteness, but it had never occurred to me that I would be alone in this wilderness, struggling to find help, to save Mike's life.

To save my own life.

To save the lives of all my friends.

Finally the road turned to the left and came out from under the canopy of trees. The moonlight seemed almost bright now considering how my eyes had tried to adjust to the darkness under the dense foliage. A waterfall cascaded down over the rocks on the right, went under the road in a large culvert, and then over another falls toward a dark valley below.

I had no idea how far I had come. For a moment, I wondered if I was still even on the right road. Could I have gotten onto a side road? Could I be heading for the border?

I stopped and took a deep breath, working to stay calm, to think clearly.

No, I had to believe I was on the right path, headed for help. Any other thought made me panic, and right now the lives of my friends depended on my thinking clearly and making the journey through this wilderness.

Lord, I prayed, *I know I'm not worthy, but please guide my steps tonight. I have never needed You more in my life. I place myself in Your hands.* That uncanny clarity of thought I'd had since I decided to make this journey alone intensified.

I didn't like being so close to the waterfall, since I couldn't hear if a truck or car was coming in the distance. I went back to jogging, putting as much distance down the hill as I could between me and the noise of the water.

With every step, it felt as if I would fall on my face, but somehow I got my heavy boots under me again for another step.

And then another.

The road finally went around a corner and into the jungle canopy and darkness. I had to slow to a walk. I could feel blisters forming on my feet from the rough treatment I was giving them. Boots like mine just weren't made for running.

As the darkness closed in around me again, my thoughts seemed to lose control, one thought flashing past on top of the one before it.

I was so far from home, I could no longer think of that home.

My only friends close by were depending on me to find my way.

It felt as if every step of the road held a danger, every curve a possible ambush.

Lorraine's face came back clear to me. She was frowning, worried, as she had been in many of our conversations about God. *Trust the still small voice of the Lord. You'll be fine.* Her words seemed to echo in my head.

I walked as fast as I dared through the almost total darkness under the jungle canopy, wanting to break into a run again, to get out of the black, to get this journey over with. A journey that had pushed me further than I'd ever wanted to go.

A journey that had left me desperate and broken before God and those I loved.

A verse in Matthew came to me as if I were hearing it for the first time: *For if you forgive men when they sin against you, your heavenly Father will also forgive you.*

I had forgiven Hollis. And others in the past. I had told them that God would always forgive the repentant sinner. But the question that was haunting me was whether I could find the strength to forgive myself.

I'd watched Hollis struggle with that very issue. I never appreciated more the courage he'd had in going forward after that night in Bangkok. If he could do it, I could do it.

I stared ahead into the darkness, forcing myself to keep moving and not think about my hurting feet or my shortness of breath. Instead, I went over my biblical teachings, making myself think calmly. Many, many people had been tested by God in the wilderness. Moses and Jesus both. They had gone out to find themselves, and their faith in Him had been tested. When I chose to go into the wilderness, perhaps God had used that opportunity to test my faith as well.

I stumbled in a hole in the road's surface and fell to my knees, scraping my legs and one hand. I stayed there for a moment, trying to catch my breath and get past the sudden pain of the fall. Then I realized that the weakness of my body had given me insight into the depths of my soul.

Dear God, I am a sinner, unworthy of your love. I stumble and fall on the path of life every day. Please help me pick myself up and struggle onward to find my way to You. Forgive me, and help me find a way to forgive myself. And help me now, as I face the duty before me. Please keep Mike and the others alive until I can bring help. Please. Help them stay alive.

I scrambled up and kept going, trying to watch the road ahead as much as I could in the darkness.

The road was climbing again. I kept going, putting one foot in front of the other, asking God to help me, asking for forgiveness for my actions, asking for the safety of my friends.

Trust the still small voice. Lorraine's face came back to me, her smile as clear as if she were walking with me.

She was with me.

God was with me.

I could hear that small voice all the way to the depths of my spirit.

I stumbled again, but this time I didn't go down. God was with me in this wilderness. I believed in Him. I believed in His ways. With His help, I would get through this.

With that thought, I felt a surge of strength go through me. And the awareness of something else. I had been so wrapped up in my thoughts, so shut off because of the pain of climbing, that I hadn't been paying attention to the road or the jungle around me.

Something was coming up the hill behind me. A car, a truck, who knew? But something.

The sound grew louder and louder by the moment.

I stood there, frozen. It seemed like an eternity before I finally made myself move. I dove off the road to the right and rolled into the brush, coming up on my hands and knees, scrambling for a tree trunk to hide behind. Like a bad movie scene, the vehicle's lights filled the jungle as it came speeding around the corner.

I got behind the tree and waited, thanking God for helping me move as fast as I had.

The vehicle didn't slow.

They didn't see me!

When the vehicle was even with me, I glanced up. The equipment van from our rafting company flashed past, kicking up a cloud of dust.

Four men were in it.

All of them had guns held at the ready.

26

Give your burdens to the LORD,
and he will take care of you.
He will not permit the godly to slip and fall.

PSALM 55:22, NLT

10:49 p.m., November 15
Somewhere in the wilderness, Northern Thailand

I WAITED, ALMOST HOLDING MY BREATH, UNTIL THE VAN had gone by and the lights had vanished completely. I couldn't hear the second van coming up the road, or any other car. The tree I hid behind had a faint smell of damp bark and mold, and a plant I had knelt on had scratched my leg. I didn't have any antiseptic to put on it, since I had given the bottle to Mike for his wound.

Lord, please give me guidance on what to do next.

I stood and eased back out onto the road in the darkness. No sounds. I strained to hear, holding my breath.

Nothing.

My watch told me I had been traveling for ninety minutes, maybe less. I might have covered six, maybe seven miles in that time, which meant I still had a good twelve miles to go, if not more.

And now there were four of the gunmen between me and my destination. I would have to be extra careful. I had to try to outthink them, even though I didn't know the terrain ahead of me at all.

I went back to an even jog, pressing on as fast as I could over the ground I knew they wouldn't be watching, since I had heard the van keep going into the distance.

Lord, please give me strength to keep going. Forgive me for what I have done. Keep my friends safe, please. Help me find them help.

As I ran, I kept talking to God, asking for His guidance, for His help.

And I also tried to calm down and think about why the four men in the van had gone by me so fast. They were either going all the way into Pai to get extra help in their search or, more likely, were following the road to set up guards along the way to intercept us.

They must have figured that all four of us had left the valley after they couldn't find their friend, the bridge guard. Or maybe the four guards in the van were just insurance, sent ahead to post watch while the others looked for their missing conspirator.

That seemed more likely to me. If they were really convinced all of us had escaped the valley, they would all be heading this way. And I knew that there were way more than four men involved in hunting us. I'd seen them. Eventually, the rest of the gang would be headed up this road too. I was convinced of that.

The thought of eight to ten men with machine guns searching for me along this road suddenly had me very scared. I slowed to a walk and let myself take some deep breaths. As I walked, I took another drink of water, then ate the last of the candy bar. I would need all the energy I could get.

I went back to running as the road leveled some on the top of a ridgeline. After a few hundred paces, I again broke out into the moonlight and stars. My eyes were so used to the darkness by now, the light from the half moon seemed almost blindingly bright.

I moved over to the edge of the road and looked down, trying to see anything ahead that might help me. In the valley, I could see a few specks of lights from some farms scattered along the valley floor. More than likely the lights were from lanterns. For a moment I considered just cutting down off the road to one of the distant farms but then realized that I wouldn't find any real help at any of them. I didn't speak the language, so I wouldn't be able to explain my situation.

No, I had to reach Pai, to get to the police and the agency called the Tourist Police, if there was an office of that organization in such a small town. Those authorities would be the only ones with enough power to help me get back to my friends with the manpower to assure our safety.

The only ones I could trust.

Then, as if coming out of a tunnel, the van appeared on the valley floor, its headlights amazingly bright in the darkness, even from such a long distance away. It looked to me as if they hadn't stopped at all on the way down. That was good. It meant that at least that much of the road ahead was clear.

I watched as the van twisted across the valley and started to climb up the hill on the other side. It had to be a good two miles away from me, if not more. I could hear only the faintest rumblings of its engine, like a distant thunderstorm.

The van didn't stop at all as it climbed, following one switchback after another. From what I could tell, that mountain ahead of me was very, very steep, and the road crossed in the open back and forth so many times, I lost count.

Finally the van made one last turn at a height that seemed as if I was looking up at it across the valley. It sent its high-beam lights out into the sky and then vanished. If they were going to set up guards waiting for us, that would be where they would do it. Right there on the top of that hill on the pass. If I was right about the distance, Pai must lay in the valley on the other side.

And I had no doubt that the others in their group would be coming along behind them, searching as they came. If I was right about their plans, I would be trapped between the groups.

I would have to figure something out quickly.

I went back to an even jog and after a few hundred yards, the road went back into jungle and darkness. The words of the Twenty-third Psalm echoed in my mind: *Even though I walk through the valley of the shadow of death, I will fear no evil, for You are with me.*

It didn't get any darker than this, any more dangerous.

Please, forgive me for what I did. I had no intention of killing. Look into my soul, Lord; please see that. Help me come to terms with it. I am a sinner. Forgive me.

I kept running. The hill's slope made each step as if I were falling forward and then managing to get a foot under me before I went face first into the dirt and gravel. It seemed to me, in the darkness, that with each step I plunged forward for the longest time, going down and down, before I finally found the road with my foot.

I tried to stay aware of the world around me, to listen for another van, but I could see so little of anything in the deep jungle that my running became a blind, nightmarish journey of one step after another. The sounds of my own breathing and my pounding footsteps were the only things I could hear in the darkness.

Finally I slowed to a walk as the road leveled. The sound of a van was coming at me again, this time from the direction of Pai, rather than from the camp.

Once more I ducked off the road and into a stand of trees, lying down and making sure my face was covered. I didn't dare look at the oncoming lights. The last thing I needed was for my eyes to reflect the lights of the van like an animal on the road.

But I had to try to look as they passed. I needed to know how many men were in it.

The roaring of the van's engine sounded like a wild animal charging. Everything around me seemed to shake, even the leaves of the trees. I could feel the power of the vehicle vibrating through the ground under my chest.

As the direct beam of the lights passed me, I looked up. The same van I'd seen before. Two men, both in the front seat. No one else with them.

More than likely, they had dropped off the other two on the pass ahead of me. That made sense. If we actually had escaped from their valley trap, they had to make sure we didn't get into Pai. So they'd left a couple of their buddies on the road ahead. And since they knew the terrain and I didn't, it seemed that I would have to go past those two to get to my destination.

I lay there despairing as the van climbed the hill I had just come down, the sound of its engine growing fainter and fainter in the night air. I was as trapped as I had been before I had killed the guard.

I was going to die out here. Mike would die in the cave. Dave and Hollis would die trying to escape. No one would ever know what happened to us. Fatigue and hopelessness swept over me. I continued to lie there, broken in my weakness and fear.

The van's noise disappeared. The silence of the jungle closed in around me.

I wanted to just close my eyes, lay my head down, take a quick nap. What would it matter? I was trapped. We were already as good as dead. "I'm sorry, Lorraine," I said, my voice hoarse and loud to my ears in the darkness. "Please forgive me."

I laid my head down and closed my eyes. Words filled my mind. That still small voice.

Give yourself over completely to the Lord. Trust Him and you will be safe.

"I'm Yours, Lord," I said into the darkness. "I'm Yours."

Saying those words broke me down and tears filled my eyes. I found myself sobbing into my hands, lying in the jungle in the darkness.

"I'm Yours."

Everything seemed to drain out of my body at that moment. I lay there, completely in God's hands.

God is with you.

The image of Mike lying on the path, bleeding, filled my mind.

Trust God. Put your life in His hands.

My duty, my very reason for living right now, was to save Mike and Hollis and Dave. I put my life in God's hands. I had gone down into the darkness both literally and emotionally. I now had to move, to allow God to help me save my friends.

I pushed myself to my feet and staggered back out onto the dark road. God was with me, God would help me. He would tell me what to do when I needed to do it.

"Thank You, Lord," I said out loud into the stillness of the night. Then I started to walk down the road in the dark, slowly at first, then faster and faster.

Mike was depending on me. God was with me. I could do this.

And for the first time since starting on this journey, I believed I could.

27

We depend on the LORD alone to save us.

Only he can help us, protecting us like a shield.

PSALM 33:20, NLT

12:07 a.m., November 16
A valley southeast of Pai, Thailand

I JOGGED MOST OF THE REST OF THE WAY DOWN THE HILL, stumbling at times, but still managing to keep running. My feet felt hot and bloody in my boots, but I didn't dare stop. Not if I planned to survive. Blisters and pain were a very small price to pay at this point.

I finally stopped at the edge of the jungle where the road started across some fields. The open road and the moonlight ahead looked inviting, but something kept me in the shadows of the trees. I moved over and leaned against a tree, working to catch my breath, listening for any sounds of a vehicle coming.

No night birds, no wind stirring the leaves, no animal calls. Nothing.

Yet something had stopped me there.

I took a few more deep breaths and tried to look at the situation as clearly as my exhausted mind would allow. In the moonlight, I could see the steep-walled mountain on the other side of the mile-wide valley. I could see dark slices in the hillside where the road snaked its way up the side of what looked almost like a rock cliff.

Two men were on top of that mountain, waiting with guns to kill us. Of that fact, I had no doubt. I had no idea how I would get past them and into Pai in the next valley.

If Pai was even in the next valley.

I glanced at my watch. I had been moving for almost two and a half hours. If I was managing about five miles an hour between running and fast walking, like I thought, I had to have traveled twelve miles or more. It was a good mile across the valley, then another mile up that mountain. That meant that Pai pretty much had to be in the next major valley on the other side of that mountain.

Suddenly it dawned on me why I had stopped here. The men with guns very well could be watching the road in the valley from up there. They had a clear line of sight from the cliff top. If they were watching, they would see me walking on it in the moonlight.

Something had told me they were watching. And if I taken another ten steps out of the darkness of the jungle and into the moonlight on the valley floor, they would have seen me, and all hope would have been lost.

God had stopped me just in time, I was sure of that.

"Thank You, Lord," I whispered into the darkness. "Thank You."

God was with me, and He was watching out for me in every way possible. That thought gave me energy, made me want to push onward at once.

But how?

Which way?

I made myself take stock of my surroundings, trying to remember the map we had spent time looking over in my dining room. That seemed so long ago, in such a different lifetime, that it felt as if I had been another person. I thought about that for a second. All this, after finally giving myself over to God completely, made me see that I *had* been another person.

For the first time, I now understood what Lorraine had meant about my faith being shallow. It had been. I hadn't yet put my entire life in God's hands. I had read of so many instances in Scripture about people being tested and finding their faith, yet until now, I had never understood those stories in any real and meaningful way.

I knew that when I told Lorraine this, she would just smile fondly at me. Somehow, she had always known I would reach this place, that I would give myself to the Lord completely. I don't think she had imagined it would take this level of testing to goad me into it, but she had always known I would do it.

I pushed the images of Lorraine's smiling face away and tried to remember the map on my dining room table. If Pai was over that mountain directly in front of me, then the river was to the right of me. That river got within a few miles of Pai, if I remembered right. I couldn't be sure, but I was willing to bet there had been a pretty good road from Pai down to the river area, since we had talked about floating the river all the way down to there.

We had eventually decided not to. Mike said he had talked to the guides about it, and they said the water was too high in this area. Or something like that. I couldn't remember exactly because it just hadn't been important then.

I knew that to the left of me was nothing but steep mountains, mountain tribes, and eventually the border with Myanmar. I remembered what had happened to the well-equipped men in WWII who'd tried to survive in the Burma theater. There was no hope for me to the left.

Nothing but death forward down that road and across the valley.

So going right it was. I needed to find the river again. I knew that as clearly as I ever knew anything because God was helping me, directing me. He had stopped me here to save me, to turn me off the wrong path and onto the correct one.

I pushed myself away from the tree. Staying in the shadows of the jungle, I worked my way to the right along the hillside, following the borders of farmers' fields. It felt very strange to be leaving the road. I had come to think of it as my lifeline back to Mike and the cave. But God was making me give up even that last strand of false security.

I kept up an ongoing conversation with God as I worked my way farther and farther away from the road. I kept asking Him for forgiveness for my sin of killing that bridge guard, asking Him to look into my heart, look at my intentions, why my actions were what they were. Asking for Him to let me forgive myself.

I also asked Him for help in directions, for help in seeing dangers, for help in continuing on even though I was as tired as I could ever remember being.

I asked for help even though I knew I was unworthy, yet I also knew that God forgave the unworthy, always had, as long as they trusted in Him and tried their hardest to follow the path He set for them.

I knew God was with me. I had no doubt. And it felt good to talk to Him. It gave me great comfort.

The traveling was slow, since there was no trail. I found myself climbing over logs and shoving my way through brush to keep going. I ended up with one cut on my arm that was bleeding enough that I had to stop and wrap a strip of my shirt around it.

Every fifteen minutes, I would move down to the edge of the jungle and check my position. I could still see where the road went up the steep face, but it was now to my left and almost behind me. What worried me was that I couldn't hear the river. If there were any rapids at all, I should be able to hear it.

I passed near one farmer's hut tucked into the edge of the jungle. It looked occupied, though dark at this time of night. I did my best to remain as silent as I could. I didn't need a farmer waking up, turning on a light, and drawing the attention of the men standing guard on the pass to this part of the valley. I wanted those men with guns to stay right where they were, not come down here and chase me to the river.

I finally reached a place where I could no longer see the road, or the cuts the switchbacks made into the cliff face. I felt safe in moving out into the open a little more and moving at a faster pace. My sidetrack along the jungle had taken a good hour, and I doubted I was any closer to Pai. More than likely, I was farther away.

A rough road, more like a wagon trail, cut up the middle of the valley. I moved along an irrigation dike and got to the trail, which allowed me to pick up my speed a lot.

Within ten minutes, I heard the river ahead. The wagon trail headed directly for it, and as I came over a little rise, it was clear why. The area was used for watering livestock, swimming, and more than likely doing laundry.

The river beyond the muddy area where the wagon track disappeared seemed wide and black and very calm. But there were clearly rapids not that far away downstream, since I could hear the rumbling of the water.

A well-used footpath ran along the banks of the river, going in both directions. I turned left and followed it. For a moment, I thought about running again, then the fear of twisting an ankle stopped me. It was one thing to run on a paved road, another on a dirt path along a riverbank.

I crossed the end of the valley going back toward the mountains that I guessed separated me from Pai. The closer I got to those steep-faced mountains, the louder the river got, the faster the water flowed in the same direction I was walking.

I had thought I might be able to find a log or some planks, or even borrow a boat, and float my way down to Pai. But there had been no boats along the bank. That meant it was too dangerous to be on the river, even for local farmers. Also, from the looks of the banks, the guide Mike had talked to had been right. The water in the river here was very, very high.

And from the sounds of the rapids ahead, floating might not be a good idea. I might be better off facing two men with guns than class-three or class-four rapids without a boat.

The sound of the river got so loud it drowned out all other

noise around me, even my footsteps. I knew my decision had been made for me. I wasn't going into that water. Not with any hope of surviving.

The river seemed to cut down through a rock canyon, slicing through a narrow gap in the mountain. I climbed off the road and up onto a flat rock to take a look. In the faint moonlight, all I could see were massive standing waves and whitewater. Class three at best. Maybe even bordering on four. Those rapids would scare me in a professional raft with Mike in control.

God didn't want me going that way.

I climbed back off the rock and kept going on the road that followed the river. It seemed to be very well traveled, which meant it went somewhere. More than likely just along the valley floor under the cliff face and back to the main road. But at the moment, it was my only choice.

In another hundred steps, the road veered right at the canyon as I had expected, but then turned back up the valley and started to climb up the mountain.

Had God shown me a different route out of this valley? A different road over the mountain? The more I climbed, the clearer the answer became—that was exactly what I had found.

Thank You, Lord.

I kept going, climbing. The road sliced across the steep hill, moving upward in the direction of the main road with every one of my steps. I kept praying that at some point, the road would cut back toward the river, but it didn't.

If this joined the main road right at the top, that would probably be where the guards would be posted. I could be walking right into an ambush.

I stayed to the inside, against the rock cliff face and in the shadows. The sounds of the river were now a distant thunder behind me. My footsteps seemed impossibly loud to my ears again.

The road crested over the top of the steep face. And turned slightly left toward Pai. So far, so good. I wasn't sure how far up the valley I had come, but my guess was that the main road wasn't that far from me.

The road wound gently, moving upward through the thick jungle that covered the top of the mountain. I walked as quietly as I could, ready to jump into the jungle and run at any moment.

Every sense I had was on high alert.

I had no idea where the two men would be stationed on the main road. I just hoped they didn't know about this secondary farm road. Or if they did, I hoped they wouldn't think I could find it, and thus would not guard it.

Suddenly, to my right, I heard a man cough. Hard, like he had a smoker's cough or maybe a bad cold.

My entire body froze. I was afraid to even take a breath.

Another man said something in a language I didn't under-stand. The first man laughed, then coughed again. Both men were together and to my right.

I must have gotten very close to the main road without knowing it. If I had tripped, or made any noise at all, they would have heard me.

I took a shallow breath and tried to listen. I had no idea how far sound traveled on such a still, windless night. But I would guess that they weren't more than a hundred paces from me directly through the jungle along the ridgeline.

My heart threatened to pound right out of my chest. I couldn't believe they couldn't hear the pounding.

The two men kept talking. Laughing, coughing, talking.

They didn't know I was here. That thought slowly sunk in. They hadn't heard me.

Yet.

I had to move, had to keep going. But I felt frozen with fear. *God, help me.*

As one man went off on a loud coughing fit again, I started forward.

Thank You.

I tiptoed down the road like a kid trying to sneak in late at night after staying out past curfew. I put each foot down like I was placing a new baby on a diaper-changing table, carefully, quietly, the sound of even the tiniest pebble underfoot echoing in my ears.

This road was angling past the two killers and toward the main road, working its way through the jungle.

They kept talking.

I kept moving, slowly, carefully, taking shallow, silent breaths.

All the while, I kept up my conversation with God in my head, asking for His guidance, His help in making my footsteps silent, His help in keeping Mike alive until I got back with help. The words were a lifeline to me.

For what seemed like hours but must have been only minutes, I worked my way past them on the side road. I wanted to break into a run to get away from them, but somehow God helped me keep my motions slow, even, and silent.

Finally I reached the area where the side road joined the main road. The two men were a good two hundred paces back toward Mike and the men's friends.

God had helped me past the men.

I stopped and crouched at the base of a tree, trying to decide if I should cut into the jungle or chance going into the open on the road, hoping neither of them came back this way.

The jungle seemed like a dangerous choice, since I was on a ridgeline. Who knew where there would be sudden drops and rocks? Not me, certainly. In the jungle, I wouldn't be able to see where I was going, and I would make a lot more noise.

On the road, there was light.

From where I was, I couldn't see the two men, but I could

still hear their voices talking about something I couldn't under-stand. What would two killers talk about in the middle of the night while they waited to get us?

Family? Murders they had committed? What? I didn't really wanted to know.

But as long as they were talking, they weren't coming back this way. And the other guys were looking for us back toward the camp, waiting for someone to pass them.

The moment I had that thought, I knew my next action.

I eased out onto the main road, turned my back on the two men, and started away from them, walking as quietly and as quickly as I could toward Pai.

Never had I done anything that took that much courage. I wanted to glance over my shoulder with every step, but instead I focused on the road under my feet, making sure I made as little noise as possible, that my footing was secure with every step. I let my ears be my warning. If the two men stopped talk-ing, I would stop walking.

I kept my back to them and kept going.

They kept talking, chatting like two old friends, for as long as I could hear them.

Finally their voices didn't even carry to my ears anymore as I started off the ridgeline and down into the next valley.

Ahead, I could see the lights of the small town of Pai. It was the best sight I had ever seen.

28

Fight the good fight of the faith. Take hold
of the eternal life to which you were called
when you made your good confession
in the presence of many witnesses.
1 TIMOTHY 6:12

4:16 a.m., November 16
Pai, Thailand

THE TINY VILLAGE OF PAI SEEMED EVEN SMALLER THAN I
had imagined it to be. I hadn't read anything about it since we
hadn't planned on getting any closer to it than our camp. So I
had no idea where to go or what I was walking into. But at that
point, I didn't much care.

It had to be better than where I'd come from.

The closer I got to the small village, the more I ran.

"Thank You, Lord.

"Thank You, Lord.

"Thank You, Lord."

I just kept repeating those words over and over.

It was so late at night that the place felt like a ghost town as I ran through it, and my footsteps echoed like thunderbolts among the low buildings. I passed a few bars, all locked up tight. I thought about banging on the door of a small guesthouse with a restaurant attached, then changed my mind.

I just kept running, even though my feet sent stabbing pains through my legs with every step. I was so close to finding help. I couldn't let anything stop me now.

The Lord had brought me here, sent me through the wilderness and out the other side.

"Thank You, Lord.

"Thank You, Lord.

"Thank You, Lord."

I came to what looked to be one of four main intersections in the small town. The international sign for *hospital* caught my attention, and I headed there. I crossed the lit stoop and burst through the door into a small entryway. There I found a small clinic with a phone number posted on the door.

The door was locked.

I banged hard on that door, but no one came and answered my pleas.

I went back outside and ran to my right, my footsteps on the wide road still echoing between the buildings as if I was back in the wilderness, as if I hadn't actually reached safety.

Was God trying to tell me something?

Was I forgetting something? This had been my goal. Had this been wrong? I could think of no other choice.

A number of older cars and newer vans and buses were parked along the street. The silence of the town felt wrong, as if no one lived here. Was I back in the cave having a bad nightmare? Or had everyone in this small village been killed as well?

My tired mind kept making up problem after problem as I ran.

I forced myself to walk for a moment to catch my breath and think. This was a small town. It was after four in the morning. Of course there wouldn't be anyone awake. There was no way to get to this town except over that impossible road I had just traveled, and by air during the day. There would be no reason for anyone to be awake now, except maybe some police.

That thought calmed me some. Not much, though. Even at four in the morning, there had to be someone around and awake, hadn't there?

I turned onto another road, and there ahead I could see the sign for *police*, shining like a blue star. "Thank You, Lord!" I shouted, my voice echoing down the empty street. Again, I broke into a run to cover the last two blocks.

As I reached the building, I slowed down and made myself not run through the open door and into the well-lighted lobby, for fear that I might scare whoever was inside. But I had been running so hard that I was panting like a dog when I finally did slow down. Sweat was running down my forehead into my eyes, and what was left of my shirt was stuck to me like a wet rag.

Two men looked up from desks behind a low counter at me. The moment they saw me, their eyes got wide.

"I need help," I said, in my mangled tourist version of Thai.

"I can see that," one man replied in almost perfect English. "Shall I call a physician?"

"No, no," I said, trying to catch my breath. "Not yet. Right now I need police help."

He looked to be about my age, with a slight gut and tanned skin. His hairline was receding and as he spoke to me, he took off his reading glasses. He didn't have a uniform on, but there was a patch on the sleeve of his tan shirt and a badge attached to his chest. I couldn't see any guns in sight at all.

He was wearing a crucifix.

I had found a Christian in what was mainly a Buddhist country. A Christian who spoke English. A sign from God, perhaps?

The other man had on the same type of shirt and badge, but he looked much smaller than the man who had spoken.

The second man couldn't have been more than twenty years old and was clearly an assistant of some type.

Not seeming to be in a hurry, the older man moved to a water bottle tipped upside down in a dispenser, filled a paper cup with water, and then turned and handed it to me over the counter. "My name is Keveh," he said. "I'm in charge of the police here in the evenings. Drink and then you can tell me what has happened to you."

I started to object, then I did as I was told, downing the coldest, freshest-tasting water I could ever remember drinking.

He indicated that I should come in behind the counter and sit down. The other man kept staring at me as if I were a creature from a horror movie. After what I had been through, I wagered I looked like it.

The chair felt odd under me, as if after so long in the caves and jungles, I had started to forget just what civilized things were all about.

Keveh pulled up his chair across the desk from me, took out a piece of paper, and got ready to listen. "Slowly," he said, "and from the beginning. What happened, and why do you need police help?"

I took a deep breath and decided it would save a lot of time in getting help if I did start almost from the beginning. I told him my name, where I was from. He wrote that down, asking for the spelling. I then gave him the names of my three friends. He wrote them all down.

"Do you still have your passport?"

"It's in my fanny pack back with my friends," I said.

He nodded and wrote that down as well.

I then gave him the name of the rafting company Mike had hired, and where we had camped.

He nodded. "I know it. A good spot for staging up the river this time of year."

Then I told him what happened, how Mike had overheard some of our guides talking about kidnapping us, how we'd snuck out of camp, how I had seen the three bodies of the men they had killed. How they had shot at us in the jungle, then set up guards so as not to let us out of the valley.

The words just poured from me. Keveh's eyes grew wider until finally he stopped writing and just listened.

"They wanted us dead, and they seemed very angry that we had escaped."

"I can imagine," Keveh said.

"We were trapped, so we finally attacked one of the guards. One of my friends got shot in the attack. I got out of the valley and came for help for us all. The guys with guns now have two armed men standing guard on the pass to the west of here."

"You got past them?" Keveh asked, surprised.

I nodded. "I went around them on a riverbank road."

"The old trail," Keveh said, nodding. "I am surprised you could find it."

"I almost didn't," I said, shuddering as I thought of that moment when I had nearly walked into my death.

"Where are your friends?" Keveh's voice had a tone of urgency.

"I left them hiding in a cave. Mike, the one who was shot, is in serious condition. We've got to get back in there and get him out and to a doctor quickly."

Keveh nodded. "I agree. How many men do you think were working together against you?"

"At least eight, maybe ten. Maybe more. I don't honestly know for sure. But I've seen that many. They're well armed."

That sat Keveh back. His face went white.

"Every man that I saw was armed with what one of my friends called an AK-47, but I don't know anything about guns. I do know they are machine guns. The gang fired at us often enough that I'm sure of that."

"It seems that they are impetuous, but well organized. So I would imagine they have what they considered to be sufficient firepower," Keveh said. With that, before I could say another word, he turned to the still wide-eyed assistant and barked a series of incomprehensible orders. Even though I didn't understand them, they sent the assistant running out the front door.

Then he turned back to me and said, "Excuse me, if you would. I have to make some phone calls."

He picked up the receiver and dialed a number, then spoke rapidly in his own language.

I sat in the brightly lit room, trying to stay calm as he made two more quick calls.

At that moment I decided that I would never, ever travel again into a country where I couldn't understand the language. I would be sure to learn the language beforehand if I wanted to be a world traveler. For all I knew, Keveh was in with the men on the hill and he had just reported that I had arrived. I was putting my life and my friends' lives into the hands of a man I couldn't understand. Mike had saved our lives by understanding what was said around us. Never again would I let this happen to me. I sat and worried.

"This is going to take a little time to get ready," Keveh said after hanging up the phone. "There's a restroom behind that door and a medical kit in the cabinet. Why don't you get cleaned up a little and take care of some of those cuts while we wait."

He then stood and went to an old metal locker. He pulled out a blue dress shirt, took it off the hanger, and tossed it at me. "You're about my size. This should fit you."

"Thank you," I said. The kindness in his eyes was reassuring. "Can I ask what your plans are? I need to go with you to get my friends out of that cave. You'll need my help to find it. It's very well hidden. And they're only going to trust me."

"I agree. I *need* you to go with me," he said, nodding.

"Thank you for understanding."

He took a deep breath. "I don't know how much you learned about our current political situation before you came."

"Very little, I'm afraid," I said. That was the last time that would happen as well. If I was going to travel to other countries, from now on I would respect their cultures and learn about the possible problems I could face. Never again would I let someone else take care of everything for me.

Keveh nodded. "We've been getting some warnings up here from the south that a group of Jemaah Islamiah were planning a kidnapping in this area. We just didn't know when or how."

"I guess my friends and I drew the unlucky straw," I said. "What did they want from us?"

The man shook his head. "Nothing, except your blood. They are trying to send a wave of terror through not only Thailand but through many other countries in this region. They hope to break free and set up an Islamic state across Southeast Asia. They have mostly stayed in the south."

"Until now," I said.

"Until now," Keveh repeated. "Perhaps. We will not know for certain until we apprehend them. I have help coming, as much help as I can get on short notice, but I need to find more. I already have soldiers coming in from Chiang Mai on two helicopters. But it's going to take time for them to get here."

"Then what?"

"Just as they tried to trap you, we'll get them locked into those canyons on both sides. Then we will go in by air. They won't get away. I can promise you that."

"Thank you," I said.

"It is a blessing that you survived," he said.

"Yes. But it is not enough. We have to rescue my friends."

Keveh nodded. "We will. At sunrise. Now take care of yourself."

"Thank you for the shirt," I said, holding it up. My dirty hands had already stained it. "I'll repay you."

"It is a gift," he said. With that, he turned and picked up the phone again.

The bathroom was a small cell directly off the main room. It smelled of urinal cake, and the sink faucet dripped. The mirror was cracked, but not enough to disguise what I looked like. Frightful. Worse than frightful. I was bloody, bruised, beaten, filthy, and haggard. I was surprised the two men here hadn't run away when I'd barged into their police station.

I left the door slightly open so I could hear if anything was going on in the main room. Then I washed up and stripped off what was left of my shirt. I was cut and scraped everywhere. A few of the older cuts looked infected.

Interestingly, I couldn't feel any of the cuts and scrapes right then. It was as if my body had turned off those nerve endings until the crisis passed. I had a hunch that when we got out of all this, I would feel everything. With a vengeance.

My face and neck were caked in dirt, and it took me a good three attempts to get it all off, uncovering a dozen scratches and a pretty deep gash in the side of my chin that I hadn't even known I'd gotten.

I dug into the cabinet and found the medical kit Keveh had mentioned. I used the bottle of hydrogen peroxide from it to clean out some of the cuts I could reach. I put a bandage on the gash under my chin, since it started bleeding the moment I tried to clean it out. More than likely, it would need stitches.

I tossed my old shirt into the garbage can, then put on Keveh's blue dress shirt. It smelled fresh and newly washed. I wondered what he had been saving it for.

There were good Samaritans everywhere in the world. God had brought me to one. I stood there at the sink and closed my eyes for a moment, thanking the Lord for helping me on my journey so far and asking Him to help me and Keveh and the others who were coming to rescue Mike and Hollis and Dave.

As I stood there, I suddenly realized what was really going to happen. The military was coming in, and they were going to trap and surround those men who had killed our driver and guides. They did not seem to be the type to surrender quietly. If they were kidnapping and killing for a cause, they would die for it when cornered. And they'd kill for it if they could.

My knees felt weak under me.

Dear God, what have I done?

I held onto the sink, trying to push the thought out of my mind. But it wouldn't leave.

My actions, by coming here to rescue my friends, were going to cause even more deaths. For our enemies, and perhaps among the friends I had recruited to our cause.

But, Lord, what other choice did I have?

I could think of no answer to that question.

29

Therefore put on the full armor of God,

so that when the day of evil comes,

you may be able to stand your ground,

and after you have done everything, to stand.

Ephesians 6:13

7:01 a.m., November 16
Pai, Thailand

TWO THAI MILITARY HELICOPTERS APPEARED OVER PAI
from the south, banked sharply, and then dropped quickly,
side by side, into a farmer's open field a block from the police
station. They were an impressive and awe-inspiring sight.

Keveh and a dozen armed men were waiting for them

beside me. We were all standing on the nearby road, blocking our eyes against the swirling dust and debris.

Both helicopters looked and felt frightening to me, with weapons hanging everywhere. Their sound was so loud, it seemed to block out even thought, and the power from their engines and the downdrafts under their blades made the ground shake and windows rattle.

It was the second time I had seen up close a military helicopter from any country. The first time had been on a golf course outside of Phoenix, Arizona. A formation of three Apache gunships had flown over us, low and fast. My friends said they were based nearby and were probably on some sort of military exercise. My foursome could hear them coming from a distance away, but when they actually appeared, flying less than a hundred feet over our heads, I felt like running and hiding. They just generated the instinctual fight-or-flight response in me. They were the most dangerous-looking things I had ever seen. Those Apache gunships stunned me with their power and danger.

The Thai helicopter gunships were also very intimidating. Not quite like the Apaches, but close enough. I sure wouldn't want one of them coming after me.

The sun was just starting to break over the mountains, tinting the sky with a light pink. The early morning air had a dampness and a chill to it that kept my tired mind as fresh as possible under the circumstances. Mostly, what I was feeling was fear. I didn't want to go back into that wilderness with those men still out there, but I had to save Mike and Hollis and Dave.

I really didn't want to ride in one of those helicopters either. I hoped that wasn't the plan for me. If it was, fine, but I didn't have to like it.

About fifteen minutes after I had told my story, the sleepy, small-town police station had turned into a riot of activity. For two hours, Keveh and his daytime counterpart, a man named Tahir, had shouted orders, made phone calls, and worked like I had never seen two men work.

Dozens of different men and women had gone in and out of the front door, many running. Every desk in the room was being used, and I had ended up in a chair against the wall.

When Tahir had first come in, he looked exhausted, but he soon lost that appearance as Keveh told him what was happening. I figured Tahir might be a brother to Keveh. They stood the same size, appeared to be about the same age, and even spoke the same way. Tahir was balder than Keveh, but other than that, they could have been twins.

After an hour, Keveh came over to the chair I was sitting in and handed me a box of four pastries and a bottle of water. "Go slow eating them," he said. "I assume you haven't had much to eat for a while."

"Part of a candy bar," I said, not telling him where or how I got it. I would tell him that later. "Thanks."

I hadn't thought about my hunger in a long time until he placed that box of pastries in my hands. "First batch of the morning from the Charlie House down the road. They are known all over for those."

As I ate slowly, forcing myself to not down all of them at once, he explained to me exactly what was happening. I would be going with him, two other armed men, and a doctor in a van, driving back up the road. We would coordinate our arrival at the post of the two guards on the ridgeline behind the arrival of the military and their helicopters.

One helicopter and its crew would confront the men, another would drop men on the ridgeline at the same time, and they would do what was necessary to take care of those guards.

"With luck, they will just surrender," he said.

"Don't count on it," I said. "They don't seem like the surrendering type to me."

Keveh nodded. "I'm afraid you are right. These are not the type of men to surrender, from everything I have heard has happened in the south."

"What about the others near our original camp?"

"The army has trucks of men coming in from Chiang Mai, moving up the highway at them. They will have the road blocked and will search all vehicles leaving the area this morning."

"But you don't expect them to have left, do you?" I asked, staring at the worried face of Keveh.

"No. After we take care of the guards on the pass, we will

push on toward the valley where you camped, with the helicopters working cover for us and the others in our caravan."

"Do you expect that we will have to fight?" I asked. The idea of more bullets flashing past me sent a shudder through my body I couldn't control.

"I hope not," he said. "I would rather leave the fighting to the men who are trained to do it. But we have to be prepared."

He stood and turned to go back toward his desk.

"Thank you for the food," I said. "And for your help."

"When this is all over, I'll join you and your friends for a full breakfast."

"On me," I said.

He smiled. "I'll hold you to that."

With that, he left me to sit and watch and pray for the safety of everyone who was helping us. My entire focus had been on coming for help. I didn't realize just what that help would entail. Now the orchestrated chaos around me made it clear what I was asking.

I spent that hour in the office sitting, talking with God, and asking for guidance from Him. I also finished the four pastries and the bottle of water.

Now I stood watching dozens of military men pour out of a helicopter. I had come to understand over the past two hours just how tough a job it would be to rescue my friends.

A man wearing a uniform and cap instead of helmet jumped from the helicopter. He wasn't carrying a rifle or anything else

as he walked toward Keveh and me. The other men, all with
weapons at the ready, spread out and took up guard positions
around the two powerful machines.

He reached us and indicated we should head down the
block to the police station, so we could talk without having to
shout over all the noise.

Around us, the town was coming quickly awake. Sleepy
people were poking their heads out of buildings, staring open-
mouthed at the helicopters and our little parade up the street.
My coming for help here was certainly going to be the talk of
this town for some time to come.

The military man introduced himself to Keveh as we entered
the police station, but all I could clearly understand was that he
was a general.

After we got inside, the general turned to me and in flaw-
less English said, "Mr. Majors, I am authorized by the government to apologize to you for your problems. It is the last thing
we like to have happen to anyone visiting our country."

"Thank you," I said. "And thank you for the help rescuing
my friends."

"We will get them out," he said. "On that much, you can
depend." He turned to the policeman. "I understand you have
a detailed topography map of the area?"

Keveh nodded and a moment later unrolled a very large
map over one desk. The map was of the area I had just managed to get through during the night. Seeing it in relief form

startled me. I had crossed over twenty miles of very rugged terrain, very quickly.

"Mr. Majors," the general said, "I understand you went around two gunmen using the old riverbank road." He pointed to an area on the map not far from Pai. Then he traced the main road and the side road coming in.

"I did," I said. I pointed to the map. "I had seen them go by while I was hiding, so I knew they were ahead of me. When I came off the hill here, I stayed in the jungle and went to the right with the idea of finding the river and going down it."

"You would have never made it through that canyon," Keveh said.

"I realized that," I said. "I was just lucky that the river road joined into the main road about a hundred paces past where the guards were watching. I managed to sneak by them without them seeing me."

"They are here?" the general asked, pointing to an exact spot on the map near where the two roads joined.

"They were four hours ago. Yes."

"They were still there thirty minutes ago," the general said, smiling at me.

His statement surprised me a great deal. "How do you know that?"

His smile got bigger, as if he was proud of having the information. "Not that we don't trust you, Mr. Majors, but we had to be sure what we were dealing with. We sent over a high altitude survey plane to take infrared images the moment Keveh called us, and high resolution photos once the sun rose. Two men are there, six here, two more here, another two here, as of the last pass of the plane."

He pointed to the map in four different places. One place I could tell was our camp, one place was back toward Chiang Mai from our camp, and the six men were beyond the canyon.

"All are heavily armed. Mr. Majors, your story was exactly as we found the situation. There are three bodies in the camp and no sign of your friends. They seem to be very well hidden, even from heat imaging."

"You'll never find that cave if I don't show it to you," I said.

"I hope you don't mind, but we also had to check on you and your friends. We could take no chances. I hope you can see that."

I nodded. I had been so wrapped up in the problems and challenges I had faced, I had just assumed that everyone would believe me. Of course, before any of these people put their lives on the line, a good leader would demand to know the exact situation, not just trust the word of some beat-up American. I suddenly had gained a great deal more respect for the general and the Thai military. He was going out of his way to rescue foreigners, risking his life and the lives of his men to save men not of his country, and not of his faith.

The general turned to Keveh. "Can six of my men borrow one of your vans? We need a force going up the road ahead of your people."

Keveh nodded, turned, and barked an order, sending one young man into the street at a run.

"He will pull it up near the helicopters," Keveh said.

"I do not want your men and volunteers engaging in fighting with these terrorists," the general said to Keveh.

Keveh nodded. "We will only be there as backup. Our job is to get to the friends of Mr. Majors and get them safely out. But consider us backup in an emergency."

The general nodded. "Good."

He seemed about to quit, but I needed to know more. "Can I ask what your exact plan is?"

"Yes, I would like to know as well," Keveh said, "so I can tell if things are going according to the plan or not."

"Nothing in this type of military operation goes as planned," the general said. "It is a truism. We hope first to take out the two guards on the ridge. Then, using mostly the helicopters, once we have ground troops in position, we will attack the main group of the terrorists."

"And the ones in the camp?" I asked.

"The second helicopter will circle around and drop troops to get the men at the western guard post," the general said, pointing to a spot on the map. "Then, with the helicopter as backup, those men will move down the road and take care of the terrorists in the camp. We will pinch all of them in the valley between the two forces."

I nodded.

"We shall see if it works," the general said. "We are very restricted by time and the terrain. May I borrow your map?"

"Of course," Keveh said.

The general rolled it up, tucked it under his arm, and then turned to face me. "Again, apologies from my government. Let us now go rescue your traveling companions."

"Thank you, General," I said.

"You are more than welcome, Mr. Majors."

With the general leading the way, we went back out into the cool morning air. The helicopters' pounding vibrations engulfed the small town. The sidewalks and streets were now filling as people watched what was happening.

Six of the soldiers climbed into a blue van that looked very much like the van the rafting company had used to take us to the camp. It seemed to be the standard vehicle of choice for this area.

The soldiers were all well armed and had full military gear. I prayed for their safety.

Keveh and I and two hard-looking men with guns and badges on their chests climbed into a second van. Keveh got behind the wheel, I took the passenger seat. A moment later a man carrying a backpack with a medical cross on it climbed in behind me.

Keveh said something to him in Thai, then in English said, "Mr. Majors, this is Dr. Dabir."

I turned around and nodded. "Doctor, thank you for helping out."

"My job," he said in a British accent. He then shook his head. "It would seem I needed to get here a little earlier. You should get some of your cuts treated."

"There will be time later," I said. "They're nothing. One of my friends was shot in the leg. We think the bullet shattered his bone, but missed any major artery."

"How was it treated?"

"Tourniquet, hydrogen peroxide on the wound, bandage to slow the bleeding, Advil for pain."

"Very good," he said. "How long ago was this?"

I glanced at my watch, stunned at how little, yet how much time had passed. "Just over ten hours ago."

The doctor nodded. "Then I hope you are right about the bullet missing the artery."

I didn't want to think about Mike dying in that cave. It couldn't happen.

Lord, please don't take Mike to Your heavenly home yet. He is too young. I know You want him with You, but he has a lot to do here yet. Please let him stay awhile longer.

I turned around as Keveh started up the van at the same time as the two helicopters lifted off. The wind from them buffeted the van and sent people back into doorways.

Keveh got the van going, dropping in behind the van driven

by the military. He followed it at a few hundred yards' distance as we picked up speed leaving town.

I would get to see the wilderness I had traveled just a few hours before in the dark. And I would help confront the evil that had attacked us. I didn't want to do either, but God's path for me was clear. I was needed to save Mike and my friends. So I would go back into the wilderness again, confront the evil again.

I hoped God's plan didn't include me killing again.

30

When the storm has swept by,

the wicked are gone,

but the righteous stand firm forever.

PROVERBS 10:25

8:14 a.m., November 16

A ridge southeast of Pai, Thailand

KEVEH DROVE THE VAN FAST, FAR FASTER THAN I WOULD
have ever felt safe driving on such a narrow, twisting road.
Even with his speed, we were slowly losing ground on the military van ahead of us. I had glanced at my watch as we left
town, then again as we neared the top of the ridge. What had
taken me almost two hours to cover on foot, running in the

dark, we had gone back over in less than ten minutes, at speeds sometimes exceeding eighty miles per hour.

Keveh was an expert driver, of that I had no doubt. He never once took his eyes off the road, and he knew exactly when to slow to go into a corner, and exactly when to power out of it. Still, the ride was harrowing at best, and I found myself holding on for dear life as we climbed up the side of the mountain toward the ridge. I always knew God had a sense of humor, but I didn't think it would be very funny if He helped me through the wilderness, only to take me in a car accident before I could get back and help my friends.

I talked to Him, asked Him to not do that.

For the entire ride, I kept talking with Him, asking Him to help those about to go into battle for me and my friends, asking Him to get the murderers to surrender instead of fight, asking Him to keep Mike with us just a little longer, asking Him to be with me.

And I felt, deep in my heart, that He was riding with me, with the troops ahead of me. Never before had I felt so completely in contact with the Lord. Even though I was afraid and very worried, my fear never reached a deep level inside me. Not as it had done before I gave myself over completely to Him last night.

I wanted to get home, to talk to Lorraine, to restart my life with her. I wanted to talk to her about what had happened to me. And I wanted my friends home safe with me. I wanted to talk to them, to tell them about what had happened to me on that road last night, to tell Hollis how much I respected him for his courage in confronting his sins.

I had done what God had needed me to do. I had made it through the wilderness, alone, at night. Now these soldiers were also doing the duty of the Lord, no matter what the outcome.

"I don't see the helicopters," Dr. Dabir said as we climbed toward the ridge.

"They are standing back, so as not to alert the two guards," Keveh said. "Using the hills to cover their sound. They will be there very suddenly when needed."

As we crested over the top of the ridge, Keveh hit the brakes and pulled the van in behind the military van, now empty. I knew the side road where I had gotten around the two guards came into the main road about a hundred yards ahead. The leading van had also stopped here so as not to alert the guards.

Everything in this area looked very different in the daylight. The jungle on top of the ridge was nowhere near as thick as I had imagined it to be in the darkness. The road itself, a wide safety line to me last night, was actually narrow, and had a deep ditch on one side of it and a rock cliff on the other.

Keveh said something in Thai to the others in the van as he shut off the engine, then to me he said, "We need to take cover. Quickly and quietly."

I opened the van door and got out onto the gravel road. Pain shot through me as the blisters on my toes and heels made themselves clearly known. I guessed I would have to get the doctor to look at those when this was all finished.

The air was warming up, though everything was deathly still at this hour. Not even a slight breeze disturbed the jungle leaves. I was surprised that I couldn't hear the helicopters. The pilots were clearly very good at knowing how their sound traveled in these hills and mountains.

I slid down off the road and into the ditch. A moment later both the doctor and Keveh joined me. The other two men fanned out, one on each side of the road. Both looked like they had military training as they positioned themselves flat on the ground, guns aimed in the direction of the pass.

Neither the doctor nor I had a gun, so it seemed that Keveh was taking it as his duty to stay with us and protect us in case we needed it. I was glad he was there. He had an air of competence about him, no matter what he did. God had sent me to a very good man for help, of that I now had no doubt.

Suddenly one of the helicopters came in low and hard over both vans, banking around the corner, following the road. The ground under me shook, and rocks tumbled off the cliff and rattled across the road. The noise was so loud and intense that it made me want to cover my ears.

A speaker in the helicopter was shouting out commands in Thai.

"They are demanding that the men surrender in the name of the government," Keveh told me.

Gunfire echoed through the trees and jungle.

My stomach clamped up. *So much for surrender.*

I couldn't believe I was back in a gunfight again. Just the idea of something like that had been crazy to me not more than two days ago. Now, it seemed, it was a part of my life. I desperately wanted to go home and never see another gun again.

I asked the Lord for the safety of those being shot at. From what I could tell, it seemed the two men had opened fire on the helicopter.

"Get down!" Keveh ordered, and I ducked my head. I spread myself out lower into the ditch, ripping on a rock the dress shirt Keveh had lent me.

The helicopter returned fire, its massive guns sounding like a freight train crawling over the pass. I could hear bullets ricocheting off of rocks, trees being shattered, branches cut down like someone had taken a chain saw to them.

Then the helicopter banked and vanished over the front of the ridge, the sound from its engines disappearing almost instantly.

A half-dozen other guns opened fire. The gunfire became a constant roar and wouldn't let up. Behind us, branches in the trees tore apart as bullets ripped through them. Neither of the two men with us fired, and both stayed in place, doing their duty to guard the doctor, Keveh, and me.

Suddenly there was only an echo of the gunfire left. It faded, joining into the faint throbbing of the distant helicopter engines.

The battle was over.

I guessed that two more human lives had been taken.

This is not my fault, I said to myself in a desperate plea, even as I wanted to be sick again. I was regretting eating those pastries.

Those men had chosen to walk the path of violence; they had chosen to die in a rain of bullets rather than surrender when they'd fired on a military helicopter. They had played a part in the deaths of three innocent people. Sometimes, even God's soldiers had to stand up and fight and kill. Now I knew that.

But I just kept feeling all this was my fault, even though I knew it wasn't. The burden of guilt was crushing. I prayed again for God to forgive me for my sins. And to let me forgive myself and find His peace in my heart.

I asked God that all those fighting on His side would remain safe. I focused on the goodness in everyone helping rescue Mike and Dave and Hollis, on how they were risking their lives purposely for people they didn't know. What greater work could God ask of a person?

Someone shouted in Thai from up ahead, and Keveh and the doctor started to stand up.

"That was the all clear," Keveh said. "The shooters are dead. We can join the soldiers now."

"I need to find out if anyone was injured," the doctor said, climbing out of the ditch with help from Keveh and starting up the road.

"We'll pick you up on the way past," Keveh said. He motioned that I should get back in the van, then signaled for the two other men to do the same.

I stood there for a moment on the road I had walked on silently last night as I had tried to get away from the two men who had just died.

I felt numb as I climbed back into my seat, ignoring the pain in my legs and feet. I wasn't sure how much more killing and death I could take. And I knew there would be more ahead before I could get to Mike and Dave and Hollis. I didn't want there to be. I asked the Lord if He could stop the deaths. If He could open the hearts of the kidnappers and let them surrender. But somehow I knew there would be bloodshed, that my request for an end to the killing wouldn't be granted.

My pastor said later that I was confusing the will of God with the world of man. Even though I had God's help, this was still the world of man, filled with evil and sinners and temptation. Here, death happened because of sin. God gave His children free will. He would let those men choose their own paths, just as He had let me choose mine.

He said that every person makes choices in life, and every person is tested by this world, that the hand of God is there for those who know to reach for it.

Keveh handed me a bottle of water from a cooler between

our seats, then took another for himself. He gave one bottle each to the men in the backseat.

The water was warm, since there was no ice in the cooler, but it helped clear my mind. I ended up downing half the bottle. It helped my breakfast settle back into place.

In the cooler we also had food for Mike and Hollis and Dave, plus more water. It would be enough to last them until we got back to Pai, if that was where we actually were heading after all this ended. I imagined it would depend on what the doctor said about Mike's wound, and what the military wanted to do with us. Or what Keveh wanted to do with me after I told him that I had killed one of the terrorists.

Too many factors to think about now. I just needed to pay attention to getting to my friends. The rest would follow as God saw fit.

One of the soldiers came running back down the road. He motioned that we should follow him, then climbed into the driver's seat of the other van and pulled out onto the road.

Keveh started up the van and followed.

As I passed the side-road entrance, I glanced ahead. Two lawn chairs were near the edge of the road. Last night, all one of those men would have had to do was turn around and see me. God had clearly been helping me, keeping me invisible to my enemies.

Where the two guards had sat on lawn chairs overlooking

the valley below the cliff face, the lead van stopped and let in the other soldiers. They were all smiling and laughing and in good spirits.

The doctor appeared from the right near the cliff face and came back to our van.

"Two terrorists dead," he said as he climbed in. "No one else hurt. So far, so good."

I didn't agree that it was good that anyone was dead, but those terrorists had made their own choices. I was very glad no soldier helping us had been hurt.

Keveh started again to follow the lead van as we passed one remaining soldier standing watch over the two bodies in the ditch on the cliff side of the road. Both of them had been covered with blankets, but I could see where their blood had splattered over nearby rocks.

One of their lawn chairs had been tipped over and was riddled with bullets as well.

I made myself look away, made myself focus on the road ahead and the fantastically beautiful valley I had walked around last night to avoid being killed by those two men.

There was more death ahead.

Both the military driver and Keveh kept their speeds down on the switchbacks going down the cliff face, something I was very grateful for.

They both picked up speed across the valley floor. Twice, we caught up to the military van because it had to slow down or stop for an oxen-pulled cart. Finally we made it to the other side of the valley and started up the hill.

I studied the thick jungle, the overhanging trees, the narrow road. It seemed so beautiful and friendly in the light of day. It had seemed so dangerous last night.

"How, in the total darkness, did you make it down this road?" Keveh asked, shaking his head in amazement.

"Yes. We had less than a half moon last night," Dr. Dabir said. "And these trees must have blocked out most of that."

"Desperation and faith can do wonders when you need them to," I said. "I asked my God for help, and I just kept going. I think I kept going because of my faith and because of the knowledge that if I didn't find help, my friends would die."

What I didn't say to them was that God clearly had been with me, guiding me every step of the way.

"I am impressed," Dr. Dabir said. "You had an amazing journey. I'm sure that people will want to hear about it."

"I think I'll just keep last night between God and me," I said.

Keveh nodded. "He was certainly watching over you."

"That He was," I said. "He still is."

Again, Keveh nodded, but this time he said nothing.

We crested over the next hill and started down, only about two hundred yards behind the lead van. I didn't recognize any of the area around me, but I knew I had walked it, and I knew that at the bottom of this hill, the road went into the rock canyon and then over the bridge where I had killed a man. At some point, I would have to tell Keveh that, tell him what happened, take my punishment both under local law and under God's law. But first, I needed to make sure my friends were rescued.

We were getting close. Very close.

Ahead, the military van pulled over and stopped. The men inside bailed out like the van was on fire, spreading out into the jungle. All but one of them completely vanished.

I was impressed. These men were well trained and very, very good at what they did. Again, the Lord had given me the best help possible to rescue my friends.

The driver came back to Keveh's window and spoke to him quickly. Then, the driver, too, went off the bank and down into the jungle, vanishing like a ghost into the green brush.

Keveh turned and spoke quickly to the two men with guns. The doctor got out to let them out. One took up a position near the rear of our van, the other took a spot near the front of the lead van. Then the doctor took his seat again, but didn't close the door.

"There are six terrorists below us," Keveh said, "where the road switches back. They seem to be searching the area along the road for you and your friends."

"Logical," I said. "The guard we overpowered was there last night."

"The helicopters and the ground troops from Chiang Mai have already killed the remaining terrorists in the valley beyond the canyon where your campsite was. Just these men remain."

"And what are the men in the van doing?" Dr. Dabir asked, clearly wanting more information than I did at the moment. I didn't like the idea that more people had been killed. I prayed for the soldiers again, and for the terrorists to find it in their hearts to surrender.

How could a simple idea hatched at a football party two months ago become so tragic? How could a rafting trip snowball into a deathtrap for so many? I knew it would take me a long time to understand the answers to those questions, if I ever did.

"They are setting a boundary on this side, between us and the terrorists. More troops will come up through the canyon on foot. When they are in position, the helicopters will come in."

"Can we stay in here?" I asked.

"I don't think we should," Keveh said. "Let's take cover in that ditch on the other side of the road. Just in case of a stray shot."

"Good idea," Dr. Dabir said. "We have no idea how far down the hill the fight will be."

I couldn't have agreed more. After seeing how those gunships could rip apart a jungle, I didn't want to be anywhere close to where one might hit again.

Just as we reached the ditch, the loud drone of the helicopters filled the valley. Again, there was a demand for surrender, followed instantly by gunfire from the terrorists.

A lot of gunfire.

The warships returned fire. From the sounds of it, both of them let rip, in a wall of noise like ten tanks crashing through the jungle, tearing down trees, uprooting brush, starting rock slides.

The valley sounded like a massive Fourth of July celebration was taking place. I doubted that I'd ever enjoy fireworks again after this. The noise was far louder, and far closer, than I had thought it would be.

Stray bullets clipped into the jungle above us.

One shattered the mirror on the military van.

"Good idea leaving the van, Keveh," Dr. Dabir shouted over the noise, covering his head as even more bullets smashed into the jungle foliage above us. One dug into the hillside about ten feet above us, sending a small cascade of dirt and rock down on Keveh's head.

The three of us kept down and covered, using the bank of the ditch beside the road as shelter from the battle. I hoped the two men stationed with the vans were doing all right. They were much more out in the open than we were.

The fight, to my tired imagination, seemed to go on for an eternity, ending finally as the only remaining sounds filling the jungle around us were the droning engines and whirring blades of the two helicopters.

And after a few seconds, even the helicopters moved off, more than likely landing in the valley on the other side of the canyon.

"Can it be over?" I asked, not wanting to believe that the men who wanted us dead were now all dead themselves.

"I hope so. All except the part of getting to your friends," Keveh said.

"Thank You, Lord," I said out loud.

"Yes, I thank our God for His goodness," Keveh said, smiling.

31

For his Holy Spirit speaks to us deep in our
hearts and tells us that we are God's children.

ROMANS 8:16, NLT

10:21 a.m., November 16
A bridge southeast of Pai, Thailand

ONLY ONE OF THE TROOPS FIGHTING THE TERRORISTS HAD
been wounded, and Dr. Dabir said it was only a flesh wound,
and that he would be fine. That was a good reason for smiles
and celebration all around among the professionals. They
thanked me. A group of terrorists, they said, had been taken
off the planet. The general pointed out that who knew how
many lives in the long run would be saved with men like those
gone. I had, he said, done a great service to Thailand.

I still wished that the terrorists had surrendered.

The general told the doctor that he would meet us at our old camp as soon as the doctor made a determination on Mike's wound. He would keep the helicopters standing by in case they were needed to evacuate Mike to a hospital.

Now, all we had to do was get to the cave and get Mike and Hollis and Dave out of there.

"Stop on the other side of the bridge," I said as we left the canyon and crossed onto the bridge. Beside us, the river was an angry torrent of whitewater. Thankfully, last night, God had kept us from thinking we could have made it through that. Seeing it by daylight, I knew that it wouldn't have been possible.

The guard's lawn chair still sat alone in the middle of the bridge, a stark reminder to me of what I had done. Being back here brought the memory vividly into focus.

Keveh pulled the van over, and the four of us got out. My legs were shaking and my feet hurt, but I tried to ignore all that. I had to get to Mike.

A moment later the military van pulled up behind us, and four more men got out of it. All were carrying guns and looked serious. Neither Keveh nor the general trusted that we had gotten all the terrorists. They were taking no chances, and I appreciated that a lot.

I stared down at the place where I had killed the man, my feet frozen.

"Will you tell me what happened here last night?" Keveh asked, stopping beside me as we waited for the doctor to get some more medical supplies out of the back of the van.

I pointed to a spot up on the hillside on the other side of the stream. "Hollis and Dave hid there. Mike and I came down here and set up to ambush the guard. After we were in position, Dave tossed a rock into that clump of brush and lured the guard off the bridge into our ambush."

"It seems like a good plan," Keveh said.

"A desperate one," I said. "Mike and I both failed to knock the guard out, so the three of us ended up wrestling on the ground. The guard's gun went off, and Mike got shot in the leg."

"And what happened to this guard?" Keveh asked, turning to look at me.

"I had my hands around his neck, trying to hold him down," I said, the feeling of his bones breaking under my hands coming back to me clearly. I wiped my hands on my pants again, trying to make the feeling go away. "The three of us kept fighting, and I ended up breaking his neck when he tried to move away from us. I didn't mean to. I swear that. All I wanted to do was knock him out."

Keveh rested a hand on my shoulder. "I understand. You did what you had to do."

Everything around me seemed to be spinning. I took a few deep breaths, but it didn't seem to help.

"You were very brave," Keveh said, "fighting a man with a gun to save yourself and your friends."

"I don't feel brave," I said. "I feel as if I have sinned against God, done the worst thing possible."

"Sometimes, we must all fight in God's name," Keveh said. "As you told me, God was with you last night. And with us today. Always remember that. He was in you, in your hands as you fought for your life. If He hadn't wanted you to win that fight, you would not have."

I nodded. Keveh clearly understood. And his words calmed me a great deal. He was right.

"Thank you," I said.

"Don't thank me. Thank the Lord."

"I've been doing that all night," I said. "And thanking Him all morning for bringing me to you for help."

He smiled at that. "I was thanking Him for keeping me on the sidelines of this adventure, instead of in its center. So what happened to the terrorist's body?"

"We put it in the river," I said, remembering the sight of the man's body floating down the stream in the moonlight.

"Good place for it," Keveh said, nodding as the doctor came up behind us. "We'll tell the general when we get back to camp that there is one more terrorist to look for."

"One more what?" Dr. Dabir asked.

"They killed one of them last night," Keveh said. "In their escape attempt that got the man we are trying to rescue shot."

"Good for you," Dr. Dabir said to me.

I didn't answer that. I didn't like being congratulated for killing anything, let alone another human being. I headed off the bridge, stepping gingerly through the area where the fight had occurred.

"We found a cave the night before to hide in. It's up on the hillside." I pointed ahead after a few dozen steps. "When Mike got shot, I decided to go for help alone, and Hollis and Dave took Mike back to the cave."

"There's no cave up in that hillside that I know of," Keveh said, "and I thought I knew them all in this area."

"It's up there, I promise. It's very old, very deep. Getting into it is a real treat for claustrophobic people. Like me. I nearly lost it every time I had to crawl through the narrow entry passage. It's worth the trip, though. It has a lot of ancient drawings on the walls."

"Cave drawings?" Dr. Dabir asked. "I look forward to seeing them. I'm something of an amateur archaeologist. Such drawings might answer a lot of questions about the early hill tribes in this region."

"I can go in instead of you, if you like," Keveh said to me as we headed up the stream bank. Six armed men spread out around us now, forming a wedge up the valley through the jungle. They were keeping a very sharp eye out, their weapons ready.

"Thanks," I said, "but I think my friends are going to be

on high alert. They need to know it's me coming through, and not under threat of gunpoint. I imagine they're jumpy. And I know that they're armed. I left them with the gun I took from the dead terrorist."

"Ah," Keveh said. "So they have the guard's weapon? I wondered where it ended up. You weren't carrying it when you came to our building last night."

"I left it with them," I said. "One of our biggest fears last night was that I would get captured and tortured and tell the killers where they were."

"I see," Dr. Dabir said. "No one can stand up to what barbarians can put a human body through. No one."

"I came to this place for adventure. I found it. And I can't tell you how glad I am that I missed *that* experience," I said.

With that, we walked in silence, the sun making the morning grow warmer and warmer. After what I figured was about the right distance, I moved to the right bank and started scanning the left hillside.

"What are we looking for?" Keveh asked. "Maybe we can help you look for it as well."

"You know," I said, starting to get a little worried. "I'm not really sure. I could find the cave at night, because it had a distinct shadow in the moonlight. But during the day, I'm not so sure what it looks like. And we rolled a rock into the opening to make sure it showed even less. I will wager Dave did the same last night."

Keveh nodded and shouted to the other men some commands in Thai. Then he turned to me. "I told them to watch for a blood trail. Especially going up the rocks."

Every nook, every indent in the rocks, every large boulder looked like the right one to me. The farther up the valley we went, the more panicked I became at not finding the cave. I didn't know what we would do if I couldn't find it.

After a half hour, I knew we had climbed too far. I turned us all around, and we started back down the stream, leaving one man to guard our upper flank.

This time I moved up through the rock slope and worked my way along there, staring down at the shape of the land below and across the narrow valley. I had looked at that shape a number of times in the moonlight. It looked very different in the bright day, but I was hoping I would recognize something.

Suddenly I was at a place I had seen before.

"Here," I said, turning and looking upward. I had climbed in this area not only to get to the cave, but to collect firewood. "It's up here somewhere."

The doctor and Keveh had both been walking slowly along the bank, looking for any signs or tracks that three men had come out of the water. They, along with three guards, scrambled up the rocks with me.

It still took another five minutes before I saw a bloodstain on a large boulder face, taller than my head. How we had gotten up that the first time, I had no idea. And how Dave and Hollis had gotten Mike up that, I didn't want to think about. It must have hurt Mike something horrible.

I climbed up the boulder, found more blood on top and a rock in the opening of the hole.

"Dave! Hollis! Mike!" I shouted into the hole. "It's me, John. I'm coming in with help."

Silence greeted me, as I knew it would.

Keveh and the doctor had both joined me on the ledge, and together, we moved aside the rock that Dave had somehow dragged in front of the hole as he went in.

"How in the world did you ever discover this?" the doctor asked, shaking his head. "And in the middle of the night to boot."

"Dave! Hollis! Mike!" I shouted again, kneeling down and looking into the dark opening. "It's John. I have a doctor with me. We're safe. I made it to Pai and got help."

Nothing.

I could feel myself starting to sweat, just staring at the blackness of that opening. I had to do this. They might open fire on anyone else coming through that hole first. I had to go in. Everyone with me knew it.

"Does it get narrower and lower than that opening?" Dr. Dabir asked.

"Yes. Crawling-on-your-stomach-like-a-worm narrow and lower," I said, still fearful at the memory.

I could do it. God was with me.

"It's going to be hard to get him out of there," Dr. Dabir said.

"There's a wide opening about two hundred feet over the road back in the canyon," I said. "If we can get some help and a lot of rope, it might be better for him to go out that way."

"And for you," Keveh said, putting his hand on my shoulder.

"And for me," I said. "But I need to go in this way. It'd take time for me to backtrack to the other entrance. Lots of it. Mike's the important one here."

Keveh turned and gave several orders to the men behind him. Three of them took off back down the valley while the other three stayed at their posts.

Then he turned and handed me a flashlight. "Keep shouting as you go in. I would hate to have one of your friends kill you by accident after all you have been through."

"So would I," I said.

I took a deep breath, then shouted into the tunnel. "Dave, Hollis, Mike, I'm coming in!"

I got down on my hands and knees and headed forward, the light helping and making the cave entrance seem very different than going through it in the complete darkness. I could see this time where it narrowed down, and that the passage where I had to crawl wasn't really that small or that long.

"Dave, Hollis, Mike, I'm coming in! It's me, John! I'm coming in, crawling through this awful space just for you guys. You guys are going to owe me for this!"

I was on my stomach, the light ahead of me, crawling as fast as I could. I could see directly ahead where the cave opened up. Dave and Hollis could be right there, or much deeper in the cave. I suspected that they were deeper, considering if the terrorists had thought they were in there, a simple bomb would have done the trick once anyone sent it inside.

"Dave, Hollis, Mike, it's me, John!"

My voice seemed fantastically loud to my ears in the tight space. I could suddenly feel the rock pressing in on my back, surrounding me. I crawled faster.

I had to get out of there before I froze and someone would have to pull me out.

I focused on the opening just ahead and as I stuck my head out, I yelled again, "Dave, Hollis, Mike!"

Nothing but the echo of my own words.

I stood, sweating, shining the flashlight around the large cavern. In the brighter light, I could see where we had tried to hide our fire. And where water was dripping from some of the fantastically colored stalactites. In one corner there was even a pillar, where a stalactite and a stalagmite had met.

"Come on out, guys! Time to go home!"

Nothing again.

A moment later Keveh stood up beside me. "Any answer?"

"Nothing," I said.

I shouted again.

Still no answer. I had no idea how well my voice would carry in this huge cave complex, but I hoped it would be far enough.

"You were right about old and big," Dr. Dabir said, joining us and then shining his flashlight around the space. "This is amazing."

"It goes off in a couple of directions," I said. "Dave and Mike followed the stream down a few caverns, and there are three main caverns between here and the opening above the canyon road."

"So they might not be hearing your call," Keveh said.

"Or they might be too busy to answer. From the looks of this bleeding," Dr. Dabir said, pointing his flashlight at the ground to show dark blood spots, "we had better be picking up the pace of our search."

"They would go to the other entrance," I said. "I'm sure of it."

I headed off, shouting my three friends' names just about every step. Into the second cavern with the stream, I could still see the blood trail on the ground. Mike clearly had lost a lot of blood getting in here. I hoped Dave had gotten that blood loss stopped, or Mike wasn't going to be alive when I found him.

That thought just scared me to death. I couldn't lose Mike, not after all this.

I kept alternately shouting to my friends and talking to God, asking for His help, praying for Mike to still be alive.

The blood trail led toward the rock pile that separated the next two caverns.

I shouted again, my voice echoing as I started to climb the rocks.

"Stay where you are," Dave's voice said from my right.

He stepped into the light from our two flashlights. He had the gun aimed at Keveh.

"Dave," I said, turning to face him. "The man you are thinking of killing is with the police in Pai. The man with him is a doctor. All the terrorists are dead, thanks to the Thai military."

"How can I believe you?" he asked, just as I knew he would.

"We are not carrying guns," Keveh said. "You are welcome to search us."

"Look at me. Except for a very long walk," I said, "I haven't been tortured. Heck, they even fed me and lent me some clothes. How is Mike doing?"

Dave looked me in the eyes.

I smiled, so glad to see him that it hurt.

He lowered his gun and almost slumped to the ground in relief. "He's still alive."

I stepped to Dave and gave him the biggest, longest hug I could ever remember giving another man.

"You actually made it?" Dave asked, pushing me away and staring at me.

"I actually made it," I said. "Now, let's take care of Mike. Where is he?"

"Beside the pool in the next room."

"Did you get the blood loss stopped?" Dr. Dabir asked as all four of us started over the rock pile. "We followed the blood trail into here."

"Getting him through the cave opening broke open his wound again. I got it stopped as soon as we got into the next cavern. He's been awake most of the time, worried about John."

As we got into the next cavern, Mike looked up from where he lay beside the pool. "Thank God."

Hollis came back in from the ledge, smiling. Then a moment later he was sitting on a rock weeping like a child into his hands. The relief was too much for him.

I knew exactly how he felt. There were tears in my eyes as well. I went over and put my arm around him. Hollis returned the gesture.

Meanwhile Dr. Dabir knelt beside Mike and opened his medical bag.

"A doctor, I presume," Mike said, wincing as the doctor touched the makeshift splint on his leg.

"Dr. Dabir," he said, shaking Mike's hand. "Oxford, class of 1992, at your service."

"Good work, John." Mike looked up at me and smiled as the doctor started to work on the leg. "But you didn't have to walk all the way to England to find me a doctor."

"I didn't," I said, letting the joy of seeing Mike alive fill my very soul. "It just felt like it."

32

Hatred stirs up strife,
But love covers all sins.
PROVERBS 10:12, NKJV

4:37 p.m., November 19
Portland, Oregon

LORRAINE'S BEAMING AND TEAR-STAINED FACE GREETED
me as I passed the security gate in the Portland airport, my
travel bag slung over my shoulder. It was the same flight we
had originally booked for the return home. We just didn't plan
the adventure we had in the middle.

Lorraine ran into my arms and held me as tight as I could
ever imagine being held. I could feel myself relaxing for the
first time in a week. I didn't care who was watching, who we

were in the way of. Nothing mattered but the feel of the woman I loved holding me tight.

What insanity had ever made me leave her, even for a rafting adventure? She had become my other half, the wonderful person that made my life whole. God had sent her to me. I had left, but God had allowed me to come home. I wasn't leaving my home again without her.

The noise of the crowds and the airport announcements surrounded us as we hugged. Lorraine was sobbing on my shoulder. I couldn't believe I was here, with her, standing in my hometown airport.

We had actually made it out alive.

Behind me, Mike had come off the plane on crutches, his shattered leg set expertly by the doctors in Chiang Mai. His bag was being carried by Dave. Dusty was trailing along after her husband. Susan met Hollis. All of them were hugging and holding each other as well.

Getting Mike through all the airports as we journeyed halfway across the world hadn't been as bad as I thought it would be. But it had been one challenging job getting him out of that cave.

Keveh had stood on the ledge and shouted orders over the roaring of the rapids down to the men on the road as the doctor checked out Mike. The men below had managed to toss Keveh a rope, and he had tied the rope on one of the trees growing in the cave mouth. He then pulled up more ropes, and with the help of a few of the general's men, they set up a fairly elaborate pulley system.

While Keveh was doing this, Dr. Dabir and Mike were bantering back and forth inside as the doctor poked and prodded and worked to clean out Mike's wound.

"John was right. Shattered bone," was his final diagnosis. "We have to keep it completely still, or you might yet puncture an artery or vein and bleed out."

"I think I've bled enough," Mike said. "Do what you have to do."

The doctor had two more splints sent up through the opening on the pulley system, then with Keveh's help and mine, he got the leg completely immobilized from Mike's waist down to his ankle, with a wooden splint protecting it on all four sides.

Then came the problem of getting him out of there.

The doctor stabilized Mike with fluids and plasma, then refused to move Mike without a proper stretcher board. The problem was, the closest stretcher board was in his office in Pai, so the general sent one of the helicopters for it, while his men worked on the other helicopter to rig up a carrier to airlift Mike to Chiang Mai.

Mike just endured and ate the food sent up for him and my famished friends as we all worked around him.

Hollis alternated between hugging me and sitting and

shaking, as if he didn't really believe it was all over. "Man," he said. "I have never prayed for anybody in my life the way I prayed for you," he said.

"I think you got through," I said. "Thank you. Friends for life, right?"

"You know it," he said.

"Are you ever going to tell us what happened last night?" Mike asked me as we waited for the stretcher.

"I will," I had told him. "I promise, after I've been home for a while and had time to digest it all."

"It's one amazing story," Dr. Dabir said.

"Very amazing," Keveh said. "You should have seen how he looked when he staggered into the police station. He looked like the monster in one of your horror movies."

"No," I said. "I looked worse."

At that, Keveh laughed and agreed and went back out onto the ledge to check on the progress there.

I turned to Mike. "God and I did a lot of talking out there. He helped me in more ways than I can ever know."

Mike nodded. "We prayed for you all night."

"I know you did. And God was listening."

Finally the stretcher arrived and was sent up from the road below. The doctor strapped Mike onto it so securely that I asked Mike twice if he could still breathe. He promised that he could. In fact, he promised that when we got to Chiang Mai to check up on him, he would still be breathing.

It was after two in the afternoon by the time we lowered Mike out of that cave and down to the road below. The soldiers rushed him into the back of a van as the doctor was lowered to the road after him.

I was disappointed that the doctor had already left Chiang Mai by the time the rest of us got there. I wanted to thank him for his help.

Before the three of us got into one of the vans to be driven to Chiang Mai, I did get to thank the man God sent me to in Pai.

Keveh just smiled at me as I shook his hand and said, "You're welcome. Come back to Pai and enjoy our real adventures. Such as sleeping late, gentle raft trips on a lazy river, great food, and wonderful sightseeing trips up into the mountains. I will take you to my church."

"I just might take you up on that," I said. "Can I bring a friend?"

"Of course," Keveh said. "Bring them all. They should see my valley in happier times."

"The friend I'm talking about is my fiancée. I'm sure she'll want to thank you in person for saving my life. And I still owe you a meal, remember? And a replacement shirt. I don't think you're going to want this one back."

"No." He looked at me with affection. "I'm going to hold you to your promise."

The drive into Chiang Mai was mostly silent. I think the three of us were all in shock that we'd survived.

I kept talking to God, thanking Him, asking Him what I could do to prove myself worthy of His trust and faith in me. He had taken me through the valley of death and had been my companion through it to the other side. I had survived.

I promised Him on that ride that I would always do my best to live out His teachings, to help others as best I could, and to never let His voice out of my head for even an instant. My life was His, to use as He wished. I gave myself completely over to Him forever.

I realized at that moment that my life ahead looked wonderful. And I had good friends to share it with, both old and new.

We were told as we got into town that Mike was doing fine and was resting. We could see him later.

The driver took us to a very fancy hotel that was being paid for by the government until our flights back in two days. The driver offered an explanation as we pulled into the fancy place. "The general said that after what you've been through, it was the least the Thai government could do for you."

It was a lovely gesture. But I have never felt so out of place as I did when I walked into that opulent lobby in my ripped and stained clothes. I hadn't taken a shower in days, and if I looked and smelled even half as bad as Hollis or Dave, I felt sorry for the van driver.

I called Lorraine after checking in and taking a long, hot shower. I told her that a few things had gone wrong and that I would explain later. I told her that Mike had broken his leg and had been airlifted to the hospital and that he was fine. I just didn't feel like telling her the entire story at that point. I would do so when I got home, or maybe sooner. But not just then. I was still too raw.

"It sounds like you had an adventure," she said.

"God and I did," I said. "You know that still small voice you talked about? I finally heard it loud and clear."

Thankfully, she let me leave it at that for the night.

Hollis, Dave, and I had a good meal. We didn't talk much about what had happened. Instead we talked a great deal about faith and friendship and forgiveness. We talked about God's grace in our lives, and how God's teaching had changed us. Our friendships had been strengthened in the crucible of our adventure. We'd come out here to test ourselves against the wilderness. Instead we had tested our mettle and our faith against the evils of the world. We'd come out of it different men.

We'd never forget what we'd been through together. It had nearly forced us apart. But it had finally drawn us together. And it had opened us up to God as we'd never been opened before. All of us felt as though we'd walked through the fire and come through refined and redeemed.

After dinner, we went to the hospital to see how Mike was doing. We hung around his room, shooting the breeze until we decided we all needed sleep.

I woke up three times that first night, screaming and sweating. I finally had to leave the light on in the bathroom to help me get back to sleep. I figured that I might be sleeping with the light on for some years to come.

God had brought me through the valley of death mostly unscathed in body and greatly enriched in spirit, but He'd left me the memories of my journey as a chastening souvenir. I hoped after we were married, Lorraine wouldn't mind too much when I slept with a night-light.

When we were all back on American soil and I held this woman I loved in my arms, I was ready to spill my guts to her when the time was right.

She gave me one more hug and then held me at arm's length. "You look like you were sent through a lawn mower. Face first."

I had to laugh. She was right. I had about two dozen cuts on my face and hands and neck and one large cut under my chin that had taken five stitches to close up after the doctor in Chiang Mai got done cleaning it out. I was taking a ton of antibiotics to fight off infections and treating the cuts I could reach with disinfectant and antibiotic salve.

Lorraine finally let go of me long enough to hug Mike, then Hollis, then Dave.

Mike's wife, Dusty, got Mike into a wheelchair, exclaiming that she wouldn't stand for any of his macho stuff around her. She was taking care of her man. Susan was there, holding onto Hollis's hand. That sight made me smile as well. He'd confided to me that he had told her what he had done, what had happened, how he had accepted God into his life, and that he hoped she would forgive him.

She had. They set their marriage date for two weeks from the day we returned. All three of us had agreed to be Hollis's best men. Lorraine and Dusty had agreed to stand up for Susan. But that was in our future.

At this moment Lorraine came back and put her hand around my waist, then smiled at the rest of the guys. "I want to tell you men right now," she said, "you four aren't leaving again for a rafting trip without us along."

Dusty and Susan were both nodding.

I glanced at Mike, then at Hollis, then we all started smiling.

"What's so funny?" Dusty asked.

"We had already decided the same exact thing before we left Chiang Mai."

At that, we all laughed.

Being back with Lorraine felt wonderful. Being completely at peace with God felt even better. Aware of His still small voice in my life.

I was whole.

I was forgiven.

I was loved.

I was home.

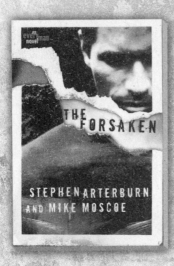